Karolinum Press

ABOUT THE AUTHOR

Karel Poláček (1892–1945) was a Jewish interwar author, journalist and screenwriter. Alongside Jaroslav Hašek and Karel Čapek, he is widely recognized as one of the three pillars of Czech literary humor.

During the First World War he enlisted in the Austro-Hungarian army, fighting on the Eastern Front. Upon his return to the newly independent Czechoslovakia, he worked for a time as an import-export clerk, and began contributing pieces to a variety of satirical magazines. After losing his job over one such story, he began working as a court reporter and feuilletonist for the prestigious Czech newspaper *Lidové noviny*. There he met the Čapek brothers and became a *Pátečník* ("Fridayist"), part of the social circle that counted leading cultural and political figures of Czechoslovakia (including the president and prime minister) as members.

While his work in the Twenties consisted of collections of satirical short stories, in the Thirties he devoted himself to humorous novels. A keen storyteller, Poláček viewed humor as a fundamental way of interacting with the world. Influenced by the small-town life that he knew so well, Poláček's idiosyncratic prose explored the fate of the common man.

In 1939 the Nazi occupation of Czechoslovakia forced Poláček out of his newspaper job. He worked as a librarian for the Jewish community of Prague until he was sent to Theresienstadt in July of 1943. In October 1944 he was transferred to Auschwitz. Both his novel *We Were a Handful* and his diary, published later as *Se žlutou hvězdou* (*With a Golden Star*), were written in the period shortly before his deportation to the camps.

MODERN CZECH CLASSICS

Karel Poláček

We Were a Handful

Translation from the Czech by Mark Corner

KAROLINUM PRESS 2016

KAROLINUM PRESS
Karolinum Press is a publishing department
of Charles University
Ovocný trh 5/560, 116 36 Prague 1
Czech Republic
www.karolinum.cz

Translation © 2016 by Mark Corner

Cover illustration by Jiří Grus
Designed by Zdeněk Ziegler
Set and printed in the Czech Republic
by Karolinum Press

Cataloging-in-Publication Data is available
from the National Library of the Czech Republic

ISBN 978-80-246-3285-8 (pbk)
ISBN 978-80-246-1449-6 (hbk)
ISBN 978-80-246-3375-6 (ebk)

Every day I head for school past a house with two storeys and a shop sign with the name Martin Bejval on it. 'Haulier and Dealer in Coal' is written underneath the name in hand printed letters. The sign is painted blue and red with a pair of crossed hammers on either side, which is something I really like. But what I like even more is the horse's head fixed between two windows on the first floor. When I was small I didn't like the head, not at all, because I was scared of it. Its mouth is always open and its teeth are bared. It grins at me as if it had something on me and was jeering: "Hold your horses, impish boy, I'm going to tell on you". I reported the fact that the head kept making faces at me and that I'd done nothing to deserve this. It started picking on me whenever I went by and it should have left me alone. Ma had to calm me down and explained that the head couldn't do anything to me since it was made of wood.

But she could say that to me over and over again and I still didn't want to believe her, because my own head was terribly empty. And whenever I went past Bejval's place I just ran like the clappers. I got the idea that the horse's head was telling people all sorts of tittle-tattle about me in a whisper. Sometimes I heard it whispering: "Why didn't you have the soup today, it was such good soup?" "I know how you tormented Honza your ginger tomcat when you tied nutshells to his paws. What a clatter he made scurrying round the house. It greatly upset him. What made you do that? Don't you realise that he feels pain just as you do? Stop making his life a misery." "And who was it that scooped the raisins out of the maid Christina's Christmas cake, eh?"

I told the head that this wasn't true and to leave it out and that sneaks ended up in hell where devils would prod them with pitchforks to stop them telling tales. But the head went on pulling faces and whispering something in a low voice. So I decided to get hold of a long stick and sock it one in order to stop it grinning at me like that.

Now, on the other hand, I've grown up and therefore I've become clever and I know that the horse's head isn't jeering at me, it's just the way it is and I've made friends with it. When I go to school I say "Hello" to the head and it says "Hello" back. In the Spring it asks me whether I'll be playing marbles today or tipcat. Or perhaps I'll be running around playing football in the playground and so it reminds me not to forget that the ball needs more air. I reply to this: "Ta for that, I shan't forget!" In the summertime it will want to know what's going to happen about swimming. Is it a day for swimming at the Trousers or a day for swimming at the Hat? In the autumn it will want to go kite flying with me or to make camp fires, and in winter to make a snowman or go tobogganing or visit the skating rink. I can see that it would like to join me, but what lad would want to go places with a wooden horse's head? Let it stay put.

We have a nice new school and a teacher called Mr. Veselík, who wears gold-rimmed specs and eats a bread roll during the break with his head in a book. When he sees a boy doing something wrong he dishes out punishment and doesn't care a hoot. During the break we go into the courtyard and several boys make an awful racket and I'm one of them. Once Mr. Potůček took a photo of us in this courtyard and they made sure that the serious swats were the ones sitting in the front. Mr. Veselík sat in the middle and country bumpkins from over the fields were standing there watching the whole scene. I have the photo in a frame, it's hanging above the settee, where no one is allowed to sit except for Aunt Angela. We will inherit from her and she's well aware of that so she's always in a terrible temper with us. That's why she always sits there and stares and looks ever so strict. Eddie Kemlink sits next to me, I'm a friend of his, and Charlie Páta sits on the left. I don't ever want to be friends with him. He's a sneak, he tells tales, but it never does him any good. He never shares anything with anyone either, he's so penny pinching, though he knows how to wheedle things out of others. But just let him try that with me!

How Ma laughed when she saw the picture! There was I with the top of my head looking like a parrot's crest. She said that it would be something nice for me to look back on one day. Pa grumbled that I wasted money on trifles and he wasn't going to put up with it. "I slave away from dawn to dusk and you throw away money to have your picture taken," he said. The teachers, he explained, all took him for a millionaire, but they did all right, they were well looked after, whereas people never paid him what they owed. "Stop complaining," said Ma, "you old grouse. Stop spoiling the child's happiness." "We'll see how he will pay me back in due course," said Pa, and went to lie down. He always sleeps after lunch and covers his face with Affairs of the Nation in order to keep the flies off.

The teacher praises me for my good behaviour and for being clever, so I carry the exercise books for him after school. I have the best handwriting in the whole class, my written work always looks very neat. I write even more nicely than Francis Kolorenč, who is top of the class but often misses school because of scrofula and mumps and suchlike. I myself came home from school with lice, my head was full of them. No one had as many as I did, not even Zilvar, who lives in the poorhouse. Ma said she despaired of me and went on combing my hair. My family say that I must go on with my studies in order to become a gentleman so that I won't end up packing boxes like Pa. Our Lawrence, he's the eldest, he was supposed to carry on with his studies too, but geometry never suited him and he smoked cigs. So they brought a student to the house to go over the subject with him, but Larry still couldn't make any sense of it. He stole sweets from our store and dished them out to girls so they'd go on dates with him. So the family hauled him out of school and put him in a grocer's in the town of Most, so that he could learn the German language. He took against that from the beginning and wrote asking them to take him home again, saying that he'd behave himself and asking them to send him his textbooks so that he could prepare on his own for the senior class. Pa wrote back saying: "Dear Lawrence, A fine thing that would be, I know you well enough, I wasn't born yesterday. We've had enough of your studying and if I hear any complaints about you I'll fetch my cane. When you've served your apprenticeship, God willing, you'll take over the business from me." I took the letter to the post office where the clerk stamped it with a thumping sound that I liked. So our Larry settled down, he sent his washing home with a letter attached saying he was happy with his situation after all, likewise his boss was happy with him. "Please send me, my dear relatives," he went on, "a little something to tide me over from time to time. I like you ever so much and little Mirabelle too. Talking of the tot, does she know how to walk yet?" I read this letter out to our tomcat. "What do you say to that, Honza? Are you happy with your situation too?" But the tom didn't say a thing, he just made a face, licked his belly and then jumped out of the window and set out on one of his jaunts.

The family thinks that when I'm grown up I'll sit in some warm office and people will come and doff their caps to me while I go on licking government stamps. And come lunchtime I'll be sending someone to fetch me a hot dog. This is not really what I'd like at all. I'd rather be working at Bejval's place with the horses, because I'd wear a leather apron and I'd wear a brass earring to ward off the evil eye, which is what Jacob does, he's the groom there. Then I'd walk beside the furniture van, a handsome fellow with a swagger in his step, and I'd whistle to myself as I gave a wave with my whip. I've tried to walk like Jacob the groom a few times and now I know how to do it. I've taught myself to whistle too, horses like that, but you must always sound a sad note. Then they turn their heads towards the coachman and they look at him with their lovely dark eyes. Sometimes Jacob tucks the handle of his whip into his high boots and stops off at Friedmann's for a tipple. First he examines the glass against the light, then he drinks the contents, shakes his head and makes a "Brr" sound. The other day Ma was surprised at the way I drank the coffee she made me. I examined the mug against the light, then I drank and then I went "Brr" and made a gesture as if I had a moustache to wipe. Ma asked: "What mischief is this, you rascally little rapscallion, how would you like me to tan your hide with the soup stirrer?" I assured her that I wouldn't like it.

Jacob is not a talker, he's a man of few words with people, the words being "Hm", "Yeah", "So", "No", "OK" and things like that. On the other hand he understands what horses say, and horses have to watch out that they don't let slip any secrets in front of him. I've seen how they whisper to each other when they're standing in front of Friedmann's and I can guess what they're saying. That Jacob is giving himself up to the bottle, which harms your health and leads to trouble. I'd also like to understand horse talk and I asked Jacob to teach me it, saying that I'd give him my collection of minerals in return. Jacob laughed and said "Some chance!" Then I said to him: "I don't care if you don't. It's all the same to me, because I already know horsetalk anyway. A moment ago I heard White Spot say to Dappled Dawn, 'Look who's coming! It's Sir Plastered.'" Jacob laughed some more and said "Sure thing!"

The name of my best friend is Anthony Bejval. Tony and I are thick as thieves. We lend each other books. He's got a suitcase full to bursting with westerns such as 'Morning Brings Plague to Prague', 'The Mercenaries from Passau Hit Town' and 'The White Lady of Rosenberg'. There's a picture on one with a caption saying: "The Prince faces a twenty-pointer'. A huge stag has its antlers at the ready to run the prince through. At that moment his trusty huntsman shoots it dead, and because of this he gains the undying gratitude of the prince. Tony's got penny dreadfuls and thrillers galore. He's got the lot, because Mr. Bejval says that he cares about learning and doesn't count the coppers.

Tony will have to take over from his father as a carter, and has promised me that he'll then take me on in the removal business. That would be great. The only problem is that Tony himself doesn't want to stay at home but plans to set off for greener pastures, because he's an inventor. He's invented glass that burns. When the sun's out he says: "Give me your hand, I'm going to show you something but you're not allowed to watch, because you'd give away the secret of my invention." So you hold out your hand and for a while nothing happens, but after another while you give a yelp from the pain and there's a red mark on your hand. Tony says that when he's grown up he'll get oodles of cash for this invention and buy himself a motorbike.

His father, Mr. Martin Bejval, is the strongest of them all. He's not afraid to stand up to anyone, he'll take on all comers. To me he's like Samson, Bonecrusher and Battering Ram all in one. It's just like I read in one of the books which our teacher lent us from the school library. The books have to be returned in good condition, otherwise the families or those who stand in for them have to pay up. Once Mr. Bejval started wrestling with Mr. Plachetka for fun. Mr. Plachetka is a brewer and also incredibly strong. He fought in the war and got the better of all his enemies. The two of them fought till they were red in the face and breathing heavily. Then Mr. Bejval hurled Mr. Plachetka to the ground. He fell with a thud. Mr. Bejval knows all the right holds. Everyone laughed and Mr. Plachetka said: "Phew! You're a crafty devil," and he had to buy everybody a beer. In the Physical Education Association Mr. Plachetka lifts hundred-kilo weights, no one but him can manage it. So I'd like to be a delivery man in order to build up my muscles. All my worst enemies will then run for their lives from me. I'll be scared of no one, even someone armed to the teeth like Horia, the Highwayman who used to go around with Gloska.

So I'm glad to be a boy, because only a man knows how to bring his enemies down so that they're begging for mercy and promising that they'll never do anything wrong again. Girls fight too, but it doesn't mean anything, all they do is giggle and cry. They don't know how to play, their games are so stupid and they want to get married. But no one will have them because it's no fun with them. When they play at weddings, a girl has to be the bridegroom because no boy will do it, so she does a wiggle and twists her mouth and that's how we're supposed to tell she's the groom.

You ought to know that I was once in great danger of staying a girl, because every boy when he's born starts off as a lassie and only later becomes a lad. I wore girls' dresses until I was four because our family wanted them used up. It made me feel really ashamed. Boys wanted nothing to do with me and my brother Lawrence, who's now an assistant shopkeeper, felt shown up by me. I can remember how some gentlemen were once passing our house and I was standing on the doorstep sucking a sweet. Lawrence was standing next to me and he was sucking a sweet too. And one of these gentlemen pointed at me and said: "What a lovely little girl."

"'snot true," Larry said back to them sulkily. "'Cos he's a boy."

"But he's wearing a dress, how can he be a boy?"

"See for yourself," said Larry, and lifted up my dress.

The men laughed and said: "He's still a girl," and Larry stuck his tongue out at them, grabbed my hand and said: "Get inside, you." But that was a long time ago now, back when I was still small. I've grown since then.

It was great luck for me that Mirabelle was born at our place, but a shame that I wasn't there at the time, because Pa had sent me to fetch a cube of yeast for baking. He said that afterwards I should go to Uncle Emil's for lunch and shouldn't be back before evening. When I got back Mrs. Štichauerová was there looking after little Mirabelle who was all wrapped up in her swaddling-clothes. Mirabelle's face wasn't very big, it was red as a tomato and inside all the baby towels she looked like a Christmas cake. Mrs. Štichauerova said: "This is your baby sister," and she told me to say "Blessed be the Lord God". I didn't want to say it. Ma was lying in bed and was ill.

From the moment Mirabelle was born I got to wear trousers and so I became a real boy. So things turned out well for me. When our Mirabelle was still quite a tiny tot, she had a button instead of a nose and believe it or not she was able to suck her big toe. I've tried to do it like her time and time again, but I always miss. All the same I must teach myself and when I've learnt how to do it I'll be famous. Then I'll get my own back on Christopher Jirsák, he's a schoolmate and his family make caps and slippers. Christopher Jirsák knows how to turn his eyelids inside out so that he looks horrible with eyes as red as a devil's. Once the bleating greengrocer saw him do this, the one who sells fruit, sweets, coconut biscuits and even oranges in the square. She spat on the ground and said: "Baah! You little brat, you gave me a fright. Someone should tan your hide, you little imp."

"And the same to you with knobs on," Christopher Jirsák answered her back as he leaped around bleating "Baah! Baah! Bleating Goat!"

"Now look here, young man," the greengrocer wagged a finger at him. "You've gone overboard, you've no fear of the Lord," and she threatened: "Just wait, you nasty urchin, I'll get the police onto you.

That made us laugh. And straight away Christopher Jirsák wrote in his notebook "I made fun of an old person", because he makes a list of all the errors of his ways so that of all the boys he can have the best sins when he goes to confession. Christopher Jirsák made a bet that if he wanted to he could break all of the commandments. In order to sin against the commandment which says: "Thou Shalt not Commit Adultery," he wrote something very rude on the wall of Herman's factory.

I don't have far to go to school. After about a quarter of an hour it's just a stone's throw away. In the morning they can't get me out of bed. Especially in winter, when snowflakes are sticking to the window and a driving wind is moaning 'Woooooh! Wooooooh!' The mornings are dark and the place is lit by a paraffin lamp. I'm dozing and listening to Christina shuffling around in the kitchen. I can hear her yawning and muttering "Oh God, oh God" and grinding coffee and there's something bubbling. Water's poppling in a pot on the stove and it seems to me as if Christina's in that pot under the lid and boiling away in a rage herself. Beneath the covers it's warm and I imagine I'm an animal inside its burrow, a mole or a badger or something like that, and I've got lots of curvy corridors and when the hunter comes I'll find another exit to make my escape. We learnt all about this in our zoology lesson. The hunter, that's to say Christina, yanks me out of bed saying: "Get up, lazybones, it's time you were off to school." I tussle with her and shout out: "Leave me be, you Rampusite," because she comes from the village of Rampus which is high up in the mountains. She can speak Czech as well as German, but with her family she speaks Double Dutch, like those men who bring tree trunks down from the mountains. Cherries grow on the sides of mountains, all tiny, red and terribly sweet. When Christina comes back from the mountains, where she's been visiting her family, she always brings a bag of these dried cherries, which I like more than anything.

What I don't like is washing in winter time, when the water is cold and stings my face. I drink down my coffee in a hurry without so much as sitting down. It's a good thing that I always pack my books away in my satchel the night before, so I can be outside in a jiffy. Christina always runs out after me shouting: "Just you wait, you loutish little imp, you haven't even said goodbye to your mother and father!" She's right about that, so I poke my tongue out at the Rampussykins. She shakes her fist at me, but I'm not scared. I say to her: "Just to make it clear, from now onwards I'm calling you a Rumpusite." She laughs like a mad thing, she's got a boyfriend and she's going to marry him.

On the way I stop to pick up Anthony Bejval and I make clear to him at once that Christina is really a Rumpusite. He likes this idea and we have a laugh together about it.

I always try to steer clear of the house where Mr. Fajst lives. He's a clerk and he's retired with nothing to do, which means that he pokes his nose into everything. Most of all he keeps an eye on all the schoolkids, whom he blames for being up to no good. He has it in for me in particular and I've never done anything to him. He suddenly comes storming out from I don't know where, grabs me by the collar and shines a torch into my ears to see whether they're clean. If the ears aren't properly scrubbed he shouts out "Ha!" and drags me back to our shop. He doesn't give a fig whether there are people in the shop or not, he just yells out: "See that, Mr. Wholesaler, see the dirt in the young master's ears, shame on him, shame." Pa quotes back to him: "You know what they say, Mr. Fajst, you can't keep children on a leash." Then he ticks me off and thanks Mr. Fajst, but I know he doesn't like doing it. It's just that we are shopkeepers which means we have to fire politeness in all directions. If he insulted Mr. Fajst then he wouldn't put any business our way. However, I don't have to be so full of respect because I'm still little and I'm not meant to understand this sort of thing. Maybe I'll spit on Mr. Fajst's window. Or I'll slip something unmentionable into his pocket, like a dead mouse. I'll go over the options very carefully with Bejval.

We go hopping on one leg down Palacký Street, seeing who can last longest, or else we run backwards, which not everybody can do, and then we come to a halt in front of Mr. Svoboda's sweetshop. There are cakes and cream horns, croissants and cookies, all pink and brown and green in the window. There are chocolate biscuits too, sprinkled with something like red and white seeds. So I'm standing in front of the shop window with Tony Bejval, where we point our fingers at the cakes and say to each other over and over again at lightning speed: "That one's mine, that's yours." It's as if we were dishing out the whole shop to each other.

I even asked Bejval whether he'd be scared to be shut inside the sweetshop overnight. Anthony Bejval came back at me saying that he wouldn't be a bit afraid, he'd just polish off everything there.

I wouldn't be scared either and I'd scoff the lot too. But I'd be scared in the cemetery. There's a part of it that's haunted. The latest person to die and go there gets no respect from the other corpses, it's like a new boy arriving at school. So a new member of the dead must sit down by the fresh grave, wrapped in a sheet, and keep guard. What a bore that must be! I wouldn't want to be on duty in a graveyard, even if someone gave me a whole sackful of peanuts, not to mention a stamp album full of foreign stamps, a blue jersey and one of those glasses that burn things.

Those of us living in Palacký Street are friends, but everywhere else we have enemies. We're the most intrepid of all, so we terrify everyone who's against us.

Who are these enemies of ours? Worst of all are the Ješiňák gang. They live in a neighbourhood called Chaloupky, they've got red hair and freckles on their faces. In fact they're so spotty that they look like those speckled beans. Their hideout is the area round a pub called Na Purku. It starts from the station and runs past the brick factory to some small labourers' cottages called Na Zavadilce. The adjacent territory belongs to the Dražák gang, a two-faced lot. They like to be in both camps at once. One time they're with us, another time they're with the Ješiňák gang. But most of all they're with themselves and jeering at everyone else. Mr. Letovský, the policeman, frogmarched one of these Dražáks before the town council because he'd hit Ducbaba's head with a stone. He was blubbing and his dad, who's a barber, said that he'd take the matter to court. The culprit, being one of these two-faced Dražáks, lied in front of the town council that no, he'd never had any stone in his hand, but I know very well that this Bednařík, who's the worst of the lot, is always causing trouble for people. The Bednařík family eats cats and dogs, and the junior version gets a double fail in practical ethics.

But our worst enemies of all are the Habrovák mob. These are the beastliest of the lot. The Habrovák mobsters even go to school with their pockets full of stones. They outnumber us, their morals are bad and their habits are mean. By nature they like to pick fights. They are often kept in detention after class as a punishment and they sit at the desks at the back which are reserved for the worst pupils, because they can never pass any of the tests. They cause trouble there too and tempt others to do the same thing. They don't wash their hands and even their necks are dirty, so the teacher sends them to the washroom. The other day he said that the Habrováks could plant potatoes behind their ears and that made us laugh so they became furious. And the religion teacher said: "You Habrováks are of the race of the Amelekites, who were abhorred by other peoples and hated by God."

The Habrovák mob rules the area on both banks of the brook which runs through a maple wood. The local population lives from raising geese and making cloth. A few of them are into smuggling, and when that happens the gendarme has them up before the district council. Many of them suffer in prison for their bad deeds. The Habrováks swear all the time. God help any strangers who dare go onto their land without being accompanied by their parents or other guardians!

The war with the Habrováks usually gets going in the autumn while the farmers are getting in the harvest, pleased with their bumper crop. From the barns comes the ratatatat of flails threshing. This is the time when we climb the hillside to where we can spy on the whole Habrovák domain which stretches right up to the sky-line where it borders another territory called Lukavice. Such a stunning sight is the eye's delight, and while we delight in it we strike up a song at the top of our voices to humiliate the Habrováks. This is how the song goes:

> In a stable one fair day
> An old mare passed away
> The Habrováks were pleased
> They were going to have a feast!
> Habrováks – hop! hop!
> They scoffed the barley crop
> They drank up all the whey
> Till stomachs went astray,
> hey hey!

As soon as they hear our war cry, they come dashing out of all their shacks and hovels and even normal houses, shaking sticks in the air and shouting wildly.

However, there are manoeuvres before any war so that our army can get used to being in the field and to the tough life of a warrior. This year we've made a ruling that we'll carry out manoeuvres on Budín Hill, which overlooks our town and where there's a marvellous view that even strangers are amazed at. Budín has a wood but no strawberries or blueberries grow there. In fact nothing grows there.

And so one morning the army formed at our house. Pa knew nothing of what was going on, because he'd actually gone to the store for paraffin. If he'd known what was happening he'd have bellowed in a terrible voice "Manoeuvres? I'll give you manoeuvres! Just get hold of a schoolbook and get down to your homework!"

The commander-in-chief of all our forces was Anthony Bejval, because he's the strongest and knows the ropes. Edward Kemlink would have wanted to be our commander, since his pa works for the Inland Revenue which means everyone has to salute him. Our dad has to salute him too, and takes his pipe out of his mouth every time he does so. Eddie Kemlink prides himself on knowing how to draw up a reconnaissance map, so he made a map of Budín and the area around it. He said that every army has to have such a map, or else it'll be crushed and will have to beat a quick retreat. He knows all about it and when he grows up he's going to join the military academy and learn to be an officer. Then he'll have a sabre with a sword knot. Bejval said that this was all right, let him draw up his maps. He himself was going to invent a weapon that would wipe out all our enemies anyway.

Zilvar, the boy from the poorhouse, came to join us because he saw that we had buns with us. He had stones in his pocket and a catapult. He said that he was bringing more boys, but Bejval told him that we'd got enough already. Eddie had a rifle, a revolver and some firecrackers. He had a wild look about him and spoke in a deep voice. I was carrying a mace, just as the Hussites used to when they set up camp in the town of Naumburk and the people sent out their maids of honour to tell the Hussites to leave them alone and not to go near them. Then the Hussites left, singing 'We are warriors of the Lord' as they went and striking fear into everyone who heard them. I read about this in a book and I'm going to whack every one of my enemies with my mace, and I don't care if they go and sneak on me afterwards.

We also had a handcart with us to put the buns on, and make sure that we didn't suffer from starvation while on the march. We were just ready to sally forth when Eve turned up, the daughter of Svoboda the Sweetmaker, to say she wanted to join us on manoeuvres. Our commander, Anthony Bejval, told her that this was a stupid idea because you couldn't have girls in an army. Eve got upset and was ready to turn on the waterworks. So I butted in and asked why she couldn't go along with us. I like Eve, because there's a fabulous smell of vanilla sugar about her.

Just when I'd spoken up on her behalf Christopher Jirsák looked at me and grinned horribly, just to spite me. While he was looking at me I started looking at him too. Then I went up to him and he went up to me as well. I made a fist, he made a fist. I said "Just try it!" and he replied "Just you try it!" The commander said that this wasn't the time to fight, there was no point in it, there'd be time enough for all that later, now was the time to be marching to war. So we left it at that for the time being, but I'll get my own back on that Christopher Jirsák. I know why he was grinning horribly. He thinks that Eve is my wife-to-be, which is a rotten fib, and he says that I'm going to be her husband, which is the biggest lie of all and anyway it's a case of pots calling kettles black. I'm not the marrying kind, and if Christopher gives me one more of those horrible grins of his I'm going to find the biggest stone ever in order to give him a hiding.

The commander decided that Eve could come with us and haul the cart stocked with buns, so she had something useful to do. Eve jumped for joy and said she'd be there at once, only could she take Josephine along with her, her best and most faithful friend, from whom she had no secrets. Bejval said: "Why not? Just make sure you're here right away."

So we waited and waited and there was no sign of the girls. The commander said "Holy smoke, will they ever come!" There was some grumbling in the ranks, and Christopher was again heard saying that he'd known all along there was no place for girls in a war, but he didn't make that horrible face of his when he looked at me, which was lucky for him. Kemlink complained that if he'd known this was going to happen he'd have gone to his uncle's, where there was a rabbit hutch and a new girl rabbit to see. The commander sent a messenger post haste to Svoboda's shop, to find out what was going on. Mr. Svoboda asked him in a stern voice: "And how may I help you?" The messenger got scared, so he bought a pennyworth of sweets and didn't say any more.

At long last Eve arrived with Josephine Hrazdíra in tow, along with someone called Bunty Šebek and yet another girl whom I didn't know. They were all giggling and Josephine had a parasol which she'd taken from her mother. The girls were drafted into the engineering corps and pulled the cart with the buns. They spent the whole time whispering and squealing like mice.

When we came near to the woods of Budín, the girls began to sing 'Oh Ramona' or some stupid girly song like that in their horribly high voices. The commander's hackles rose at this and he yelled out: "Silence! Don't you know anything about discipline? Our foes could be lying in wait not far from here, ready to ambush us, while these girls cluck away as if nothing was happening."

The girls just giggled at him. Bejval flew into a rage and said that this was the last time they'd be taken along and they could go and poke fun at their grandmothers but not at his army. The girls giggled even more, which is all they ever do, seeing that they're stupid.

On the edge of the woods we struck camp in order to take a break and drink in the fine view. Eddie Kemlink showed us his beautifully sketched map which he pulled out with a flourish. It was truly beautiful, drawn in a special ink and even touched up in colour. Every tree, rock and footpath could be made out, so we all admired it. Christopher Jirsák was the only one who said "Big deal!"

When we'd had a rest and got our strength back, the commander ordered us to sneak round the edge of the woods and report anything suspicious. So we went on the prowl looking on all sides. Eddie Kemlink walked ahead saying that he was an officer. He had the map in his hand and kept on looking at it. He went on saying "Eyes right! Turn left!" without let-up. Then suddenly he was hit by a stone and gave a shriek.

We looked to see what was happening. We could hear something rustling in the undergrowth. Then one of the Ješiňák gang came rushing out waving a stick and shouting "Wipe them out! Slaughter them!" And lo and behold, behind him there were two, three, at least a million of those Ješiňáks, all of them yelling like the Assyrian hordes and waving sticks. I could see plainly that they'd attacked us in a very unfair manner and I tried to save myself by running away.

The commander wanted to run away too and hid in a ditch. I thought that they wouldn't spot him, but the Ješiňáks found him, yanked him out by his hair and beat him, while one of them spat on his trousers from behind. The girls started to cry. Squealing and shrieking, they left the cart to fend for itself and ran off. The Ješiňáks wolfed down our buns before chasing us across the fields shouting that they'd have to wipe us out for good so we didn't get any more big ideas.

God knows how it could have ended. Maybe we'd all have been at death's door if some angry farmer hadn't come on the scene. The farmer had a whip with him as he shouted: "What a bloody rabble. I'll tan your hides! I won't have you scaring my cattle!"

Our foes took fright at this, because the farmer struck them as being a great ruffian who could give them a good going-over. So the yellow-bellied Ješiňáks turned and fled, and the farmer said he was going to break everyone's legs, it didn't matter whose. And the Ješiňáks kept running away. When they were far enough away they swore at the farmer, but no one could catch what they were saying.

Then we went home and Eddie Kemlink lost the map. Christopher Jirsák was spitting blood saying "There you are, just as I thought. I didn't want girls coming along, it's no fun with them." If it hadn't been for them, he said, he would have smashed the Ješiňáks to smithereens. He said he could have taken them on a dozen at a time. He asked me whether I knew that four of them had attacked him and he'd given them each a beating in turn. I said that I didn't know anything about it and he gave me one of his filthy looks.

I said: "Stop making faces at me," but he came back at me with: "I will make faces, I'll make as many faces as I like." So I said: "If you make faces, it means you're a monkey," and I followed up by bashing him across the bonce. He bashed me back across the bonce and so we set to scrapping.

Commander Anthony Bejval declared "Count me out! I don't want any part of this," and went off. Eddie Kemlink said that he had to go to a violin lesson which he'd already missed twice. Zilvar of the Dražáks had already gone. He left the moment he saw that the Ješiňáks were getting close to us. The others had scarpered already too.

So I was left with Jirsák and we scrapped the whole way back. When we reached the village of 'Dlouhá Ves' Mr. Fajst came across us and said: "What a charming example of youth today!" So we stopped scrapping and went our separate ways home.

I've already told you how Anthony Bejval is a great inventor, the best there's ever been and no doubt about it. The other day he said to me that he'd invented something new, but he wouldn't let me in on the secret unless I swore never to tell anyone about it. So I said "cross my heart and hope to die" and spat three times.

Anthony Bejval said: "Just remember that you've taken an oath." Then he said that he'd invented a game called 'The Fire-Raiser from Mostrava, a town dedicated to St. Cecilia'. The idea behind the game is that you build a village in the middle of the fields. Then you set it on fire and the people of the village have to put it out.

I liked this very much and said that Eddie Kemlink should be told about it, for he'd certainly be able to play a villager.

Bejval said OK to this and I pointed out that Zilvar, the boy from the poorhouse, could also play a villager. Bejval agreed. But I went on to say that nothing should be said to Christopher about it, because he spoilt every game.

"You bet," declared Anthony Bejval.

Then he said that he'd need boxes for the game. Out of the boxes he was going to make houses. He asked me whether I could provide him with some.

"Yes, I can," I replied. I told him I'd filch them from my uncle by sneaking into his place without being seen.

"That'll be spot on," declared Anthony Bejval.

Now this uncle in my family is called Silas Vařeka. He has a house in the square and runs a business dealing in fabrics and textiles in general. He sells collars, shirts and ties.

This uncle is stingy and Mrs. Vařeka, my aunt, is just the same. Her name is Emily. They never give anyone anything. We're not on speaking terms with them.

Whenever my uncle sees me, he asks: "What did you have for lunch today?" and I always reply "Potatoes". Uncle continues his inquiry. "With butter on the potatoes?" "Without," I tell him. I tell him this on Pa's orders. Pa said that when I went to see the Vařekas I was never to let it be known that we'd been eating cabbage soup or sweet pastries or a thick mushroom and potato soup. Nor should I tell him we'd had mixed pickles, omelette surprise, hairy dumplings, mashed potatoes with barley grains, pancakes or even meat. If I had told Uncle he'd have said "Well then, how are you supposed to keep a penny of your savings if you insist on spending all you've got on food?" And then my aunt would certainly have added "First comes the Wow!, then comes the Ow!" Followed by "Waste not, want not." Topped off with "You should always have a spare wheel to fall back on."

Pa said that the Vařekas were afraid that we'd come to rely on them, but they could go whistle for the day anything like that happened. Pa knows that we can't expect any favours from anyone, and that we have to look after ourselves. Ma said: "Does Emily think that I should stint on food for my own children, that I should give them nothing but a few sorry scraps?"

Uncle Vařeka is awfully rich. He has millions of gold coins buried in his cellar. He goes to the cellar at night carrying a lantern, and when he gets there he calls out in a loud voice: "Abracadabra, open sesame!" At these words the wall opens up to reveal a secret chamber where there's a chest full of coins. Uncle puts the lamp down on the ground and counts his money.

I heard all this from Francis Voborník whose family are tenants of the Vařekas. I asked him whether he'd ever seen this treasure chest, and he told me that actually he hadn't, but once during the night he'd woken up and heard a jingling sound coming from the cellar and the words: "One and twenty – two and twenty." Francis swore such a terrible oath that what he was saying was true that I knew he couldn't be fibbing. When I told Pa about all this he laughed saying "Ho! Ho! Ho!" and gave me a minty sugar-plum.

The Vařekas also have a grandpa who is really ancient. Last year he was two hundred years old. He's always sitting in an armchair. On his head he wears a round cap with a tassel and there are hairs growing out of his nose, eyes and ears, while there's moss growing on his back. There's a droplet hanging off his nose too. He sits in the dark taking snuff and then sneezing badly. It sounds like a firecracker going off. Legend has it that Emperor Franz Joseph was once passing the Vařekas' house in a coach and Grandpa knelt down in the mud holding up a written application for a tobacconist's licence. The emperor took the opportunity to stop, gave a kindly smile and said "What a good fellow!"

Grandpa can't see anything now, but his hearing is still sharp. When Uncle Vařeka tells the apprentice in his shop to get cracking and take some money to the post office, Grandpa taps on the floor with his stick and shouts out in a fury: "I won't allow money to be thrown away on nothing!" That's why when the talk at the Vařekas is about money it all happens in whispers.

I chose the early afternoon for stealing the boxes, the time when they'd just had their lunch. This is the moment for Aunt Emily to scold the maid in the kitchen and for the maid to answer back, while the apprentice has gone off to play cards with the others on the tree trunks next to the building site. Uncle Vařeka stretches himself out on the shop counter, puts a bale of fabric underneath his head, finds some other piece of fabric to cover himself with and then says: "Well now, the business is all worth peanuts, but if anyone comes, wake me up," but no customers arrive at this time of day. Then comes his fabulous snoring and he's away with the fairies.

So I sneaked into the shop, carefully looking to all sides, making sure there was no suspicious noise. I'm familiar with the shop and I know where everything is. So I crawled under the counter, where boxes of shirts and other things are kept. I emptied everything onto the floor before seizing hold of a pile of boxes and I was back outside in a jiffy. Anthony Bejval was there waiting to give me a hand, so he grabbed hold of part of the loot and we scarpered so as to get as far away as possible or else my uncle, if he found out, would kick up a fuss about it, claiming he'd suffered a huge loss and after that there'd be ructions at home.

Then we set off to the fields. Eddie Kemlink came along with us and Christopher Jirsák wanted to come too, but no one invited him. So he made out that he wasn't with us, but I knew perfectly well that he wasn't just wandering around on his own but would tag along. When we got to the fields we used the boxes to make a village. I wrote 'School' on one of the buildings, 'Town Hall' on another, 'Grocer's' on a third and nothing on the rest. Christopher Jirsák stood there ogling what we were doing and then he said that we should write 'Church' on one of the boxes, but I told him: "No one asked your opinion." He answered back with: "No one asked your opinion either," so I pointed out to him: "That's what I said and you either ought to think of something to say for yourself or shut up." Then he went quiet and I was pleased that I'd got the better of him.

I went on to write 'The Thirsty Raven' on one of the boxes. We squatted down in front of this box as if we were in the pub ourselves, sitting and chatting together. Then Christopher Jirsák said in a sad voice: "It's a shame that I've just been to confession. If I hadn't just been to confession I could pretend to be sitting with you in the pub, drinking beer and being one of the people. But because I've just been to confession I'm not allowed to. I mustn't commit any sins, not by word and not by deed."

"Clear off then, you little git" I said.

He scowled horribly and said: "You brainless boy, if I hadn't just come from confession I would tear a strip off you." He waved his fist at me and said: "Just you wait, you dimwit. When I've not just come from confession I'm going to smash your nose in."

But we took no notice of this stupid talk. We just sat in our pub and went on chatting.

"You know what?" said Eddie Kemlink. "I'm going to be the mayor."

Anthony Bejval laughed at this and answered: "The mayor? But that's what I am."

I laughed at the idea too and said: "No doubt about it."

"What am I going to be, then?" asked Eddie Kemlink.

"You're a town crier and your job is to tell everyone about the fire." This was Tony's reply.

Eddie seemed pleased by this and said: "Right then. I'm the town crier and I will make an announcement about the fire."

"Right. Enough of all that. Now we have to get chatting," said Tony.

"So get on with it," I invited him.

"Now then, neighbours," Tony began, "The Lord be praised that the harvest has been gathered in and all is well." He put on a deep voice while speaking.

I made my voice deeper too. "'Tis as you say, neighbour, 'tis a good harvest. Could be better, a' course, but there be a good yield a' barley and the tatties 'ave turned out well. Now we'll see how it be with the sugar-beet. There be no shortage a' fodder and we've plenty a' geese."

"Well now, neighbour, I would like to interest you in the purchase of a heifer. A real bargain, this beauty is," said Tony.

"'ow much be ye asking?" I inquired.

"Fifty thousand and I'll be the one to lose out on the deal." And so we shook hands on it.

We carried on chewing the fat, but we started talking about how children should not play with matches. It would be very bad luck if that were to happen, seeing as how the wind was blowing towards the village. This was the moment for Zilvar to set light to one of the buildings. The people living there started shouting 'Fire!' I was a fireman so I had to make a 'Waaaah! Waaaah!' noise like a siren, while Kemlink started drumming and said: "Let it be known to all members of the public that an outbreak of fire has occurred." The locals were rushing around taking their furniture and cattle with them while the victims of the fire cried out: "We've got nothing left!"

When the fire was raging more than ever, Anthony Bejval said: "Good people, keep your cool, for this is the worst disaster in living memory."

Christopher Jirsák was standing a short way off and making faces, though not very bad ones. He said that it wasn't a real fire unless someone sounded the alarm. The other day when the count's granary was on fire, all the bells rang out and several people went rushing outside in their nightclothes, given the fact that it was after their bedtime.

Bejval owned up that this was so. I owned up too, we all owned up and then Bejval said: "Sound the alarm then." And so Christopher Jirsák sounded the alarm and that meant he was playing with us, though no one had wanted him to be part of our game.

The whole village was reduced to ashes. Eddie Kemlink burnt a hole in his trousers and wailed that he couldn't go home looking like that.

Bejval said: "What can we do about it? You should have been more careful."

Eddie replied: "You led me astray and I'm going to tell on you."

While we were making our way home Bejval said that it wasn't any fun playing with Eddie and I said the same thing in return.

Because he's not nice, I'm not on speaking terms with Christopher Jirsák. When he's not nice to me, I'm not nice to him either.

We call Jirsák 'Krakonoš', which is the name of a mountain sprite. Tony Bejval thought this name up, which isn't surprising since he's invented everything there is. Because of him everyone calls Jirsák Krakonoš, and the name has even stuck to his brother, the one who works in a factory.

Jirsák's dad makes caps and slippers and he's called Old Krakonoš. His mum bakes wafers and sells them at village fêtes. She's called Old Mrs. Krakonoš. Even grown-ups use these names about them. They don't mean to laugh at them, but that's the way it is. The Jirsák family don't seem to mind.

When someone comes to the shop and says: "Glad to see you in such good health, Mr. Krakonoš. Now we'd really like a pair of slippers," he replies "What sort of slippers would they be, if you please? We have a great many to choose from."

The Jirsáks are very pious. Mr. Jirsák heads the religious procession to the town of Vambeřice. He leads them in the singing of 'Hail Mary, Morning Star of Victory, Eternal Mother, Pray for Us, Queen Supernal, Pray for Us.' He has his glasses on while he does all this, looking through them with a stern expression on his face while he makes sure the procession stays in line, that there are no stragglers and no one is lagging behind. When the procession stops for a change of footwear he waits for them while he sings a holy song to himself and peers through his spectacles to check whether they've changed their shoes yet.

Mr. Jirsák is also a verger in his local church, the Church of Our Lord. This is where the good father says "Krakonoš, do this" or "Krakonoš, do that" and he does it. When some boy starts pushing and shoving in church, Mr. Jirsák leads him outside by his ear and says to him: "You Roman mercenary, learn the fear of God in His Holy Temple! You're not out in the fields playing now."

Christopher Jirsák is a server in the church and wears priestly vestments. Big deal! I'd be just as good at serving. He also carries the cross at funerals, which makes him swell with pride. He won't let anyone else hold the cross, not for a single moment.

Another thing Mr. Jirsák does is play the trombone. He does this in a very melancholy manner at funerals. His elder son Ferdinand plays too. In his case it's a carrynet, but he plays it in the same sad way.

Christopher Jirsák is pious just like his pa. On high days and holy days nothing can make him get into a scrap. He's afraid of being prodded by the pitchforks of the devils in hell, which wouldn't be nice for him. That's why on each of those high and holy days he plots his revenge for the days on which he's allowed to fight and throw stones. But I can fight all the time with anyone who won't leave me alone.

When there's a procession going to Vamběřice, it makes us happy. That's because we boys set off together and wait until it's on the way back. We can hear it coming from far away, because they're singing hymns and kicking up the dust. Some of the pilgrims walk barefoot with their shoes slung across their shoulders.

Then when we see that the procession's coming close, we kneel down in the road and put our hands together. When they get level with us, we start praying in a loud voice, the loudest we can manage, so that they can hear our prayers, because it's on the return journey that the procession performs acts of charity. When the procession hears us praying, they all shower us with praise: "Such good little boys, see how they walk in the paths of righteousness." And as a reward they toss a few hellers at us, sometimes even a crown or two. This makes us pray in an even louder voice in order to reap an even bigger reward.

Anthony Bejval knows how to beg better than any of us, and then I come a close second. Zilvar from the poorhouse also knows how to beg, but his skills are a far cry from ours.

With the fruits of our begging we buy pickled cucumbers, coconut biscuits and firecrackers that go off with a bang when you step on them. We also buy prints that you can make transfers with, and anything else that our takings will stretch to. Zilvar, the boy from the poorhouse, once bought himself a cigar and smoked it under the viaduct, scowling and spitting. He knows how to take a drag and it doesn't make him sick. I tried it once and everything seemed to go green, but Zilvar said: "It's nothing. You're just not used to it."

Little Otto Soumar came along with us once. He asked us to try him out, saying that he could plead nicely too. We would much rather not have had him, being afraid that he might get us into trouble.

And that's just what happened.

His pa owns a factory in our town where they make knitwear and hosiery, and my pa says that Mr. Soumar is one of the fat cats. Otto is always trailed by a governess who speaks to him in a foreign language without a break, telling him to walk upright and look straight ahead. He wears a blue coat with gold buttons and a sailor cap with the word 'Miramare' on it. He's not supposed to go out with boys in case they teach him bad language.

So he came along with us and knelt down on the highway and put his hands together and his prayers were more ardent than any of ours. He shouted the loudest and received the most praise from the pilgrims and got the most money.

Then he went off to the man who has an orchard down the lane and bought a huge bag of cherries, the black ones. He was scoffing them all the way home, saying how good they tasted and that he was going to go back and beg some more and that when he was grown up he'd become a real beggar and then he'd make lots of money.

He messed up his clothes and then he was ill. At home they called the doctor and Otto owned up that he'd been begging for money.

Mrs. Soumar said: "Oh my goodness gracious!", while Mr. Soumar demanded to know of the governess: "Is this what you call doing your job, Miss?" Otto was grounded and had to do all his lessons again until his brain couldn't work any more. He was also made to lie down in bed and drink tea. And he had a visit from the doctor who prescribed some medicine for him. All the money which Otto had managed to beg from the pilgrims was presented by Mr. Soumar to a soup kitchen run by St. Ludmila's Church. It was in the papers too, where they wrote about "a thousand thanks to a donor with a big heart."

None of it makes any sense to me. Just because the Soumars are rich, Otto isn't allowed to go begging – why is that? What good does it do one to be rich, then? I spoke to Bejval about this and he said that Otto could get stuffed and he'd better not try to wheedle his way into our group again. Not if we weren't going to be allowed to beg any more just because of him.

Tony's dead right there.

When those of us who are on speaking terms go swimming, we choose between going to the Trousers and going to the Hat.

Strangers ask where these names come from. I tell them that they come from time out of mind. The point is that all the boys who want to go for a swim have to strip first and carry their clothes to the far bank in their arms. The point is also that the far bank is high and unlike the near bank doesn't have so many stinging nettles and all sorts of brushwood.

Once in the dim and distant past it so happened that a boy dropped his trousers on the way across. He never noticed and the trousers floated away. His name was Rudy Venclík. He's a strapping young man now, has finished his apprenticeship in the cutlery-making trade and sells jack-knives at markets. And that's why this spot is called the Trousers.

Exactly the same thing happened to Johnny Pivec, but in a different place. In this case it was his hat that floated away during the crossing. Johnny Pivec now has a wife. He has a business making soda water which is carbonated water and he also sells carbide. And that's why the other spot is called the Hat.

We don't like the Trousers because it's next to a circular brickworks and you don't get much sun there. And there's a lot of slime which makes bubbles when you tread in it. Once when I went swimming there something yanked at my leg. Tony Bejval said that it might have been a water sprite, because it grabbed hold of me with a cold and slippery hand. The Trousers also has leeches which suck your blood.

That's why we'd rather go to the Hat, where there's plenty of sun, the water is clean and there are none of those blood-sucking leeches.

The Hat is a wonderful place with weeping willows that grow coat-hooks for hanging your clothes on. Anyone who's got a swimsuit puts it on. I've got a stripey one in red and white.

Damselflies hover above the water with sheet metal wings in strips of blue. There are also dragonflies. No one can catch them, because they're off in a flash, like a streak of lightning. Below the bank grow leaves of burdock which we wear on our heads as hats to ward off sunstroke. The one bad thing about the Hat is that there are thieves living in the forest all around it. Only the gamekeeper dares go into that forest. He's armed with a rifle and whenever he spots a thief he shoots him and takes him bound and tied to the mayor's office, so that the man doesn't steal any more.

Whoever's got a swimsuit wears it. Zilvar, the boy from the poorhouse, doesn't have a swimsuit, so he goes skinny dipping. In any case we all jump into the water together with a cheer.

So here we were, four of us, off to the Hat for a swim. I was there, and then there was Anthony Bejval, Eddie Kemlink and Zilvar from the poorhouse. It was hot when we went and a little chap called Victor Štěpánek mingled with us as if he wanted to tag along. We didn't want this, because he was small and that meant if anything happened to him, who'd get the fallout? We would! So Bejval shouted to him 'Buzz off!' I shouted 'Buzz off!' to him too, but he wouldn't buzz off, he kept buzzing round us instead. And he kept saying 'I come too, me too!' So we stopped speaking to him and talked among ourselves. And that's how we came to be a handful.

When we got to the factory, then who should tag along as if nothing had happened but Christopher Jirsák. He acted as if he wasn't tagging along but we could all see that he was tagging along like mad.

I asked him: "What are you pushing in for, Krakonosh?"

He replied that he wasn't pushing in and he wasn't any mountain sprite.

So I came back at him sharply with "So where are you off to, then?"

He answered that he was off to the Hat for a swim.

"Ah-ha!" I said in a loud voice "We're going for a swim at the Hat, not you."

"But I'm going on my own to swim at the Hat," said Jirsák as he made one of his terrible faces.

"We were the ones to think of it."

"I thought of it too."

"Leave him be," said Anthony Bejval, "if he wants to go there alone, let him go there alone. The point is he's not going with us. Don't take any notice of him."

So I took no notice of him but I kept an eye out on purpose to make sure that he was going there on his own and not with us. He made out that he was going there alone, but I knew that he was really going with us, even though he acted as if he wasn't, spoke to no one and whistled loudly.

When you go to the Hat, you go via an embankment where hazel trees grow. We go there in autumn for nuts and fill our pockets with them. Down below lies the railway track leading to town.

Jirsák, who was walking ahead of us, suddenly stopped and called out: "Dare me to jump down!"

The thing is that he's full of pride and likes to show off.

I said that he shouldn't have such a big mouth and in any case I'd bet that he wouldn't jump.

He said that we'd see about that. Then he quickly climbed up and when he was at the top of the embankment called out: "Just watch me!" and raised his arms.

We watched.

"Don't jump, you idiot," I shouted at him, "You'll break your legs."

"Just watch me!" he shouted for a second time, "One, two and one makes – makes – three!" Then he crossed himself and launched into the jump.

I shut my eyes to avoid seeing what happened. When I opened them again, he was already down below. Nothing had happened to him apart from a grazed knee.

We all gasped and started talking to him.

"Why did you cross yourself first?" I asked him.

"I have to do that," said Christopher Jirsák, "so that my guardian angel will protect me and deliver me from all evil."

"You've committed a mortal sin," I said.

"What mortal sin, you little twerp?" came his answer.

"Because when you jump off the embankment onto the railway line, then you put God to the test."

He gave a start at the thought of such a bad sin applying to himself. But then he said: "I haven't sinned, because putting God to the test is something that we haven't yet done in our Religion classes."

"Aha!' I came back at him in a determined voice, "as luck would have it we have done it. The catechism teacher told us all about it."

"When was that?" came the reply from Christopher Jirsák.

"Wednesday of last week," I said, "I've got Tony as a witness to the fact."

Bejval said he was a witness, and Eddie Kemlink said he was another witness.

"I was absent on Wednesday," said Christopher Jirsák, "so the worst I did was sin without knowing it. That's only a venial sin and can be put right with an Our Father and a Hail Mary."

"Oh, very nice!" I said. "The heathen also sin without knowing it and they get the full works. They all end up in hell, and when they plead that the light of true faith never reached them, the Lord God tells them: "You should have made sure that it did, you muttonheads. Off to hell with you pronto!'

Christopher Jirsák made no reply and kept silent from that point on. He spent a long time thinking over what to say and how he could avoid everybody seeing that I'd turned the tables on him totally.

Eventually he said in a proud voice: "It wasn't a case of putting God to the test. It was a sports activity."

I didn't like his proud manner and I said: "On the contrary. It was putting God to the test and I'd bet on it."

"Go ahead and bet on it!" said Christopher Jirsák.

"I'll bet anything you like!" I said.

Christopher Jirsák said that if what I'd said were true, then every athlete would end up in hell. Sprinters, in fact all track-and-field athletes, boxers and wrestlers, those in volleyball and handball, swimmers and anyone in racing, whether bikes or cars, weightlifters who got huge loads off the ground, even footballers. Indeed the Reverend Father himself would have to make his way into the eternal darkness if this was true, because it was well-known that he was once a dab hand at the game in his younger days and used to play for his seminary against the Strahov team and selflessly defended his holy net as goalie.

"That would mean hell was so full that there'd be no room to move," he said.

"I couldn't give a damn about that," I said.

So we talked and quarrelled all the way there while we went across the meadow, speaking about nothing else until we reached the Hat. Anthony Bejval said that we were a pair of twerps and it was time to put a sock in it. So we put a sock in it.

The sun was out at the Hat and it was hot. I like it when the sun's shining, because when I half close my eyes they make rainbow-coloured rings. When I was little I tried to catch the rings. I wanted to keep them in a drawer, because this was a time when I didn't have any sense. Now the sense has got into me, but I still like seeing rainbow-coloured rings through half-closed eyes.

So we stripped off and some horseflies nibbled at us, because the Hat's swarming with them. Some people say that when horseflies bite it means it's going to rain, but I've looked into all that and it's not true, because the monsters bite whatever the weather. These animals are clever. They don't drown even if you hold them underwater for an hour.

Once you let go of them the little brutes just rise to the surface and fly off as if nothing has happened. They're covered in some kind of grease which means that the water can't do anything to them. The best way of stopping these bites is to rub yourself all over with mud, but we would do that in any case so that we could be taken for Africans. Anthony Bejval painted himself with stripes that made him look like a zebra, but I gave myself a moustache so that I looked like Mr. Kordule the constable, who bangs up vagabonds and highwaymen. Everyone thought this was good so they all copied me and little Victor Štěpánek copied me too, even though he's too young to know what he's doing.

We rolled about in the grass on our way through the meadow. Some of the others were talking but I was watching the haymaking instead. Then I saw a train heading towards us from the distance, and that made me think: "I wonder if there are any travelling salesmen on it." I like it when a travelling salesman arrives, because it means he'll come to our shop and Pa will have a row with him. All he says on every occasion is: "Don't bother me, you have nothing I want, it would all end up remaindered, no one buys anything in these hard times." The traveller will also say that these are hard times and that there's nothing to be done about it. They will spend a long while arguing like this, after which the travelling salesman will take out a notebook and take down Pa's order. Then he'll put the notebook away, shake Pa's hand and say: "I remain, Sir, your most obedient servant."

I like the travelling salesman because he's always wearing new clothes and there's a sweet whiff coming from his beard and moustache and his hair too. When Ma arrives in the shop the travelling salesman showers her hand with kisses and says that she's forever fresh and beautiful like a rose. Then Ma laughs and wags a finger at him saying: "What's he like!"

That's why I'm fond of the train. I like it because it brings travelling salesmen and also because you can get a good view of the wide open spaces of our countryside from it. When I grow up I'm going to take a leather suitcase with me and go travelling all the time.

When we had messed around enough in the meadow I said: "Who dares go first?"

Everyone shouted: "I do!" But the first to dare was Eddie Kemlink. Let me tell you that when he jumps it's like watching someone in a swimming competition. Bejval and I went down with a splash like frogs. Christopher Jirsák dived backwards, being the show-off he is. Even so he crossed himself before he did it.

The little chap called Victor Štěpánek was another one to shout "I do!" before he jumped into the water just as he'd seen us doing.

At the Hat there's a patch of deep water and we hadn't thought of the fact that little Victor Štěpánek might not have learned to swim yet. And sure as hell he hadn't.

He vanished beneath the surface. Then he came back up. Then he shouted something and disappeared once more, gulping down water as he went.

"Heavens above!" we cried to one another, "he's going to drown!"

There's a whirlpool, you see, and the water is always swirling around. And your legs can get tangled up because it's full of roots. So we stood there shrieking and scared out of our wits, because we just didn't know what to do.

Zilvar from the poorhouse was the only one who didn't shriek. He said nothing to anyone and jumped into the depths. He dived down, groped around, surfaced, coughed up some water and said:

"I've got him. I'm holding him by the hair!"

We all yelled: "Don't let go of him!"

He replied: "I'm not going to let go of him, 'cos I'm holding him tight."

We helped him to haul little Victor onto the bank. When we'd got him there Zilvar said: "That was a close one!" and blew his nose.

Little Victor was lying down. He didn't move at all and we couldn't tell whether he was breathing. We were out of our minds because we thought he'd had it. "See what you've done," I said with a snivel, "I never wanted him to come with us."

Anthony Bejval said that he hadn't wanted the boy with us either, but I told him: "That's not true, fibber. 'Leave him alone,' you said. 'Let him come along,' you said."

Bejval told me I was the one fibbing, which was a dirty trick, but Christopher Jirsák said: "Stop arguing. It'll get us nowhere. What we've got to do is revive him."

Eddie Kemlink said Jirsák was right in what he was saying, but how were we going to do it?

Christopher Jirsák said that in the corridor of the school we went to there was a picture which showed you how to revive a drowned corpse and we'd have to do it in the same way.

So he acted like they did in the picture and moved little Victor's arms and legs. Then he pressed the boy's tummy so that the water started to empty from him.

All of a sudden the lad heaved a sigh. Then he sat up and looked around, not knowing where he was. At first he felt ill but in a while he was better and we jumped around shouting "Hooray!" because we weren't half happy.

Christopher Jirsák crossed himself and said: "It was touch and go."

Little Victor kept smiling at us and told us what had happened. He said that the water had been all around him, that he'd had a wonderful time, feeling as light as a balloon, that there'd been bubbles popping in a funny way in his ears. When he'd opened his eyes everything around him had been green as if he was in a meadow, a meadow where big red strawberries grew that he'd wanted to pick, though somehow he couldn't get at them.

He talked like this for a long time, but everything came out in a higgledy-piggledy manner and we couldn't catch what he was saying.

Eddie Kemlink said: "Nice strawberries all right, but you could have been nicely dead."

"No, I couldn't," said little Victor, "I couldn't have been dead, but I did want to pick those strawberries, a whole bunch of them, and take them home to Mummy."

"Leave him alone," I said, "he's still small and he doesn't know what he's saying."

Then we showered Zilvar from the poorhouse with praise for the fearless way he'd flung himself into the water in order to save the drowning boy.

Zilvar went red because he was annoyed and he said: "Get stuffed, you servile creeps. Just leave off, will you." But I could see that he was just shy because we'd praised him, so we kept on telling him how great he was and he kept swearing back at us in a really dirty way.

Then we put our clothes on because we'd had enough of swimming, and we walked home with our swimming costumes slung over our backs to get them dry. Zilvar from the poorhouse took little Victor Štěpánek by the hand and told him how to swim. First he should learn to doggy paddle and then he could learn how to swim properly. He showed him how to do breast stroke and swim underwater before instructing him in the crawl for advanced swimmers. He used his arms to show the lad and made him do the strokes after him.

Then he said to him: "You'll remember what I've said, won't you?"

"Yes, I will," said little Victor.

Zilvar praised him for that: "I'm glad to hear it. At least you're not going to drown all over again!"

The following week I was happy all the time larking about, and got a lecture from the grown-ups telling me not to fidget so much. That's because it was the end of the school year. Wednesday was when I was happiest of all, because that's when we got our school reports and Christina said: "You're a real mischief-maker these days."

On the morning of this particular day I did not burrow away in the bedclothes. In fact I didn't even pretend to be an animal. Instead I jumped out of bed yelling: "School Report – Docked in port! Be this as it may, dinner's every day!"

Christina made a face and said: "Just you wait and see! When you fail you'll be beaten black and blue and left without any dinner at all."

I said: "You'll be the one to fail, you Rampusite, Rampussykins, I'm not going to fail."

She went after me with a broom. We were both shouting and laughing and Ma said: "Christina, I sometimes think you've got even less between the ears than the child has."

Christina said: "If you please, Madam, he start-ed it."

When our teacher gave out the reports he called us up one by one and he looked like someone else because he was in his Sunday best. The pupils themselves were dressed up to the nines too. Zilvar from the poorhouse was wearing his dad's trousers and Mr. Stádník, who lives in the poorhouse too, lent him a cap so that Zilvar could catch the holiday mood as well. His coat came from his brother, who had gone off to serve in the army. The sleeves were too long for him but he didn't mind that and used them to wipe his nose. Otto Soumar had been brought by his governess and was wearing his sailor's outfit again. Eddie Kemlink had scrunchy shoes which made him happy. Anthony Bejval wore a blue tie and had a machine haircut. I had a watch but I wasn't allowed to open it up in case I tried to have a look at all the cogwheels.

Before our teacher handed out the reports, he urged us not to forget that we were Czechs born and bred and should be good sons of our proud nation, meaning that we should not spend the holidays with our hands in our pockets but should help out in the home. We should set an example that didn't bring shame on our school. We should greet any adults and avoid eating unripe fruit, which only gives you horrible illnesses with the runs. We shouldn't break the branches off trees, because they were part of nature. We should keep our bodies clean and not think that just because it was the holidays we could behave like pigs. And we should keep up with our reading.

I enjoyed the speech and I made my mind up to rush off and borrow a detective story from Eddie Kemlink. He said it was a great thriller called 'The Body in the Intercontinental Express', and I needed something new to read, seeing that I'd read everything so far.

When we'd got our reports, we were all able to proceed to a higher class. Just two boys failed. One was called Arnold Vosáhlo. He comes from the village of Dubinka. He has no father and a mother who cleans houses and is always at the brandy. The other was Francis Klema, a fat boy who smokes ciggies. His dad runs a pub and he knows how to play bar billiards. But they're not people I go around with, and nor does anyone else. They didn't mind the fact that they'd failed too much. I'd have been in a fury if I'd had to stay sitting in the class below.

I only had two B grades. All the others were top grades. I'd got better in sums, civics and drawing. I was pleased about this, because when I take a good report home I get a crown from Pa and a crown from Ma which Pa mustn't know about. I put them in the piggybank and then when I've got plenty of money in it I can buy tobacco for Pa.

Charlie Páta is the best of our class. He has top marks in everything, because he sits up straight and pays attention and always has his hand up to speak. So when we were leaving the classroom someone tripped him up and he started snivelling. I got blamed for it but it wasn't me that did it. I think it was Zilvar, because all at once he looked the other way.

We poured out of the school, dashing about and shouting our heads off. Charlie Páta was the only one to walk home in the proper manner, because he's a twerp. Mr. Fajst was standing in front of the school, watching out to see whether we touched our caps to him. If we didn't touch our caps he'd report us, no one tells tales like he does. So we touched our caps to him, even Christopher Jirsák did so. He took the cap off his head and said: "Your honour." Then he made one of his horrible faces. Mr. Fajst was at a loss to know whether he made this face out of politeness or in order to insult him and so he just kept staring.

Only Zilvar, the poorhouse boy, failed to touch his cap and Mr. Fajst stared after him before saying in a loud voice: "Don't you know how to show respect, you rude boy?"

There was no response from Zilvar who just carried on walking. Mr. Fajst went after him and asked him in his booming voice whether he didn't know how to touch his cap and what was amiss with his upbringing. Zilvar still said nothing and walked faster. Mr. Fajst walked faster too. Then Zilvar broke into a run, but Mr. Fajst couldn't keep up with him. When Zilvar was a long way off, he started shouting out: "Mr. Fajst ate all the pork, munch, munch, munch. Then he bought his family horse meat for their lunch."

Mr. Fajst went awfully red and boomed out: "You roguish little ragamuffin, you'll come to a sticky end, you will!" But Zilvar carried on home and several people laughed.

Mr. Fajst turned back and looked all around him, but especially at me, to see whether I was sniggering. I looked away. But Mr. Fajst kept his eyes on me, making sure that I wasn't thinking "Mr. Fajst ate all the pork, munch, munch, munch. Then he bought his family horse meat for their lunch." I was thinking it, but he couldn't see that I was, because I didn't say the words. He just told me: "You'd better watch out too. I've been keeping an eye on you."

I knew that he was going to report me but I thought nothing of it, because I also knew that Ma and Pa wouldn't hold it against me as Mr. Fajst never puts any business our way anyhow.

So I went off and the other boys went off too. Mr. Fajst stayed with the bleating greengrocer and we could hear him saying to her: "All those boys are growing up to embrace a crinoline career. Remember these words of mine, dear lady, when I am here no more."

Chris Jirsák is now a friend of mine. We're back on speaking terms and I've told everybody that this is so. That's because I've seen that he's not false and that, on the contrary, he's all right. One thing that definitely isn't true at all is Anthony Bejval's remark that Chris only cares about himself. That's what Anthony himself is like. I know this because I asked him to lend me his bike, so I could ride round the square just once, and he said he wouldn't let me have it. I said it surely wasn't such a big deal to let me have it for a while, it wouldn't be the end of the world, Lord love a duck! But he replied that it was up to my pa to get me a bike to ride, seeing that his pa had bought him his. So I said to him: "Just you bear in mind that I won't forget how mean you are. Just you wait till you want something from me." He said: "Even if you don't forget I'm still not letting my bike suffer wear and tear from the rest of you."

I told Chris Jirsák about all this and he said that Tony had always been like that. He said he'd noticed it ages ago but had never mentioned it so that no one could say that he did people down. But he said he'd always wondered what I saw in Anthony and why I always went trailing after him like a little tail. I said that from now on there'd be no more trailing after him like a little tail and I swore that this would be so.

Then Chris said: "Never mind about that, I've got an idea. Come up to the attic with me and I'll tell you what I'm thinking up there."

We went up to the attic, sat down by the skylight and Chris said: "We'll start a club for going to Italy. Don't tell that Anthony about this or he'll want to go with us."

I said that of course I wouldn't breathe a word of this to Bejval. I told Chris he didn't know anything about me if he thought I would. Then I said that Eddie Kemlink should also be told so that he could come to Italy too.

Chris said by all means speak to Eddie Kemlink and he fetched a box so that we could put money into it. When we'd put together enough, off we'd go. Once we were in Italy we'd send Anthony a card and he'd be furious that we were setting eyes on a foreign land without him. I'd say to Bejval as soon as we got back: "Who saw Mt. Vesuvius with its flames and boiling sulphur and who didn't see it? Who was in the cave whose poisonous fumes kill a dog almost instantly, and who was never there? Aha! And who didn't want to lend me his bike? Aha!" That would really turn the tables on him.

We went to Kemlink's place to hold a conference. Once Eddie had passed on the news that we were going to Italy, Mrs. Kemlink made us coffee and buns to make us strong for the long journey ahead. Mr. Kemlink was fixing the electrics, because when he's not in his office he's always fixing the electrics. He said that he was once in Italy as a soldier serving in the heavy artillery, and that you could get baked chestnuts there.

Eddie Kemlink has two sisters whose names are Victoria and Roberta. They looked into the box where there were already a couple of crowns and laughed at us because a few coppers like these wouldn't even get us as far as the next town. Eddie Kemlink said each sister was just like the other in being as thick as two short planks. He also said that they were each thinking of marrying an aviator, but they should realise that no airman would be that daft. Any modern pilot can just board his plane and go to places like India, so what would he want to be doing with a wife? They wanted to scrap with him so we drank up our coffee and said we were off to Jirsák's, so that we could make our escape from the girls and have some peace.

Eddie has some kind of book for learning Italian. In fact he's picked some up from the book already. He already knows the exercise called 'Love – Engagement – Marriage' by heart and knows how to say "Give us a kiss, miss, when are we getting hitched?" in Italian. We were really surprised at how quickly he could say this.

When we left Kemlink's we were a three because Patch came along. Patch is Kemlink's dog, a very long one though with short bandy legs. But he knows how to scurry around so no one can catch up with him. And he laughs as he runs off, poking his tongue out while his ears go flapping around his head like a couple of flyswatters. Patch is a very clever dog who'll chomp anything. He'll even eat a pickled cucumber and then come back for more. When he wants to be let inside he taps on the door with his tail.

Eddie said: "No, Patch, you can't come with us because our club's got a meeting about going to Italy and that's not a thing to concern you."

Patch listened to this and stood there looking sad with one of his ears inside out. Then Chris said: "Why can't he come along? He's not going to get in our hair like these girls do, because there's some sense in him."

So Eddie said: "Come on, then Patch," and Patch was a happy dog, barking loudly and bounding around and licking Eddie on the nose. Then he rolled over on his back and straight after that jumped up and kept running around, having a good sniff at everyone. Whenever he was far ahead of us he'd wait with his paw in the air, as if to say: "Can't you speed up a bit?"

We all praised Patch but Eddie said that Patch was nothing like he seemed to be. He said that whenever there was trouble and Patch was sworn at, he always looked like Snivelling Saint Snottynose, but this was utter tommyrot. That's why there had been so many complaints about the dog. He goes around with another dog called Arnie, who's supposed to protect the building site for the masons. But he doesn't guard it. Instead he looks around for something to steal, being a well-known thief himself. Best of all Arnie and Patch like to steal things from Mr. Štverák the butcher. They watch for when Mr. Štverák is out of the shop, which he often is because he has to spend a lot of time making passes at Angelica, the maid serving in the chief accountant's household. So he stands leaning out of the window from where he can see the kitchen where Angelica is ironing and calls out: "Always working so hard, dear Angelica. When can we go off for a little walk together?"

When the dogs spot Mr. Štverák making more passes, Arnie slips into the shop because he's big and can reach the counter. Patch is small and so he stays outside to make sure no one's coming. Then Arnie jumps onto the counter, grabs hold of a string of sausages and they both hop it at a rate of knots. They scoff what they can and bury what they can't in a dung heap, because a dog is a clever animal and knows that there can be bad times as well as good.

We were surprised at this and said: "Stop kidding us," but Eddie swore that he was telling the truth. And he told us that Mr. Fajst went past Štverák's shop once and caught the two dogs in the act of thieving and said: "Well there's a sight for sore eyes." He went round to Kemlink's place right away, said: "You'll never guess what I've just seen, Mr. Kemlink," and explained what had happened.

Mr. Kemlink came back with "It can't be true, our Patch is not like that, he's not one to steal. You make it seem as if we don't give him enough to eat." But Mr. Fajst kept saying otherwise, so Mr. Kemlink told him that he envied the dogs their sausages and would rather have eaten them himself.

Mr. Fajst went red as a beetroot and said: "That's what comes of trying to do you a favour." Then he left.

So off we went chatting non-stop together. Patch knew we were talking about him and kept jumping about and barking loudly and whirling around and that's how we got to Jirsák's. Mr. Jirsák wore specs and was stitching a cap as he began with "A warm welcome to you, young sirs!" and then said nothing more. Patch gave him a sniff and wagged his tail and Mr. Jirsák said: "Who's been a bad boy, then?" and gave a laugh.

Mrs. Jirsák said we shouldn't mill about because there wasn't room to swing a cat and we should go into the garden so she didn't have to have us indoors. So we went into the garden, where there was a gnome with a long beard filling a pipe. Eddie Kemlink said that we had to have a conference with regard to our trip to Italy and so we held a meeting. Each of us was to take a rucksack and fill it with food to stave off hunger. I said I'd fetch some fizzy sweets from the shop and we'd make lemonade so we didn't get thirsty, seeing that Italy had a hot climate. Everyone told me this was a great idea and that made me happy. Jirsák said that we ought to pay careful attention to everything there, so that we'd know how high each mountain was and which rivers flowed into which other rivers. Then we'd be able to give the right answer if our teacher asked us about it.

While he was telling us this we heard a terrible roar from Mr. Jirsák as he cried out: "Holy Mackerel, he's eaten my cap!" A moment later Patch came flying out of the door with a mouth full of morsels of shredded cap and Mr. Jirsák came rushing after him, stomping about and asking how he'd come to deserve this.

Eddie urged the dog not to eat caps and Patch made eyes at him with his tail down. Then Eddie told us he'd got a map of Italy which he was going to study so that we'd know where we had to change buses or trains. We agreed that he should definitely take a good look at this map and then we went home.

When I got home Ma asked me where I was forever hanging around and I said "Nowhere". She told me to take some shoes to the cobbler's because the heels had worn down and ordered me to make sure that I passed on her best wishes and asked when the shoes would be ready. So I took the shoes and repeated her words on the way there so that I wouldn't get mixed up.

As I was going over her words Anthony Bejval turned up and said: "Hallo, where are you off to?"

I saw that he was trying to be nice so I told him that I wasn't talking to just anyone.

He asked me whether I was in a strop because of the bike. I told him I didn't care a hoot about his wretched bike and wanted to be left alone. He said that there was no need to be angry on account of the bike because he would let me borrow it whenever I liked.

When I didn't reply he said that he'd invented something fabulous which would have everyone's eyes popping in wonder. I didn't ever want to talk to him, seeing what he was like, but even so I asked him about the invention.

In a hushed voice he told me that he had been in the fields the other day. Sure enough he'd discovered a wasps' nest in the grassy patch that runs along the edge. He even said that we could scoop out the nest and then take home the honeycomb with the young wasps to make a wasp hive. He was surprised that people only kept bees, because wasps also made honey. We'd get loads of honey and sell it to make pots of money.

I said that this was true, but the wasps had to be tamed in order to make honey.

Bejval said that taming the wasps was the least of our worries. Wasps would listen to what he said to them. He asked me if I'd go into business with him.

I liked the idea but I didn't want to seem too keen, so I said that I'd see, but just at that moment I had to go to the cobbler's on account of some worn-down heels so I didn't know.

Then Bejval said that I should take his bike. I'd get there quickly and besides it would look better going to a cobbler's on account of worn-out heels by bike than if I just went on foot.

I said that he was right about that. He brought over the bike at once. I sat on the saddle, said "See you!" to Bejval and set off like a lord in his carriage, watching to see whether the people were looking my way.

When I got to the cobbler's I said: "Mr. Šafka, my mum conveys her best regards and would you repair these shoes and when could the aforesaid shoes be ready in order that it might not take an eternity as it has in the past?"

Mr. Šafka replied, "Young man, say that I send my best wishes too and the shoes will be ready by Sunday. My word is my bond."

So I was back on the bike and off again, but I didn't go straight home because I wanted to make good use of it. So I went past the school where the caretaker was working in the garden. He dropped everything and looked at me and I was happy to have his attention.

When I'd been home I went out again with Ma saying to me: "Where are you off to? Can't you spare a moment to sit at home?" I said that I had to go for violin practice, but I didn't go to any violin practice. Instead I went to Jirsák's.

Chris Jirsák already knew about going to see the wasps and so he told everyone that he had a violin lesson too.

There are three of us who go to violin practice – Chris Jirsák, Eddie Kemlink and I. We're all taught by Mr. Rektorys who runs a music school. Jirsák is already one of the pupils at advanced level. He already knows how to do double stops and practises the second position. At Christmas he played with the other members of the 'Dalibor' club. I only know how to play the tunes of 'As I was Dressing Flax' and 'When Once I Tended Geese' and that's it. No one's allowed to watch me playing. If they do I go a half tone too low and then a half tone too high on purpose. When Pa hears how awful my pitch is, he gets terribly annoyed and says: "You're definitely never going to be a Kubelík. It's money down the drain."

So off we went to see the wasps and now we were a three. And while we were on our way we came across Zilvar from the poorhouse and he asked us where we were heading. When we told him we were off to see the wasps he said he'd join us. So now we were a four. When we'd got a bit further we looked back and saw Patch bounding after us with a smile, his ears dangling. So that made it a handful.

When we arrived Bejval led us to the edge of the field where wasps were flying out of a hollow. So we started to sound each other out on ways of making the nest ours, but just then Patch let out a terrible howl because he'd sat on a wasp. Eddie Kemlink told Patch to calm down. He said he didn't have to make a song and dance about everything, but Patch was howling all the time. Eddie said that he didn't have to come with us and that no one had asked him to do so.

Then he told us that Patch was always prone to bad luck. He explained that once he'd sat on a bee which had stung him and made him squeal horribly. Eddie's mother had said: "This dog will drive me mad!" She'd rubbed some oil they used for the lamp into him, which ended the squeals. But then he ate her sewing-kit and they had to pull thread out of him. Eddie also had to help, given that this was no easy task.

We were all amazed by this tale, and when Eddie saw how amazed we were he said that one gentleman offered him a lot of money for Patch, saying that he was a wonder of the natural world. However, we could see that he'd put this in of his own accord, just to add to our amazement, so we told him not to make fun of us.

This made Bejval say that we should consider how to get the better of the wasps, seeing that it wasn't so easy. Jirsák said: "You know what, we'll pile up some dry grass and set light to it. We'll smoke them out and then they'll go away and we can dig up the nest and take it home."

Bejval said "Good idea" to this, so we went after the dried grass. There was plenty of it about. Then we set light to it.

However we soon realised that this was a mistake. We now know that wasps are not stupid and have even more nous than boys have. They probably already knew that we were planning to smoke them out, and they always seemed to have one more hole than we knew about. In this way they turned the tables on us.

So when there was fire on top of one hole they'd be flying out through the other hole in a jiffy and circle about in the air above, buzzing furiously because they were in a mighty rage. There was a great army of them and they danced round and round, searching out the enemy. As soon as they spotted us they began to count how many of us there were and reached the figure five.

Then the swarm split into five battalions and each battalion had one of us in its sights in order to give us what for.

We screamed and scurried off in all directions, running like the clappers but to no avail, because wasps are a million times faster than boys. They chased us hither and thither through the fields, stinging us from head to foot. Patch was stung on the nose at one point and his howling was remarkable as he thrust his nose into the mud in order to cool it. The farther we went the more we yelped, and we tried fending them off with branches, but this seemed to enrage the wasps even more, so all we could do was whimper.

So we kept running until we reached our street and came across the horse and removal waggon which Jacob was bringing from the Bejvals. When he saw how we looked after a wasp attack he laughed even louder than usual and said: "Just what have we here!"

When I got home Pa asked me where I'd been. I told him I'd been at violin practice.

He said: "So how come you've got a twisted mouth, if you've been playing the violin?"

This was true. I had a twisted mouth and a swollen nose and a narrow slit where my eyes had been. In fact I looked as if I'd turned Chinese.

When my father kept on asking I kept on lying by saying I'd been at violin practice but not for long, because Pa removed his belt and I got six of the best to stop me fibbing any more.

After that I wasn't allowed out of the house for three days so that the swelling didn't stay forever and I wouldn't have to spend my whole life with a twisted mouth and that's what I got for all my pains.

I'm never going back to those wasps again. There's no fun in it, and I'd rather help out at home so people can see how I've turned over a new leaf. And I'm going to tell Anthony Bejval to his face that he isn't a great inventor but a buffoon, a prize one.

I actually told Bejval after three days that he was an idiot, and he came back at me saying I was an even bigger one. I told him that I got what for because of him, and he replied that the what for was his and that he'd got it on account of me. And he said that if I came to borrow his bike again I could go and take a running jump. I said I couldn't care less and I was never going to speak to him again till death us did part.

Eddie Kemlink was packed off to his grandmother's in Moravia. She lives in a retirement flat on a farm there and is very poorly, so she wants to have someone with her. Eddie also got what for on account of the wasps.

Christopher Jirsák said that on account of the wasps his mother shut him in the goat shed and he missed out on dinner. He thought things over in the goat shed and decided that he'd committed a great sin by oppressing the wasps. The Lord God in His Righteousness had punished him, as the wasps hadn't deserved to be smoked out by street urchins and if someone had tried the same trick on us we wouldn't have liked it any more than the wasps did.

He wasn't allowed to be friends with me any more, but had to help out in the home mending slippers and caps. He also had to work hard on his music lessons, so that one day Mr. Rektorys would recruit him to play at funerals just as his father does. He said this in a very quiet voice, fixing his eyes on the heavens as he spoke.

I was furious at him for speaking like this and pointed out to him: "It's clear that you're nothing but a Krakonosh, your brother's a Krakonosh, your pa's a Krakonosh and your mother's a Mrs. Krakonosh. And for all I care the Krakonoshes can go and get stuffed."

Came the reply: "You little swine, I'd give you such a thrashing you wouldn't know your arse from your elbow, but I'm not allowed to commit another sin, luckily for you."

Zilvar from the poorhouse was now going round with the Habrováks, so there was nothing doing with him.

So I'm very well-behaved at present and spend my time with myself and no one complains about me and I read everything, most of all thrillers, so as to become educated. I don't get into any fights, or if I do it's only with the Rampusite, but only for fun and we laugh about it.

Also I have to look after Mirabelle and I carry her from room to room wrapped in her swaddling clothes and sing to her: "His name was Billy Harward, Nevada's little drunkard, His poor wife was a gonna, down there in Arizona, so Billy just drank harder, lost his gold in Canada." She really likes this song. When she nods off I prop her up against the wall in the corner and she sleeps, looking sweet while I read a book.

My family is happy to see me looking after my baby sister, because Ma has to help Pa out serving people in the shop. We run a small general store where you can buy anything. Coffee, chicory, sugar, dry spirit for burning, whips, brushes, teas and spirits of all kinds, as well as lemons, not to mention chocolate. We've got the lot. And loads of people come to us. They even come from the villages round about.

Best of all is when Bejval's waggon stops at our door bringing things which Pa has ordered from Prague and even from lands overseas. For me this is always a reason to jump for joy and celebrate. The first thing that happens is that Jacob comes into the shop and says: "Hello there! So here we are, right as rain and dead on time." Next the delivery men start taking down boxes and when that's all done they get a tot of brandy which they drink up saying "God's bounty". Then off they go.

Straight away I start jumping around and pestering Pa to get started on the boxes. Pa hums and hahs about it and says: "All in good time, give me room to breathe. The best thing would be for you to take hold of a school book and get some ideas into your head." But that doesn't stop me pestering and when Pa is pestered into submission he seizes hold of a cleaver, a hammer and a pair of pliers and starts opening a box. He's very slow about doing this and has his eye on me all the time he's working, so I know he's teasing me about the fact I'm totally impatient.

It's true that I'm impatient because I'm greedy to know whether there are pictures inside and maybe even lots of them. I'll know at once if there are pictures inside the box or even maybe fairy tales. How will I know? If the box is all dirty and grubby, then there'll definitely be nothing in it for me and I leave it alone because it doesn't interest me. But if there's a box that's white all over with a lovely smell of fresh wood about it, then no doubt about it there'll be pictures and fairy tales and also posters inside it.

There's a squeak and a crack as Pa opens the lid. There's paper underneath and then wood shavings with a poster on top. Pa unwraps the poster, on which there's a picture of a beautiful lady. She's very pink and has blue eyes and is drinking coffee with a merry smile that's rare to see. Underneath her picture there's a caption in block capitals: "In every place it's what they say – we drink coffee the Falcon way." Pa looks at the picture fondly and then says: "Mother, come over here." Up comes Ma wiping her hands. She looks at the picture too before going "Ahh!" Then it's Christina's turn from the kitchen. She also has a look and goes "Ahh!" because both of them really like it. Then Pa hangs the poster in the window, so that everyone will see it and come to buy chicory.

Then comes the main event, because underneath the poster there are fairy tales and plenty of them. I start reading the stories about witches, dwarves and giants, upright kings and a princess who is downright bad and would never want to drink Falcon coffee. So she's bewitched and turns into a frog until she's released by a prince who would love to while away all his time with Falcon coffee, and who for just this reason is terribly strong and amazingly valiant and will take the princess's hand in marriage, and later they'll drink Falcon coffee in perfect harmony until death do them part.

When I grow up I'll be a shopkeeper too, because these people have the best life of all. Shopkeepers never have to buy anything. They just go to their shop and take whatever they want. Pa said: "Listen here, I'm hoping that you'll take over the shop. I won't be here forever. So pay attention, so that one day you can step into my shoes, because our Larry will do his own thing." So I pay attention and stand behind the counter greeting people in a firm voice, in order to behave like a proper shopkeeper.

But what I like best of all is going to chase up people who owe us money for goods. What happens is that I call on them at home, greet them politely and say that Pa sends his regards and then I tell them how much they owe and that we can't wait any longer. The people get into a strop and say there's no need to get so up tight about it and they'll pay in good time. But I don't budge. I say that no one waits for us to pay either and that I'm not allowed to go home without the money. Then they decide they'd better let me have the money, before telling me to buzz off.

However what I really don't like at all is going to chase up Svoboda the Sweetmaker who gets sugar, chocolate, cocoa and all sorts of things like that from us. Mr. Svoboda is waspish and always throws me out of his shop saying that he's never yet run away from anyone owing them money. I like the way he gets into a strop and I'd be happy to raise my voice and argue with him, but Eve Svoboda is there with him, looking so wretched that my voice goes all weak. Then I go back home and Pa has to send Mr. Svoboda a reminder in writing.

The other day I again had to take him a letter on which the words 'The Honourable Mr. and Mrs. Svoboda at their Place of Residence' were written. When Mr. Svoboda caught sight of the envelope, he went bright red and exclaimed: "Tell that father of yours that my name is Jaromír Svoboda the Sweetmaker and that I'm no one's Honourable Mr. Svoboda.

So back home I went and told Pa that Mr. Svoboda is Svoboda the Sweetmaker and not the Honourable Mr. Svoboda.

Pa replied: "Tell Mr. Svoboda that as far as I'm concerned he is the Honourable Mr. Svoboda whether he likes it or not and that I know what I'm doing."

So back I went and said to Mr. Svoboda that so far as Pa was concerned he'd always be the Honourable Svoboda whether he liked it or not.

Mr. Svoboda went an even brighter red than he had the last time. On his forehead a vein stood out shaped like the catapult we use to fire at sparrows.

"Just wait here!" he said.

Then he sat down and wrote something. When he'd finished writing he licked the envelope, banged it with his fist and said: "Take this and say that I send my regards. This is nothing for your father to boast about."

Pa read the message. When he had finished reading it the notary's maid arrived saying she wanted a quarter of a litre of vinegar. "I'm at your service," said Pa and put down the letter. As soon as he'd done so I quickly picked it up so that I could read it for myself.

The message in the letter was as follows: 'The Honourable Mr. Victor Bajza, Holesaler, At His Plaice of Residence'. Highly esteemed Mr. Holesaler! If you use a mode of address such as The Honourable Mr. and Mrs. Svoboda' – if you pleas! – just once more, despite the fact that I have made it clear time and time again that the people in question have no wish to be adressed in that way, seeing that business is conducted in my name only and in no way in that of my wife, then in future I shall be taking my business elsewhere.'

When I read the letter I found lots of howlers in it, so I took a red pencil and underlined the spelling mistakes. Then I added the words: 'Presentation of Written Assignment: Lacks Neatness – Spelling: Very Poor' and took the letter back to Mr. Svoboda so that he could correct it.

Mr. Svoboda looked at it, went bright red and said in an unusually strong voice: "That takes the biscuit! I'm no one's fool and I won't let anyone treat me like some whippersnapper. I'm a man who pays his taxes on time."

From that point on he never bought a thing from us. Pa was surprised at this and said: "I don't understand what Mr. Svoboda has against me that makes him go to my rivals."

I said: "I don't understand it either," but I knew perfectly well, only I couldn't say because I'd get a thrashing.

Pa said: "The seasons are changing," and Ma said: "To be sure they are, there's a wind blowing from the fields of stubble," and they watched as a gale worked itself up outside. Autumn will arrive at a stroke, there'll be no more bathing and plop! plop! down will come the apples in the garden. For sure the water is still warm, but no one likes to bathe now. The wind will tear the shirt out of our hands while we're getting dressed and then wilfully play with it so that we can't fit into the sleeves. There'll be goose-pimples on our bodies and no one wants to go into the water at a time like that.

So we go kite-flying, which is a real sport. The kites are made by Jacob, who works for the Bejvals. He's the one who does it best. We wait until Jacob's unharnessed the horse and tidied up the stable and done all that he has to do, and then we start pestering him: "Go on, Jacob, make a kite for us." His face clouds over and in a sulky voice he comes back at us: "Get out of my sight, you bratlings, I've no time for you." But we keep on pestering and he says in a heavy voice: "If only I could be left in peace."

Then he sits down on a log used for chopping wood and gets down to work while we stand around watching how he does it. First he makes a strip of wood, making sure that it is straight and smooth. Then right in the middle of this strip he fastens a cane rod which bends so as to work like a bow.

Then he uses a cord to bind the two together at the lower end of the strip. He makes a couple of small holes in the strip and through these he threads some string. And now you have the kite in skeleton form. Then he checks to see if it's balanced. If it is, then he says: "That'll do the trick." He then adds paper flesh to the skeleton. Jacob doesn't talk a lot while he's working. The most we get out of him is an occasional "Pass this" or "Pass that", and we always know just what we have to pass him, whether it's scissors or paper or a pot of glue or whatever. While he's working we have to keep silent if we're to avoid him chucking it all over us. He doesn't like talking. Only when he's finished are we allowed a "Spiffing!" to say we're happy.

He fastens pom-poms to each side of the kite in order to give it extra balance, and then he uses coloured paper to cut out little bows which we thread into the kite's tail. Another pom-pom is put right through the tip of the tail as well in order to keep everything balanced. The thing is that if a kite doesn't have balance, it pulls to one side like a mulish horse and does several swift somersaults in the air and then plunges straight into the mud. And then no one can do anything with it.

But a kite must also be given eyes and a beard with some red paint. This is the job of Eddie Kemlink, because he does it best. Now the kite looks down at us from on high to see whether we're flying it properly, while it sways hither and thither depending on the way the wind's blowing. Meanwhile we sit on the edge of the field and chat about this and that. And sometimes we send messages to the kite asking what it's like up there. We tie these notes to the string of the kite and then the wind drives them higher and higher until they're right up high and there they stay.

What we like even more though is making bonfires. This is the best thing of all. First of all we go to Jirsák's and wait until Chris Jirsák is ready to put the goats out to graze and then we go with him. When we get to the field, we start running around and gathering dry grass and even old potato stalks in order to get a lot of inflammables. When we've found enough we set light to them. The fire crackles and blazes high up into the air, while the thick smoke stings our eyes. And we sit around the fire feeling happy and chatting about this and that.

And while we're sitting on the edge of the blaze each one of us pulls out a pipe that's called a 'calumet' in Red Indian dialect. Each boy makes one out of a chestnut, scooping out the insides in order to make the bowl of the pipe. A goose quill is attached to the bowl and through this you draw the smoke. We have a bout of heavy smoking with potato leaves in our pipes. They're not allowed to know about this at home or I'd never hear the end of it.

Our teacher doesn't know about it either because he says that smoking is a noxious habit which ruins your health and sends you to an early grave. But smoking is one thing I can do better then anyone. I know how to blow smoke rings, and everyone else tries to do it the way I do.

Smoking by the fire is something you must do if you're going to pow-wow about Red Indians who went on the warpath and laid siege to log cabins or one of the trains belonging to the Pacific Railroad with loud war cries and much spilling of blood. Or else we chat about Barbara Ubryková, who was once a nun in the olden days and was walled up although she was innocent. Otherwise we tell stories about a ghost who terrified people by going around with his head under his arms and howling horribly. When we talk about the headless spectre we do it in a hushed voice and keep looking around while the goats go on grazing.

Patch is always keen to come to the fields with us and so Eddie Kemlink brings him along and he barks at the goats and they want to butt him in return. Patch is wise to this and he always jumps out of the way in time, while his clever antics make us laugh. Eddie Kemlink says: "Patch, go fetch the goat." That gets Patch barking more and more.

Eve Svoboda asked me many times to take her along to the fire with us. I told her that I didn't know, I really didn't know about this and it's true that I hadn't a clue what to do, because making fires is a lad's thing, it's not for lasses. I was afraid that the boys would stare and Chris Jirsák might pull one of his horrible faces, even though I'm now on speaking terms with him.

But after a lot of pestering and her telling me she'd never have guessed I was so nasty, I said: "All right, come along then." But I didn't tell the lads anything about it and went straight to the fields with Eve after they were already there. When I got there with her I looked straight away to see whether the boys were going to stare and Chris make one of his horrible faces. He was already preparing a horrible face, but at that very moment Eve pulled out a paper cone full of roasted almonds and offered them to everyone. I realised from this that Eve was no fool, and everyone praised her for the almonds and said that she should come again pinching a few more from home, because roasted almonds are a treat for any boy. And Eve said that she'd filch more of the same, because she knew where they were kept, and no one at home knew that she was an almond thief.

Anthony Bejval offered her his pipe so that she could have a smoke too. She tried it and the first drag had her starting to cough and saying: "Yuk! That stuff will be the death of me." I told her she just wasn't used to it, because Red Indian wives smoked too and so did gypsy women and nothing happened to them. But Eve said she'd rather fetch some old grass and stalks and she baked potatoes in the ash and made sure that the fire didn't go out and this let us just sit there and have the time of our lives because we had someone to look after us. So sitting round the fire we were a six now, and Patch was pleased to see so many of us.

There are walnut-trees growing in the squire's garden. This year there were loads of walnuts on them and so a handful of us crept in there. When we got inside the gardener waved a stick and shouted at us: "You little urchins! It's time someone sorted you out good and proper." So off we ran, but with pocketfuls of walnuts which tasted really great. The only thing was that by the time the walnuts grew ripe in the squire's garden it was the end of the holidays and we couldn't take full advantage of them. Ma said that she was happy in some ways that school was starting again. At least she'd be rid of me, her little nuisance. Pa also claimed that it was time for school to resume. He said the holidays were nothing but trouble and they should be abolished, seeing that they made young people uppity and unruly. He said it was good that our teacher would have us under his control again, but on the other hand there would be a strain on the wallet paying for books and school equipment and those who passed the laws never asked themselves where he was supposed to get the money from for all this.

Christina teased me saying: "Little bumpkin, little bandit, now the holidays are ended," and I replied: "Wretched Rampusite, your last hour's come, I'll take your life." And we got into a big scuffle which could be heard as far away as the shop, which meant Ma arrived and said: "Christina, you've got even less sense than the child has. And to think that you're engaged to be married. I wonder who's going to wed someone as silly as you."

Christina laughed and went to wash the dishes while I was furious that I would soon have school again, which meant I would be going round in shoes and things like that. So I went to have a look at Bašta's bookshop, because students are always standing in front of the shop selling used textbooks. One of them was shouting: "Latin grammar, perfect condition, only three crowns," so I shouted: "Latin grammar, perfect condition, only three crowns," too, so that I could be like one of these students. Mr. Fajst was also there watching out to see whether the students touched their caps to him, but they didn't take any notice of him. This put him into a terrible rage and he spat and said: "So much for our young scholars, the hope of the nation."

We didn't learn anything during our first day back in school. All that happened was that the teacher had a roll call to see that we were all there. Our teacher was Mr. Veselík once again. He said to us: "Welcome back from your holidays, boys, I hope you are refreshed in body and soul in order to take your place as the pride of our nation and our local community, as well as of your parents and guardians." Then he had a whip-round to take a crown off those of us who were from better-off families. This is so the better-off can help poor pupils living out of town, and it's going to pay for soup to be dished out to them in winter. Charlie Páta is back in position at the front, looking pious with his hands on the desk. We were already supposed to be going home, but then someone wrote 'Muggins lives here' on Charlie Páta's back in chalk and at once I knew I was going to get blamed, though it was nothing to do with me. I know who did it, it was Michael Hanzal, because he was looking inside his pencil case and making out that he was counting his pens to make sure he had lots of them. I was kept in detention on the very first day back at school and I was thinking just let Charlie Páta wait, he'll have something coming to him from me for this.

When I got home Christina teased me with a song: "Birdie is a fool, he got detained at school, naughty little lout with his shirt hanging out." I said to her: "I'll make you pay for that, you rampaging Rampusite." And I thought hard about how I could get my own back on her but nothing came to me because I'd done everything I could to her already and she knew all my tricks. So this put me in a grump.

But then our tomcat Honza came to my rescue and so I was able to come up with my revenge. Our Honza is a clever ginger tom, the cleverest cat in town. Our Pa says that Honza definitely has a degree from the cat's college. He often has him in his lap and we all give him bones which he likes to suck dry.

I like to watch him when he's in a mood for catching the sparrows which fly into our courtyard in the hunt for scraps. Honza just sits there with eyes half-closed until they look like a couple of slashes on a page. He makes out that he's not watching, but he's watching all right. He lurks in wait for a sparrow that settles without taking care of itself. When such a sparrow arrives Honza crouches down till his stomach is trailing along the ground. He crawls along to the far side of the sparrow in order to outflank it and then all of a sudden springs on top of it. When, on the other hand, the sparrow spots him and flies off, Honza makes no display of annoyance, so that the sparrow doesn't think it was anything that mattered. He just licks himself and goes off without a care.

He only rarely catches a sparrow, it's more likely to be a mouse. He knows all about doing that. We've got a cesspit in the courtyard which has loads of mice in it. Honza sits right here by the hole where he doesn't move an inch. You can call out "Here, pussy!" and he won't so much as look up. When he spies a mouse he dives head first into the hole and grabs the mouse which can't escape. He likes catching it, though he doesn't eat it.

On one occasion we were sitting together for a lunch of potato dumplings with poppy seeds. I don't like them and so Pa always says they are good for the brain and that whoever eats potato dumplings fills his head with learning and becomes a scholar. The window was open and Honza jumped in with an enormous mouse in his teeth which he dumped on the table right in front of my father. This was his way of bragging about being a great hunter. Pa was startled and lashed out with his napkin while yelling in a terrible voice: "Ugh! Get that thing away from me!" Ma was startled too and yelled even more but the biggest screams of all came from Christina who said that it would be the death of her. Honza couldn't make out why they were yelling at him for catching mice so he picked the mouse up again and took it away with him, thinking to himself: "That's what I get for all the good I do you." We didn't see him again for a whole day because he was offended. He's very proud and left the mouse lying in the courtyard.

While the Rampusite was screaming her head off, I said to myself: "Now I've got you!" because I'd just thought up the perfect revenge. I took the dead mouse and stuffed it into the Rampusite's suitcase, the one that has pictures, laundry and papers of all sorts in it. Then I walked round her and made a face to look mysterious and took hold of a school book and made myself look busy studying the tributaries of the River Elbe. To Christina it was strange that I'd all of a sudden started learning about the tributaries of the Elbe, and so she went to look at her case.

I left the house and was outside when I heard the grisly sound of screaming and her terrified voice saying to Ma: "I'm giving in my notice, Ma'am. I'm not staying here a minute longer. It's more than I deserve."

Then they spent a while talking together. Christina was blubbering while Ma was calling out in a soft voice: "Peter! Where are you, little Pete. Your mother's got something to give you."

I heard her calling, went inside and asked: "What have you got for me?"

And Ma said, though without such a soft voice this time, in fact in quite a firm one: "Come here!"

So I went in, but bit by bit and stopping at the door.

Ma said: "Just come here." I asked why I had to go even nearer when I was already there, and took another step forwards. But Ma wanted me as near to her as possible and pointed with her finger to where I had to go and stand. But I didn't want to because I was thinking that this was all to do with the mouse and I was certainly going to be blamed for it.

Pa had been listening to all this in the shop and came into the room. He also wanted me to come nearer. Seeing that I didn't want to make a move, he caught hold of me by the ear and pulled me over to where he was standing. Then he asked: "Who put the mouse into Christina's case?"

I answered in a pitiful voice that it wasn't me and that yet again I was being blamed for everything.

"So it was me that did it, was it?" Pa asked.

I answered that he didn't do it either and started snivelling.

"So it must have been your mother after all?" said Pa.

I said that it wasn't Ma either.

Christina was standing there all this while and with such a grin on her face that I would have knocked her down and thumped her if Pa hadn't hold of me by the ears.

And Pa kept pressing me to say who the culprit was, asking whether Christina herself might have done it.

But I said nothing because I could see that all my denials were in vain. Ma said that lying was a great sin and that whoever tells a fib is also a thief.

"That's not true!" I said, "I don't steal things."

"Aha!" the Rampusite cried out, "That's caught him out!"

Then Pa took off his belt and holding my head between his knees gave me a thrashing on the back of my body that went on for ages. He stopped when Ma said that it was time to let me go and I then had to do my violin practice. I cried a lot and played 'The bagpipe song' and made terrible scraping sounds on purpose, grinding the bow against the strings until Pa yelled at me to stop saying that it was mashing up his brains and fiddling like that kept the customers away. Ma also said: "No more violin practice or I'll need serious medication."

So I left off and went outside and didn't cry any more.

I really like winter and can't wait for it to begin. I look out of the window every morning to see whether the ground is white but it never is. All it does is rain. It falls from the sky like pieces of string being twisted into plaits and there's a kind of grumpiness about the weather. When people call in at the shop they say: "Some weather, eh, Mr. Bajza?" Pa tells them: "What am I supposed to do about it? If it doesn't want to get any better, it won't."

I have to stay at home the whole time, and when Pa shuts up shop he checks whether I know the multiplication table or the catechism. If I get mixed up he takes me by the ear and says: "I shall instil some wisdom in you, you young rapscallion," and goes on to say that I've got to be more educated than he is even if he has to tear both my ears off to achieve this. Honza is lolling about under the stove in a constant doze. Nothing amuses him; not mouse, not bird, not anything. Sometimes I play ludo with Christina. If she wins she laughs until she can't get her breath back. Losing also makes her laugh because she's a silly goose and so it's no fun playing with her at all.

I was bored stiff because I'd read all my books, so I made friends with Otto Soumar. It happened like this. Mrs. Soumar was in the shop with Otto and bought some spirit for polishing metal and some vanilla. Otto said that he wanted to go round with me and that he had all the novels of Jules Verne. Mrs. Soumar asked me whether I'd like to be little Otto's friend. I replied: "Why not, it's all the same to me," and this made her laugh. She said that I could go to their place so I went there and Otto lent me 'Across the ocean on an ice floe' which is a great read with stupendous illustrations.

Pa said that he liked to see me going round to the Soumars, because they were better sorts and that meant I'd learn good manners, which would stand me in good stead in business circles. Then Ma told me that I should always say "At your service" at the Soumars, so that they'd know I was well brought up. I promised to do so, but I didn't say "At your service" and I wouldn't even say it if you offered me a bag of monkey nuts, because it causes me embarrassment.

The Soumars have a really nice place. It's like a chateau with one room leading to the next and the next to yet another and so on forever. They've got a sofa with coloured cushions and a dresser full of gold and silver and little cups. There's a jaguar skin on the floor and pictures and everything you can think of.

And Otto has a gynormous amount of toys. The best is an electric train set, which runs of its own accord when you switch on the current. So off we go in the train. I'm the conductor which means I shout "All aboard!" in a loud voice. Little Otto is the driver and keeps ringing his bell. The only thing is that the governess keeps sitting in the same room knitting a sweater and keeping an eye on us all the time, making sure that we don't cause any trouble and always lecturing us about keeping quiet. Finally I lost my temper and said: "Strike a light, Miss, what makes you think we're yelling?" after which she had a word with Mrs. Soumar in case her little Otto picked up bad habits from me. Mrs. Soumar replied to her in some strange dialect and patted me on the head.

On the whole it's pretty fantastic at the Soumars and I always get tea with raspberry syrup and sweet cakes there. I can help myself whenever I want, which is terrific. Chris Jirsák told me that I suck up to Otto because he's rich, but I said to him: "That's not true, you puddingheaded Krakonosh. Besides, you'd like to be mates with him yourself." And sure enough, when he heard that Otto had lent me his Jules Verne novels he made out that he was my best friend and started sucking up himself.

The only fly in the ointment is that little Otto keeps having to stay in bed while they put a thermometer in his armpit to check that he hasn't caught any colds and he has to take his medicine. I got fed up with this and I don't go there any more. Besides, I've read all his Jules Vernes.

Now I go round to the Zilvars, the people from the poorhouse. That's the most fabulous place of all, but I don't say anything about it at home because they'd only be against it. Mr. Zilvar was in the Great War, during which he was wounded by enemy gunfire. So he goes begging from house to house and has a wooden leg. I'd like to have a leg like that and I long for one so much that it gives me dreams in which I go around with a wooden leg that makes a heavy 'Plonk! Plonk!' sound and people come running out of their homes, each one of them marvelling at my wooden leg, with me feeling very proud. I've set my heart on mending my ways, and when they're mended I'll ask the family to give me a wooden leg for Christmas, and then the lads will really have something to see.

The poorhouse also has some ladies who go begging and they spend every evening counting what they've been able to beg during the day, and then they get into arguments. Mr. Zilvar can't stand it when they argue a lot. He unfastens his leg and flings it at the old hags and then they stop arguing. Zilvar boasted that his pa's the chief beggar because he gets the most money and so the others have to listen to what he says. He coughs a lot in the night because of a blood clot. He told me this and was very proud of it.

All the time I wanted to get hold of this leg, if only just to be able to touch it, and Zilvar said "Wait till Dad's asleep. I'll take the leg off and we can play with it."

So that's what happened. When Mr. Zilvar was asleep he removed the leg and I was overjoyed. We played at begging and I was the cripple. Zilvar was everyone else. I walked around asking people for alms. Zilvar played someone who gave help and then someone who didn't. What he did best was play someone who didn't. When he played a big shot with a plaque on his door saying 'Helping the local needy', he always put on a swagger, rolled his eyes about in a horrible way and said: "The answer for the workshy is to do some work" or "Be off with you, there's far too many of your sort round here." Or else he played a policeman and said: "Hop it, you tramp. I've warned you twice already. Get out of my sight and don't let me have to tell you again or I'll be taking you somewhere you don't like." And then he took hold of me and hauled me up before the village authorities.

What a game that was! We had a great time with the leg while Mr. Zilvar slumbered on and coughed in his sleep. When I told Bejval all about it he was full of envy and said that he wanted to play with us too. I said to him: "I don't know about that. It all depends."

But he was all eager and went on about it. He made out he wanted to see whether we played the game properly.

I told him that we weren't worried about that, and that Zilvar must surely know how to play a beggar properly because his pa was the top beggar in town.

Bejval asked whether we stopped off for a drop of the hard stuff if we managed to beg something. I told him we didn't and he said that was a mistake.

Then he asked whether we played a musical instrument while begging and I said no. Then he said that was our second mistake.

So I told him to come to the poorhouse and he said that he'd come to show us how to beg and that the real Mr. Zilvar would be reaching into his own pocket at the sight of Tony's begging and would be wide-eyed in amazement at the way Bejval played the beggar just right. This awful boasting of his went on all the time and I didn't like it.

But when we got to the poorhouse Zilvar said to us there'd be no more begging because his pa had found out that he'd taken his leg. He'd yelled at him that he wasn't going to let his leg be messed about with and he'd thrashed him a few times. Then he'd taken the leg and gone begging.

Winter is now here. Snow is falling, the ground is white all over and the crested larks inspect the horse droppings. Beautiful frosty stars appear on the windowpanes. And our shop is full of people buying almonds and raisins because Christmas is coming. Ma and Pa see to them and they say: "Winter's come again then, Mr. Bajza," and Pa says: "Right enough. It's bitterly cold out there. Who's next, please?"

If you ask me I don't really look forward to Christmas presents because I never get what I want. They always give me something I need, which is a swizz because they'd have to buy it for me anyway, so there's nothing to be over the moon about. Besides I've got everything already – winter shoes, sweater with a zip, tracksuit, a sled and a hockey stick. And if they were to ask me seriously what I'd like then I'd have to tell them that most of all I'd like a wooden leg like the one Mr. Zilvar has, because that would make everyone envy me, most of all Anthony Bejval. And if they didn't want to put a leg under the Christmas tree for me then I'd ask whether I could be let off violin lessons and if that wasn't possible either then could I at least have an album full of foreign stamps.

On the other hand I never say what I want, seeing that they'd call me a spoilt urchin and a mischief-maker and would say I was never going to make anything of myself and Pa would scream at me in a horrible voice that I must leave the house and that he didn't want to set eyes on me and then I'd have to spend a whole hour scraping the violin. I've already skipped three violin lessons because the teacher's been giving me stick for having a bow that was dirty as a boot and asking me why I haven't cleaned it.

I love everything else about Christmas, though. We always have a bathtub with carp swimming about in it opening their mouths. Dad keeps coming back from the shop, looking at them and saying "They're real whoppers." Mum slices the almonds, Christina sorts the raisins and I nick them while they keep telling me to clear off. Our Honza goes round the kitchen with his tail up in the air like a magic wand while he sniffs at everything. Mum and Dad and the Rampusite stamp their feet at the sight of him and say in a loud voice: "There's no need to go sniffing everything. No one asked you in here. Be off with you, there's nothing here for the likes of you. Scarper!" And off Honza goes. As he picks his way across the courtyard he steers clear of the snow because it freezes his paws.

On Christmas Eve the shop shuts early and if anyone's forgotten to buy something they go round the back door. When evening comes everyone speaks in soft tones, with only Mirabelle crying at the top of her voice, but she cries whether it's a holiday or not, having no idea of the difference. But as for me, I do hardly anything wrong at all, seeing that I'm no longer a baby.

Whatever he gets as presents, Pa is full of Christmas spirit and game for anything. This year, just like the other years, he was given slippers and said: "What a surprise, just look at these!" and kissed Ma. Ma got a woollen shawl and said "You shouldn't have!" and kissed Pa. I knew that I'd get mittens and so I did. In return I had to say "Thank you" in a loud voice while to myself I said: "That didn't break the bank, did it?" And Christina got cloth for a dress and a bowl of apples, figs and nuts, just like the ones we have in the shop, and kissed Ma on the hand. She sat in the kitchen cracking nuts and crying, because she was depressed. Then she borrowed pen and ink from me and wrote a letter home.

Then we had carp, strudel and tea, and played cards for nuts afterwards, a game I always won. Honza went out on the prowl and Dad grumbled that the cat wouldn't even stay in on Christmas Eve and I had to go to bed early.

Our Lawrence came to see us at Christmas . He wore a blue sweater and asked everyone "How much do you think this sweater set me back?" and was overjoyed that no one guessed correctly. He had yellow gloves too, not to mention white gaiters on his legs and he stank of something fragrant. When he spoke to someone he screwed up his left eye and Pa told him off for doing this. He brought me a box of water colours which had two sets of eight colours inside, including silver and gold paint. He talked like a grown-up, reminding me to keep studying hard so that I would have a better life than he, seeing that he had to work hard all the time. And he said that he had to go to the barber because his beard grew too quickly.

He was always hanging around the shop to see how we were doing and whether business was brisk. People said: "What a grown-up lad you have, Mr. Bajza," and Pa replied: "Time flies, right enough." Then the people came back with "At least you'll have someone to take over from you one day" and Pa said "That'll be the day!"

Whenever Christina saw him she burst out laughing and couldn't drink her coffee in front of him because she started choking on it and ran outside and Ma said: "When will that girl get some brains inside her head!" Larry kept asking how I was doing at school. He had his nose in my exercise books and he also wanted me to play something on the violin to him and asked me whether I knew about double stops. I told him that we were already playing in three sharps and three flats, but I didn't want to play to him. He spoke with a deep voice and walked around at a slow pace and kept saying that his beard grew quickly and did so faster than that of the senior shop assistant. I didn't like the fact he was so vain and told him that he didn't have any beard at all. He said "Touch it and see," but that was something I didn't want to do and I told him once more that there was nothing growing and he didn't need to visit any barber. He felt insulted and wanted me to give back the water colours as a punishment, but Pa said: "Once given, forever gone. Leave off and stop arguing." On Christmas afternoon Pa gave Larry a cigar and told him to go with him to the pub, because he wanted to show people what a grown-up son he had. They smoked their cigars and went off to the pub while Ma stared after them.

We had goose for lunch on St. Stephen's Day, and it was getting on for noon when Christina looked out of the window and shouted in a loud voice: "Goodness gracious! My lady, I do believe that it's the Vařekas coming to see us."

So Ma looked out of the window too and said: "So it is. You mustn't say a word about the goose we're having for lunch."

Shortly afterwards Uncle Silas and Aunt Emily arrived to wish us Merry Christmas. Ma sat them down at the table and treated them to home-made brandy and almond cakes which they went on eating. They started by talking about the freezing weather which was not going to go on but would ease off. They said this would be a good thing because otherwise they'd burn too much coal. They went on to talk about various illnesses and the fact that everything cost more than it used to. Then Aunt Emily asked what we were having for lunch.

Ma said "Well I've done some potatoes. It's really hard to know what to put into the pot nowadays."

"Potatoes?" came the reply from Uncle and Aunt, while they looked at each other as if surprised.

Pa said it was no surprise, since business was just so bad.

At that moment I went to the stove and opened the oven which released a strong scent. My aunt got to her feet and went to the kitchen to have a look. Then she said in a thin voice: "So that's potatoes. I'm a Dutchman."

I was pleased that they were furious. Uncle said: "So much for your sincerity. If you think we came here to eat you out of house and home, then you can think again. We don't need anything like that. In fact we don't need or want anything from anyone." His whiskers twitched while he was speaking.

Aunt Emily also said that they never asked for anything from anyone, because there was nothing to be expected from them. She said they'd come to pay a visit to their relatives, but now it was plain as a pikestaff what we were like and besides we'd never given them anything worth having.

She made quite a speech but then Uncle said "Come on, my dear, it's just not worth it."

Then Aunt Emily said "Shame on you," and off they went.

As they went, Ma looked out of the window and saw how they stopped to talk to Mr. Fajst. They spoke and he nodded and they all nodded towards our house and made all sorts of movements with their hands.

Then Ma turned back from the window and when she looked at Pa she had to laugh, and when Pa looked at her he had to laugh too and they both started laughing more and more and then I started laughing because they were laughing and then Christina in the kitchen was laughing and squealing and having coughing fits and shouting: "Oh dear, you'll be the death of me."

And we were still laughing over lunch, until Pa said in a stern voice: "That's enough. Moderation in all things," and after lunch he went to lie down. And Ma was still tittering while she tidied some clothes in the wardrobe.

But our Lawrence didn't laugh at all. In the evening he walked around the town square with a girl, smoking a cigar, speaking in a deep voice and feeling very proud of himself.

And as he was taking his shoes off when he got back home he said that he'd been through thick and thin in his life but now the course of his career was clear. I wanted to say to him "You still can't grow a beard," but I felt sleepy so I nodded off instead.

A lot of snow came down. There was more and more of it and this made me glad. So I got out my toboggan and popped round to see Eve Svoboda, because she'd asked me to pick her up. Then we went to Budín, a place where there's great sledging. Loads of boys were there already, as well as other children. When we were right up at the top we sat on the toboggan. I was in front and Eve was behind holding on to me.

We went downhill really quickly, faster and faster until we were bombing down really fast, Eve clinging to me tight-ly. It was fantastic. We sprayed frozen snow in all directions and I could hear the wind howling 'Woooo!' Eve gave fright-ened whoops but I told her not to be afraid when I was at the helm, for nothing could go wrong then. She said that she'd never again be scared when she was with me, but she'd whoop all the same because we were going so fast.

Anthony Bejval said that so much snow was a good thing. It meant that we could play at Eskimoes. So we made igloos and Bejval said: "I am Nanook, man of nature." We all recognised him as Nanook and paid him homage. Then we made out that we were hunting whales and seals and polar bears. Otto Soumar joined us and we told him that he was a polar bear and had been shot. So he lay down and played dead. We cut off his paws and roasted them over a fire and said they were very tasty. But then his governess came to get him, took hold of his hand and said that if little Otto caught pneumonia she wasn't going to take the blame for it. We said that it wouldn't be our fault either, seeing that Otto chose of his own accord to be a bear, play dead and have his paws cut off which we'd pretend to eat. And Bejval added that it was no fun playing with Otto and anyway there were others queuing to take his place as a dead polar bear.

One after another we said "Count me out! I'm not playing!" and we stopped the game and went home and I was afraid that Otto might catch a chill and once again I'd get blamed for it all. On the way back Bejval said to us: "Folks, I've invented a brilliant game, a terrific game, something you've never ever seen before."

We asked him at once what sort of game it was, but he said that he was not going to tell us on purpose, seeing that we'd only shout about it from the rooftops. We said that we'd never do any such thing, but Bejval didn't want to say a word about it until we'd sworn ourselves to secrecy in a loud voice.

Then he said: "OK then." He went on to say that he was going to visit Johnny Pivec, who sold carbide. He and Johnny were thick as thieves and Johnny would give him whatever he wanted in the way of carbide.

We asked him what he was going to do with the carbide and he replied with a knowing wink: "You'll see." We gave knowing winks back but we didn't really know why. The next thing that happened was that Bejval told us to turn up at his house in the evening and we told him we'd be there.

When evening came along we arrived at Bejval's place. We were a four: besides me there was Eddie Kemlink, Chris Jirsák and Zilvar.

Zilvar stuck two fingers into his mouth and whistled really loudly. This brought Bejval to the window and he told us he'd be down straight away.

He came out and I said to him: "Got the stuff?" "You bet," he replied, and showed me a bag full of carbide. There was ever so much of it.

Then we set off. Bejval said nothing and we kept quiet too as he led us off to the fields. When we got there Bejval asked us if we knew that when carbide mixes with water it produces a gas which gives off a bright light when you set fire to it.

We told him that we knew this and I said that I'd once seen a carbide lamp at a fun fair, where the Turkish delight seller was using one.

Bejval said it was good that we knew this and then explained to us all about this invention of his which was going to give us such a good time.

There was loads of snow lying in the fields. We buried the carbide in the snow and when it was just about covered we struck a match and held it to the carbide for a while. In a short while it began to hiss sharply. Then it caught light and burnt with a bright flame. Whoever didn't know that there was carbide beneath would have thought that the snow was burning and that would have struck him as very odd.

Then we stood back and when we stood back the flames blazed right up and made it light all around us and we had a great time.

I have to point out that we were on the route Mr. Fajst always follows in the early evening when it is getting dark and he is off to a certain farmhouse in the village of Dlouhá Ves. He gets milk there which he uses to make gruel since he lives alone and has no one to cook for him. So we lay in wait for Mr. Fajst to come along.

And so it was. Mr. Fajst came along, holding his jug of milk and he looked around and saw the flames blazing up from the snow and gave a loud shriek and dropped his jug and we heard him saying: "By all the heavenly hosts, this is a sight to lay me low."

So we laughed ourselves silly and leaped high into the air. We were laughing the whole way home about Mr. Fajst being laid low and when I went to bed I was still laughing. When I came round in the morning Ma asked me what I had been dreaming about to make me laugh in my sleep.

From that time forth Mr. Fajst spread it far and wide that the path to Dlouhá Ves was haunted, telling the tale of when he went for milk and met Mr. Humpál, the tippler who'd died the year before because the spirits inside him caught fire. He said that the dead body stood in his way with flames coming out of its mouth and supposedly took hold of Mr. Fajst by a button and said "Oh Fajst, Fajst, remember and repent, you old sinner."

And Mr. Fajst said that after the fright he'd had he went down with gripe and had to take to his bed and because of this he's never been right since.

There are two picture halls in our town and both put on great shows. One is in 'The National Institute' while the other is in 'The People's Institute.' On Saturday and Sunday they both have something on. In the National they show silent films and it always looks as if it's drizzling on the screen and Mr. Stuchlík, who keeps the books in a factory, puts something on the gramophone to accompany them. There are cowboys in these films and they're always on horseback lassoing and firing their evolvers and going after robbers. Or else there's some man who loves a woman, and then there's yet another man who loves this woman too, but she doesn't want him and this man, he would like to be rich, and because he hasn't got any money he murders someone to get some and therefore he has to go to the electric chair and this is the point where Mr. Stuchlík changes the record and plays something very solemn.

Still better are those films which are set in the jungle where there's a maharajah who rides an elephant where he sits beneath some kind of canopy and his army follows him. These are Indian soldiers who have turbans on their heads and some kind of rag round their waists. Otherwise they're stark naked making their way through a jungle full of pythons and tigers and other wild animals.

Then there are those great comedies where some man is always falling into water and getting drenched from head to foot or else a man hits another man in the face with a custard pie and this other man doesn't like it and hits the first man in the face with a custard pie too and their eyes are covered in whipped cream so they can't see. It has us in stitches!

Sometimes our teacher takes a crown off each of us and then the whole class goes to the picture house but only to see films like how to get logs downstream or how to do highland dancing in circles or how to blow glass. There's no point in going to see such stuff really, but at least it's better than having lessons.

We boys, or those of us who are on speaking terms, don't go to the National because the windows there are high up. We'd rather go to the People where the windows are low. One of us pays the entrance fee, and then when the lights go out in the cinema he can help the rest in through a window so that they don't have to pay. We prefer to spend the money they gave us at home for the tickets to buy liquorice or those suckable candy sticks or sugar sticks or sweet shoe laces as well as salami sticks.

It was Zilvar who thought up this way of going to the pictures because his pa would never give him a crown to pay the entrance fee. So we sit inside the playhouse really pleased about the fact we're there for free. We did this many times and we were a handful who crept in through the window. Besides me there was Zilvar, Bejval, Jirsák and Kemlink. Once we took Victor Štěpánek with us but he couldn't make head nor tail of the film because he's still too little.

But once a boy was mad at us because he paid for his ticket and we didn't, and he ratted on us to Mr. Maule who checks the tickets. In a stern voice Mr. Maule asked us to show him our tickets. We told him we'd already shown them to him and he said we had to show them to him again. Bejval told him loftily that there was no law requiring us to keep showing our tickets and Mr. Maule became cross and shouted at the top of his voice: "Hop it! Get out right now." Bejval said that we were on our way and there was no need for him to start yelling.

So out we went, but when the intermission was over and the cinema was dark we climbed in once again, eager to discover how things had turned out in the film. So when the lights went up again and Mr. Maule spotted us he cried out in a shrieking voice: "Jesus Christ, when wilt thou take this cup of sorrows away from me, wherefore must I always be wasting my time on these reprobates?" and he roared at us: "Out of my sight now, you little bastards, or I will hand you over to the police for a hiding."

Bejval said to him that there was no need to fly off the handle at the drop of a hat. Besides, he should mind his language because we were not bastards and if Mr. Maule was going to say a thing like that again then the matter would have to be passed on to a lawyer.

Mr. Maule opened his eyes wide and said simply: "Well I never! Did you hear that? This is what you get from young people today!" while we ran for it.

But this didn't stop us doing it again and one day I told Eve Svoboda about it. She looked at me all astonished and I liked her being all astonished by me, so I told her about it all over again and I kept telling her and she said that she'd like to try it herself and I came back with "I don't know about that, I really don't, you need a lot of courage for something like this," and she begged me to take her with me and get her into the playhouse through the window.

So I did what she wanted after she'd done a lot of begging, but later I was sorry that I'd done so. One of us offered her a hand from inside the cinema while I pushed her from behind and with this massive effort she finally made it through. If only she'd at least kept quiet, but no, she had to laugh all the time while people went "Shhh!" and turned in their seats.

And this was a time when it was a really smashing film. There was this actor who flew in an aeroplane to California because he had to free his beautiful beloved from the clutches of some robbers. He had to fly really quickly in order to get there before an express train. There was a storm and forked lightning and the wind was blowing a gale and our eyes were glued to the screen. And that was the moment when Mr. Maule chucked us out.

Then we stood outside the picture house waiting until people came out from the film. Mr. Lokvenc and his wife came out and Bejval went up to them and said "Hello sir" politely and asked: "If you please, Mr. Lokvenc, did the actor manage to free his beloved from the clutches of those robbers?" But Mr. Lokvenc gave a nasty chuckle and said nothing.

But we found out what happened anyway: the actor really did free his beloved from the clutches of the robbers and shot them all dead and then the beautiful beloved became his wife.

The winter was a very long one this year. Neither I nor boys who were much older than me could remember such a long winter. The daft snow stayed for ever, there was always a hard nip in the air from the frost and it was terribly dark all the time. I didn't like it at all and nor did the other boys and we all said that things were much better in the spring.

But one day I woke up and heard a rat-a-tat-tat and a drumming sound on the roof and all at once I knew that the seasons were changing. This made me so happy that I jumped out of bed all on my own without needing to be dragged out by the Rampusite and in a terrifying voice I started singing 'Here's the spring, it's coming.' Dad heard me from inside the shop and told me to leave it out.

And when I went off to school there was a strong wind which wanted to blow my cap away and I came across the Bejvals' furniture waggon. Jacob was striding beside the waggon with a runny nose. He made a face at me and said: "Look who it isn't – clever clogs," and I said to him: "Jacob, give me a ride," and he said "Sure thing" and found me a place.

So I went to school by waggon and Jacob let me take the reins and I called out: "Gee up!" in a really deep voice and glanced around to see whether the boys were looking my way. When I saw that they were I felt proud.

' I hardly paid any attention at school, because I was thinking that it would be so nice if I could go up and away, far and wide in a furniture waggon and visit other lands, and so I was in disgrace and made to stand in the corner.

And then the clouds parted and everywhere it was really blue and the sun shone fiercely and when we left school we ran quickly making a lot of noise and the birds were noisy too and kept messing around with each other. Streams of water poured along the streets and small children were making mud cakes but we were big children and so we sailed boats in the stream or built water-mills. Or else we played hide-and-seek and I hid inside a concrete pipe and no one could find me. And I climbed a tree with Eve Svoboda and there we read a book about sailors together and her pa came out of his shop and shouted "Eve! Eve!" but she didn't respond as it was such a good read. And our Honza started to go out on the prowl and was forever away and after something and when he came home he was black all over because he'd been climbing high and far and he had a torn ear.

Soon after this it became really pleasant. Cabbage white butterflies played on the mud and everything started turning green and our teacher told us that we should pay close attention to nature and learn to give the right names to all the plants and animals.

One day Anthony Bejval came to pick me up and said that we had to go to the river and see the ice floes and I said to him: "Wait a mo," and then I sneaked off secretly so that I didn't have to look after Mirabelle because Christina was unable to, owing to her being away at the big wooden wash-tub rinsing the laundry. So off we went and Eddie Kemlink was with us, though he couldn't bring Patch along. This is because Patch was always hanging around the building site and scrounging titbits from the bricklayers and he ended up falling into lime and his coat was singed and now he's not so well. Chris Jirsák and Zilvar, the boy from the poorhouse, joined us too, and so we were a four.

When we got to the river we found it making a ter-rible racket with the ice breaking and a grisly whining sound coming from the depths. This was great fun and we watched it all from the bridge and when we lifted our heads back up we felt as if the ground and everything on it was flying backwards at great speed.

And then the boys from across the fields failed to arrive at school because the way there was covered in water. The train didn't run either because the track was under water, and the meadow turned into a gigantic lake.

One day Mr. Světelský, who is a caretaker in the factory, came dashing into the town in his fireman's uniform. He ran as far as our house and sounded a bugle. Then he rushed off to another house and again sounded the bugle and then he kept on bugling. And people shouted out: "The floods are coming!" I shouted the same thing and so did all the lads.

There was a great posse of us now and we ran to the river and when we got there we saw that the town slaugh-terhouse was already under water and many homes were in water up to their waists and a few had water up to their necks. Then we saw some dead hens, some cupboards and beds carried by the current and the fire brigade were moving from house to house in boats, sailing in through windows in order to rescue people and their possessions. And we, being already grown-up lads with strength in our limbs, also helped to prevent people drowning. And we helped one little old lady into a boat and two children who were howling horribly and the old lady was complaining that her goat would drown so we went to the goat-shed to find it. We were in water up to the chin but we freed the goat which tried to resist but there was nothing doing and we got it into the boat. I noticed Chris Jirsák over-acting about being brave. He was always crossing himself and then plunging into danger and so I said to him: "Stop showing off, Krakonosh the mountain sprite," and he told me that he wasn't showing off and that once the water level had fallen he'd give me what for because I'd called him names. And he seemed very proud of himself, being so vain.

Everybody praised us for being so brave and we also got praise from our teacher when he said that our actions were words written in golden letters and Chris Jirsák put his hand up to say he'd written the most because he'd saved all his neighbours. The teacher laughed at this and we all joined him in loud laughter which put Jirsák into a huge strop.

And when the flood was over we started throwing stones at each other. Jirsák started it and then we moved on to fighting each other with pencil cases and the grown-ups said: "Just look at you, and you are supposed to be young scholars!" and so we went further away and then started fighting some more.

And when we were off to violin practice Jirsák swiped me across the head with his violin-case and said: "That's for calling me Krakonosh," and I swiped him across the head with my violin-case in return. And we would have repeated this exercise several times but Mr. Rektorys, the one who was going to give us the violin lesson, saw what we were doing from his window and shouted: "Wretched boys, if you don't stop this pushing and shoving straight away I'm going to be getting in touch with your parents." So we left off and I said to Jirsák: "You've got it coming," and he said that I'd got it coming too and we both knew that we'd have to have another scrap another time so this could finally get sorted out.

So I vowed I'd no longer go round with Jirsák because of what he was like, and when I told Bejval he said that he wouldn't go round with him either and that none of the boys was going to do so. He could go round on his own, and if he tried to suck up to the others then we'd tell him to stop toadying.

And the weather got better and better. Everything turned green, the cherry trees blossomed and the students took off their coats while they were playing pool in the pub. And one time, it was just before noon, Mr. Dušánek, who works for the local council, was going around town with posters under his arm, a mug full of paste and a brush. He stopped at every corner and those of us who went round together followed behind him because we were eager to know what was going on. Anthony Bejval was keenest of all and he asked: "Mr. Dušánek, what's it all about?" and Mr. Dušánek replied: "Pipe down and buzz off home so Mum can deal with your fleas," and he said other things that were really nasty because the wind was catching hold of his posters.

And when he'd pasted up a poster it turned out to be a fantastically big one full of pictures and we read the words:

NOT TO BE MISSED!
ONLY HERE FOR A FEW DAYS!
THE GRAND CIRCUS RUDOLPHI!
INTERNATIONAL SENSATION!

Then came more information in capitals saying that the Grand Circus Rudolphi was letting it be known to everyone in this most worthy and esteemed locality that this was the greatest act in the world, guaranteeing the most varied of programmes and leaving all those who were connoisseurs of circus entirely satisfied.

The Grand Circus Rudolphi had performed before all sorts of emperors and kings, not to mention presidents and ministers of state, winning accolades and appreciation from the aristocracy, the high and mighty and even the mayors of towns and villages.

And then it went on to say that this illustrious audience will be able to set eyes on the King of the Desert, a huge Nubian lion, whose terrifying roar tears the natives in Africa from their slumbers. Moreover everyone will stand aghast as a Bengal tiger, terror of the jungle, is put through its paces, or stare goggle-eyed at a fearsome serpent, known also as an Indian rock python, devourer of live rabbits and other creatures, the devouring to be witnessed during a live show.

Devotees of daredevil derring-do will have a rare opportunity to see that world-famous acrobatic troupe the Abaldini brothers, who were awarded a gold medal at a world exhibition in San Francisco for their top-notch performances.

The programme is enriched still further by freestyle Graeco-Roman wrestling. The masked man, master of the world and all its colonies, will challenge all-comers in the ring and anyone who is able to beat him will receive a most worthy prize.

The world famous circus rider Miss Arabella will display examples of her artistry which have dazzled audiences the world over. This is her Bohemian debut! You will never have a chance like this again!

Also Jumbo the Indian elephant! And a troupe of performing dogs, darlings of every audience!

The circus owner Signor Rudolphi will make a personal appearance riding his thoroughbred mare Kismet.

In the intervals between performances the most distinguished audience will be entertained by the side-splitting antics of those jesters extraordinaires, Pif and Paf.

At the bottom of the poster there was a note to say that schoolchildren and servicemen could get in for half price.

We went on following Mr. Dušánek so that we could see all the posters and the exotic animals that were being pasted up, the clowns and the circus rider, the elephant, giraffe and lion and other creatures. So I was late for lunch and Pa said that he was not going to wait at the beck and call of His Lordship before starting.

I said nothing to these words of his but simply drank my soup which had drops of batter in it, even though I don't like it, and looked a picture of virtue. When I'd finished eating lunch I said in a loud voice: "Thank you, God, for these thy blessings," and Pa looked at Ma and Ma looked at Pa and then for a while each looked at the other.

After lunch I looked after Mirabelle and sang to her 'Youth's magic never returns' and I went on singing for a long time, till Ma said I should leave off and go get the newspaper for Pa. I didn't answer her back and ran off at a fair pace.

Eddie Kemlink called in the afternoon and wanted me to go off with him because all the boys were waiting for me. I answered in a voice loud enough for Pa to hear me in the shop that I wasn't going anywhere because I had to do an exercise with fractions in order to make sure I knew them.

I didn't have even a tincy wincy scrap with the Rampusite, although she tried to start one herself. But I answered back in a soft voice with "Dear Christina, pray let me alone and I'll do the same to you."

I practised on the violin of my own accord and I tried a double-stop and some trills and I tried to play without scraping it and Pa heard me in the shop and gave a murmur of content.

Every now and then I went to the shop and said "Hello" to the customers in a loud voice, winning the praise of one farmer's wife for being well brought up. Pa was pleased, and so I started greeting everyone in a louder and louder voice until Pa told me that there was no need to shout so much. I also helped out in the shop and one gentleman said: "Such a wee scrap, you can hardly see him behind the counter and he's already full of business sense."

At school I sat up straight and didn't even fidget much and kept my hands on my desk. I was careful to pay attention and kept putting my hand up. I was nice when I spoke to Charlie Páta and Christopher Jirsák made one of his faces at me to say that I was sucking up. And Zilvar said that I was no fun at all and I said that I wasn't going to go round with him any more since he would only get me to depart from the straight and narrow.

I walked slowly feeling righteous and looking pious, because I wanted to be extra good and the best behaved of all. Every evening I searched my conscience to make sure that I was the best behaved, and it always seemed to me that I wasn't the best behaved yet and must improve my behaviour still more. And when I met Mrs. Soumar I bellowed at her "I beg the pleasure of your acquaintance" in such a fearsome voice that everyone turned round.

On one occasion Pa was drinking coffee and when he'd finished it he put down his mug and said: "Mother, there's something about our Peter that concerns me. Do you think perhaps he's unwell? He never makes a noise nowadays."

Ma replied: "I don't think there's anything wrong with him. He's not gone off his food."

"If you ask me it's some piece of mischief and he's afraid of it coming out into the open," said Pa.

But I hadn't done anything and I wasn't going to do anything either, although I could have made mischief galore. I could have dragged away the fruit cart belonging to the bleating goat of a greengrocer, something Zilvar from the poorhouse egged me on to do, and pushed it down the hill. She would have screamed her head off. I had every chance of doing this because nobody was looking. I had good opportunities for all kinds of mischief, but I did nothing on purpose. I got it into my head that I would be a model of good behaviour in everything.

I was sorry now that we'd frittered away the money we'd been saving for our trip to Italy! Though I was against it, Eddie Kemlink kept pushing us to buy firecrackers, saying that they wouldn't do any harm. So we bought them and then Eddie said that there was nothing we could do with the bits of change left so we bought a thriller called 'Murder in the Strongroom', more suckable candy sticks and carob bread and then we went to a friendly between the Soumar XI and the Summer away team made up of clerks from Herman's Factory. So when the circus came along we didn't have a penny and so we had to be good all the time. I had become so good that I used proper language and said things like 'notwithstanding' and 'in consequence' all the time. Pa said: "Leave it out with the 'notwithstanding', I find it gets on my nerves."

So I walked here and there sadly thinking to myself that in the end the circus would move on and I wouldn't be seeing it. Every evening I said a prayer which I'd made up myself: "Dear Lord, please let me see all the circus acts, as well as feeding time for the beasts of prey, which is half-price. Must all the boys be there and only I forbidden to go? I promise Thee that I will go to church with zeal and that if I have a writing exercise I will be careful to get an 'excellent' for presentation and not to make a single smudge."

"Do not, O Lord God, permit Pa to say: 'Forget about going to any circus, it's throwing money out of the window and anyway where's one supposed to get the money from? You'll only pick up bad habits there, nothing else. It'll stuff your head full of mischievous ideas.'"

"But rather let him say: 'Do go to the circus. Here's the money and have a good time.'"

"For this, O Lord, thou mayest do with me what thou wilt. I will always be good, even if the boys grumble that I've turned into Little Lord Fauntleroy. Not once will I dodge my violin practice or get into a scrap or throw stones and I will take care not to spill anything at lunch. And I will be a picture of virtue and walk in the correct manner and think good thoughts and speak properly and speak up when I greet people. And I don't care who, so that even includes Mr. Fajst."

"And I will not become pals with anyone who'll egg me on to mischief, and I will not get chummy with street urchins. When there's something going on I won't join in. And I will never make war but I will love my neighbours, even the Habrováks and the Ješiňáks."

"When Ma says: 'Fetch this, Pass that, Hold this, Serve that,' then I will fetch, pass, hold and serve and I will never carp."

"Upon my soul this is the truth."

"This is the prayer which I have made up because we haven't have got that far in our Religious Education lessons. Amen."

When I'd finished praying, I slept badly, and in my sleep I had a hideous dream. I dreamed that I was locked in a cage with a Bengal tiger which made horrible faces at me because it wasn't really a Bengal tiger, it was Christopher Jirsák, but I couldn't know this because I was asleep. The Bengal tiger said: "Oh yes siree, young man, we're off to the circus! That'll be the day! Off you go to do your lessons!"

And we boys, who go round together, went to New Square every day to see whether the circus had come and the wait was getting really long.

Until one day five circus waggons arrived. They were red, yellow, blue and green and they had flowers all over them which were carved and beautifully painted.

They had little rooms in the waggons and inside the rooms were tiny little stoves, pictures, mirrors, beds and even kitchen things.

They also had a goat and loads of dogs and masses of squabbling kids.

Then there were still more waggons of a different kind and you could hear a terrible roaring sound from them because wild animals were locked inside and there was a strange pong around these waggons.

And men came out of the waggons, all of them with lots of hair, smoking fags and talking loudly. They wore stripey T-shirts and sported bare arms with all sorts of figures, flowers and symbols tattooed on them – and yes, they even had some sayings tattooed on their arms, which was something I specially liked.

And they brought the cages out of the waggons. There were really sweet little monkeys in them searching for fleas in their fur, looking really worried with lots of wrinkles on their foreheads. Christopher Jirsák learned to furrow his forehead just as they did, and this made us all laugh.

There was also a huge bear with a shaggy coat which shuffled around and grumbled something we couldn't follow.

All the time we were standing and watching to see what would happen, while the hairy men put up a tent and yelled at each other as they did so. It was an incredibly big tent. You could fit all the boys from the junior school into it and even those in the middle school. You could get the girls' school in as well. And in one waggon a woman was sitting at the window and she was supposed to be selling tickets.

I told them all about it at home and I went on telling them and then I told them again and I said that going to the circus was a must. I said I needed to see the animals from other parts of the world so that I could learn about them for my natural history class and I said that all the boys would be there.

Pa said: "There's no question of it being a must to go to the circus. It's not a must for me to go, or your mother, or Christina either. We'll all survive without it."

I started snivelling.

And I asked Ma and Pa whether this was where being on my best behaviour all the time got me.

Pa said that I ought to be good for the sake of being good and not in order to go to the circus. I said that this wasn't true, no one was good just for the sake of it. And I flew into a rage at the fact I'd been good and nothing had come of it and I made up my mind to become the worst behaved of all and a policeman would come to take me away and it would bring shame on my parents and do harm to business in the shop. And I snivelled all the more and then some more again.

Then Ma spoke to Pa in a very soft voice, after which Pa spoke up in a very loud one: "All right then, have your own way, we'll go to the circus and now give me some peace and quiet because I've had you up to here."

I was over the moon, but not totally over because I wanted to be at the circus every day so that we could see all the acts, but I knew that my parents wouldn't want anything like that and would go on and on about it. So therefore I was a bit worried.

I said that many children had come with the circus and that one boy from the circus was coming to our class to have lessons with us. We were very proud of this and the whole school envied us the fact we had a schoolmate from the circus.

I really wanted him to sit next to me. I'd whisper all the right answers to him and the rest of the class would be furious and full of envy. But the teacher sat him at the back of the classroom next to Šabata, because he was big. He was bigger than any of us but with nothing in his head. He wrote as if he was still in the tiny tots' preparatory class, made inky smudges all his own and didn't even know his multiplication table, or what mortal sins were, or how to work out ratios and fractions. The thing was that he acted in the circus and so didn't have time for lessons.

He was called Alphonse Kasalický, but his father was Signor Rudolphi who was the leading figure in the circus because he was in charge of all the circus riders, clowns, caramels, monkeys and other wild animals. I asked him how come he was called Kasalický and his pa Signor Rudolphi, and he told me that in the circus all the artists took other names in order to make themselves better known, and that it was called advertising. I found this really strange.

But he was better than any of us at PE. He knew how to climb, leap over a vaulting-horse, work the parallel bars, do a full circle on the horizontal bar, stand on his hands and head and do lots of other things that they don't teach in school. During the break he did three somersaults in the air and he knew how to tangle himself up so that he had his head where other people have their legs and his legs where they have their head so he looked as if he'd got himself into a knot that he could never untie. The teacher saw this and said: "Kasalický, Kasalický, you're not in a circus but a school building," and at this we all laughed a lot and the teacher laughed too. But when the teacher saw us laughing he added: "Everything in moderation," and took hold of Kasalický by the ear and so we laughed even more.

All of us boys went round with Kasalický and he with us. Anthony Bejval sucked up to him because he wanted to be the one who went round with him most. He said that the two of them should go round together because the Bejvals had horses too, just like the circus. But Kasalický went round with me most of all because I promised him that I'd get him some tobacco which Pa kept in a tin box in his cupboard. After school we always made sure he was in the middle when we were all together and boys from other classes wanted to join us but we said to them: "On your way and we'll go on ours." And we talked to him for ages, mainly about the circus. We wanted to know all about it and he told us. We asked him how long the circus would be in town and he said it would depend, they would see what the takings were. His pa had said he thought our town would not be a good port of call because it had too many pubs in it, not to mention two picture halls and an amateur theatre. That meant the people here were too educated and wouldn't appreciate art of the first rank. I said this wasn't true. I told him that the people in our town weren't educated at all and they'd all be going to the circus. This made Kasalický say: "I'm glad to hear that. It's high time business was looking up."

When I got home I told everyone about this. First I told Christina, then Ma and then Pa. I told them about it again when they were all together and Pa said: "This circus is the work of the Devil. It's driving you even further out of your head." But Ma said: "Leave him alone. We were no better in our day."

When I went to bed that evening Ma sat on the edge of the bed. It was dark and we chatted together in just the way I really like. And Ma began to tell me about Pa and about what he used to do when he was my age, how he and some other boys ran away from home because they wanted to get to Africa. They took food and adventure stories with them and Pa nicked some sugar and a book called 'A Guide for Growing Girls or How to Win Rare and Lasting Affection from a Man.' They also took with them a fishing rod and tackle, because they wanted to live on fish. They spent a whole week roaming around, sleeping in haystacks and brickworks. The police scoured the area looking for them and made inquiries everywhere. But then they turned up of their own accord, famished, scruffy and dirty as tinkers.

Pa overheard Ma telling this tale and told her off for talking about it to me. He said that this would stop the boy having respect for his elders, but then he laughed himself and said: "Well, that was then. Those were the days."

I wanted him to tell me how he had walked to Africa, and he told me more about it and he kept adding to it, because I couldn't get enough of his story. And I asked him why he took 'A Guide for Growing Girls' with him. What help would the book be among all the wild tribes? And Pa said: "What could I do, my lad, when I didn't have any other book and the boys would do me down for turning up empty-handed? Anything's better than nothing."

I liked Pa more after that, because I'd always thought that my father had his head screwed on all the time, but now I realised that it hadn't always been as screwed on as all that.

On the day when the circus was to have its first performance, the whole place was in a tizzwozz, because the circus artists went on a procession through the town and there were horses and elephants and caramels and clowns and giraffes and from everyone there was lots of trumpeting and drumming, so the people of the town came running out of their homes to see what was happening.

The procession came past our house and the whole family stood in front of the shop and Ma had Mirabelle in her arms and Mirabelle was clapping her hands and saying in her own language "Oss, Oss!" which means horse and Pa was smiling and said proudly: "There's always something happening in this town of ours so just let anyone call us the back of beyond now."

One of the circus riders, who was sitting on a tiny little horse, heard him say this and blew him a kiss. Pa raised his cap to her and said: "What would you say, Mother, if I was to run off with a circus artiste?" Ma gave him a slap and said: "Aren't you even a little ashamed to talk like that in front of the children, you old prattler?" Pa laughed and said: "Oho!"

I caught sight of Alphonse Kasalický in the procession. He was sitting on a caramel and wearing an amazing jacket laced with gold. He had one hand on his hip and looked very proud and I pulled Ma and Pa by the sleeve and shouted: "That's Alphonse who's in our class," and I followed the procession and kept shouting "That's Alphonse, who's in our class," so that all the people around would know about it, and I kept pointing at Kasalický. And the boys, both those of us who went round together and those we had nothing to do with, were running behind the procession, and so were the Ješiňáks and Habrováks and our other enemies and a great shout went up that could be heard all around.

And while I was running I suddenly spotted Eve Svoboda running next to me, so I at once stopped pointing at Alphonse in case she got too keen on his jacket laced with gold and instead I pointed at the elephant. Some girl was sitting on it with gold coins in her ears and a turban on her head. Eve Svoboda said: "You know what, Peter, we'll both be going to the circus together," and I replied: "Whatever, but I have to go with my family today," and she said that she'd be going today with her ma and pa too, which suited us fine, because at least we'd see each other at the circus. I even said "You bet!" and then I was again running and shouting. Eve ran and shouted too, so we were both yelling our heads off.

And we laughed them off too when we saw the clowns, who had such tiny wee hats and huge baggy trousers into which you could have fitted at least five of the boys in our class. They also had red noses and white faces with thick lips and they stumbled as they went along and babbled and when they saw some girl or other they doffed their hats and the girls squealed frightfully as only girls can.

Mr. Fajst was standing in the square without a smile on his face. Instead he was nodding his head gloomily and talking in a low and slow voice to the bleating greengrocer who was sitting beneath a parasol selling apples. "This is an act of abomination," he was saying, and the Bleating Goat replied: "Let no one think that the Lord God will suffer such lascivious behaviour to last long. His wrath will be kindled at this pandemonium."

And as she spoke the procession came to a halt and one of the musicians sounded the trumpet with extra power and one of the comedians announced in a pleading voice that he was drawing the attention of these esteemed citizens to the fact that today would see the first performance in their town and that things would be on show that had never been seen before anywhere in the world. He praised the animals from far-off lands for being strong and fierce and of great educational value for all lovers of nature, and said that everyone should come to see a top-notch programme. Then there was another blast of the trumpet and a really loud roll on the drums by another musician and that was it.

What a spectacular! No one was paying attention in school that day, even the wash-behind-the-ears good boys who got the top marks, and the teacher said: "What's happening here? I take a good deal of trouble to teach you something but your mind goes wandering away from the classroom. I welcome anything in the way of general entertainment but bear in mind, boys, that duty comes before pleasure." But we went on thinking all the time about the circus anyway, and no one who was asked to speak could put two words together.

When Pa shut up shop in the evening, he put some new clothes on and took a bowler hat out of a box and put two cigars into a cigar case. I felt as if it was a Sunday even though it was only Wednesday. Then he looked into a mirror and gave his moustache a twist, making himself look specially serious. Then he went from room to room singing "ta-ra-ra-boom-de-ay." But Ma took a terribly long time putting on her glad rags, twirling around in front of the mirror and looking at herself from all angles, until I started whining that we'd miss the performance and I stamped my feet, while she kept urging Christina to take care of Mirabelle and kept unlocking and then relocking the wardrobe and wandering off here and there until Pa said: "Mother, you're acting as if we've got all the time in the world." And then we were off and when we were on our way Ma wanted to go back because she was afraid about whether she'd locked everything up and she started to worry her head over whether Christina would start a fire by knocking over a lamp. So I kept asking her not to go back and I said that our house wouldn't catch fire and anyway if it did the fire brigade would come and hose everything down until the fire was out. And I added: "You'll see, Ma, by the time we get home from the circus the fire will have gone and we'll just go to bed." Pa laughed heartily at this and said that I was a clever clogs, but Ma said to Pa: "You men always stick up for each other," and I said: "You bet."

There was a huge crowd of people on display in New Square marching up and down, seeing that the circus was playing music that you could march to followed by a polka and other dance music. On top of that you could hear the wild animals roaring. Pa went to the waggon where they were selling tickets and bought some. He gave them to me to look after and I showed them to some official standing at the entrance who was putting a tear in the tickets and showing visitors their seats. The official sported a beautiful red coat with a huge mass of silver buttons on it and wore knee-high boots with spurs and he also had a wonderful great moustache.

We sat down in the seats we'd been given. We put Ma in the middle so that there was a man on each side of her and I looked all around and the first person I saw was Eddie Kemlink. So I said to him "Hi there!" and he said "Hi there!" back and I shouted: "I'm here!" and he replied: "I'm here too!" and we both shouted "Everyone's here." Tony Bejval was there and so was Chris Jirsák and all the boys who formed our gang and even the ones we didn't mix with and even some of the pupils from way over the fields. We all said "Hi!" to one another and were happy as sandboys.

I couldn't wait for it to begin. I couldn't sit down even for a second and Ma told me that I had ants in my pants and went on to say: "The way the child goes on, I'm afraid he'll do himself a mischief." This made me say: "I'm not a child and I'm certainly not going to do myself any mischief." I thought the bell rang for the start at this moment, so I went "Ooooh," but it wasn't the start because people were still streaming in and the official was telling them "This way, please!" and showing them their places. There was the sound of another bell a moment later but it turned out to be another swindle, because nothing started.

When the bell sounded for the third time nothing happened yet again and Pa looked at his watch and said: "They're taking their time," and someone started to clap and then all the boys started clapping and then everyone there was clapping and me too and I was yelling: "Come on!" But at that very moment the curtains moved, there was a stamping sound and then a girl appeared in the arena riding a horse. She was beautifully painted like a picture in a book. And there was a man cracking a whip loudly making a sound like a cap-gun going off and the girl smiled to us and blew kisses at the audience and the man cracked his whip even more. She was juggling with her legs in all manner of ways and had lovely high and shiny boots. At one moment she was hanging head down but this didn't bother her at all and she went on smiling and the horse started going faster and faster until it was all over and as much as we could take and everyone clapped and I clapped more than anyone.

Then they brought on the horse again and one of the clowns wanted to do what the girl had done. He thought he knew how to do it but he didn't have the first idea and fell over to roars of laughter from people who bellowed out at the top of their voices "Tally ho!" I laughed more than anyone and threw my arms around Ma's neck and shouted: "He's falling over, he's so daft! Look Ma, look what a pudding-head he is." And Ma told me off, saying that I couldn't even mind my Ps and Qs in a circus and was showing her up in front of other people.

Before I could come back at her saying that I knew exactly how to mind my Ps and Qs in a circus, three clowns appeared and it seemed to me that one of them was the official who had been tearing the tickets earlier. The three clowns threw red, blue and yellow hoops at each other with such speed that the colours seemed to flicker and all the audience was gawping and all the boys were open-mouthed and each and every one of them was amazed at their skill, until one of the clowns got tangled up and fell on his nose and shouted "Ooops!" and everyone laughed their heads off and they played some music to go with it.

Then they lowered a trapeze from up above and three boys appeared, all dressed in the same way in black, a tall one, a not so tall one and the smallest one. When I looked at them I saw that the smallest one was Alphonse Kasalický, the boy who went to my class. This made all the boys shout

out: "Kasalický!" and I shouted "Kasalický!" as well so he'd know I was there too. But Kasalický took no notice at all. He stood rooted to the spot and the pair of bigger boys didn't move an inch either.

And then they were joined by the ringmaster Signor Rudolphi who said in a loud voice to his esteemed audience that the three boys were the famous Abaldini brothers, whose performances of the highest rank were the wonder of the world, and whose exploits were written up in the newspapers of other lands and after these words he bowed and went off to one side. Then one of the bigger boys flung himself onto the trapeze and caught hold of Alphonse Kasalický and threw him to the biggest boy, and Kasalický did three flying somersaults in the air while they were all swinging about madly and then Alphonse flew across to the biggest boy who threw him back to the bigger boy and they kept doing this and suddenly the music stopped, the audience was all agog, I was the most agog of all, and Ma said she couldn't watch, she was afraid they'd do themselves a mischief, and Pa said she shouldn't be afraid and they knew what they were doing. When it was over we clapped madly and they thanked us and I said to everyone that one of the trio was Alphonse Kasalický from my class and I was very proud of this fact.

After they left the ringmaster asked in a clear voice whether everyone might contribute a little something for the Abaldini brothers. He said that he wasn't forcing anyone to do so, everyone could give according to their means. The thing was that the Albadini brothers had to go abroad to study new acts. And Pa said in a grumpy voice that they certainly knew how to pick the money out of people's pockets and straight away Alphonse Kasalický went round with a plate and I asked Pa to give me a crown and he said: "Do you think I'm made of money?" but he gave me a crown all the same and I said "Hi there!" to Alphonse in a very loud voice so that everyone could hear me and he said "Hi there!" back to me.

Then a clown appeared and wanted to do what the three boys had done but he didn't know the first thing about it and before long he'd fallen on his nose over and over again and we were all in stitches laughing and I thought to myself: where is he stumbling off to, he's daft as a brush. And yet he wasn't so daft, he suddenly straightened his legs and sprang up onto the trapeze, twisting himself like a snake making several turns in the air and everyone was gawking at him and I was gawking too and I saw that he knew what he was doing and how he had to play the fool in order to get people laughing. Pa said: "Some fellow that, I must admit," and Ma said: "Where do these people get their ideas from?"

Then I went up to Eve Svoboda and praised the clown to her, but she said that she didn't like him at all because of his red hooter and I said: "You're crackers. I'll explain it all to you, his hooter is just stuck on. Otherwise he looks just like anyone else." But she kept laughing and saying that she wouldn't want to be seen with the likes of him, oh no, not for all the tea in China.

When I lay down to sleep that evening I took a postcard of a female circus rider to bed with me so that I'd find it there in the morning. The girl in the picture had been going round during the interval selling postcards which Pa didn't want to buy because he said: "Another piece of cheek to pick our pockets with. I'm not going to be had this time." But I wore him down and badgered Pa for so long that he bought me a postcard so that I could have it. And when I bragged about the postcard to Eve Svoboda she went into a sulk and said that she didn't know what I saw in the circus rider anyway.

It took me a long time to get to sleep. Whenever I looked at the ceiling or the wall I kept seeing the brilliant circus programme all over again. Such as when they led in an enormous Indian elephant called Jumbo who had a huge trunk with two fingers on it and such tiny eyes with which he gave a knowing twinkle. He could do any trick you could think of, every single one. He stood on his hind legs and then used his front ones to beg as if he were a small dog. Everyone looked on in amazement and Pa said to Ma: "You've no idea how much such an elephant eats. Where elephants are concerned, it's better to clothe them than to feed them."

And then I saw a man appear with a troupe of dogs. Some were shaggy and some were smooth, some were common breeds and some were strange-looking, but they all wore little skirts and caps on their heads. The man pointed with a stick, music started up and the dogs began to dance. Then he fetched some tiny steps and the dogs went up and down on their back legs and then they did the same going backwards. The dogs that knew how to do it barked happily, but those who got their steps mixed up were told off by the circus artist so that they paid proper attention next time and didn't let their minds wander away from the classroom.

And the clowns carried on with their comic capers and silly riddles at which everyone laughed, and made out that they were slapping each other really hard but I could see that they never slapped each other at all and so I thought to myself, what if boys could also manage to slap each other like that, then they could spend the whole day fighting and no one would be able to say anything about it, not the teacher and not even the constable.

Then I thought again of Eve Svoboda and of how we went up to each other between the circus acts and told each other how great it all was. And she gave me a lollipop stick which was in four colours: red, pink, yellow and chocolate. I took the stick from her and said: "Thanks!" and she told me that I could have a lollipop stick from her whenever I liked so long as I talked to her and I said: "Why not, it's all the same to me," and this answer made her happy.

And we boys who go round together told each other how much we liked the circus and Chris Jirsák said that he was looking forward to seeing the Nubian lion most, because he was the King of the Beasts, but Eddie Kemlink said that he was keener on seeing the Bengal tiger, because it was known to be specially bloodthirsty. But no lion appeared and no tiger turned up and Pa said he should have known this all along, that circus people always managed to pull the wool over Joe Public's eyes, that the circus was a swindle and you could never rely on the people working for it. But it shouldn't be left that way, someone should do something about it. Ma said: "Don't start putting your oar in," and Pa replied: "I've no wish to put my oar in. Even so you must admit that it's as if some customer came wanting a pound of sugar and was given a piece of wood instead. If word got around about such a thing I'd have to close the shop at once, but I couldn't behave like that because I know about satisfying my customers and that's something circus folk don't know about."

But what surprised me was the fact that Zilvar from the poorhouse was there, and I asked him where he'd got the money for the circus from because he was poor. He replied that he got it from nowhere and so straight away I asked him how come he was there. He replied that anyone could come and ask him but he couldn't say, because it was a big secret. So I said to him, as if it was just by the by, that I'd got hold of a book called 'Among the Mongolian Tribes' and it was a fabulous read. He took the bait at once, and said that he wanted to read the book too. So I thumbed my nose at him and said: "Out with it!" and he said he'd spill the beans but not at once, only later. I came back at him saying later was no good, it had to be right now or I'd lend the book to Bejval instead, he'd been asking me about it.

So out it came, he'd been working an artful dodge to get into the circus for free. He helped the circus people fetch water for the wild animals and horses. If I came along to the circus the following afternoon he'd tell them I was also a water carrier.

This was good to hear and I said that I'd be there, no doubt about it. But he said that I mustn't let anyone know about this dodge and I swore not to tell anyone and while I swore I pulled my ear and stuck out my tongue, just to make it certain. So at home I kept mum and the very next day I ran to the circus but whom did I find? Whom did I not find! There was Anthony Bejval and Eddie Kemlink and even Christopher Jirsák. Zilvar had blabbed to them because they'd given him enough peanuts to fill a pocket, a jackknife, a knitted whip handle and two screwdrivers.

But I didn't say anything because it was all the same to me. Each of us grabbed a can or a pail and ran off to the standpipe for water. And while we were fetching water little Otto Soumar turned up saying that he wanted to be a water-bearer too. We told him that he shouldn't because his was a family of means and if it came out that he'd been doing this he'd be in trouble at home. But we could see the floodgates were about to open so we let him join us.

And while we were carrying water I saw the female circus rider who was on my postcard but she didn't look a picture any more. Her bobbed hair was ruffled and looked like a bird's nest and she was walking around in ordinary togs and rinsing clothes in a wash-tub, which really amazed me. And the circus official was just in breeches, smoking a fag and chopping wood. As for Signor Rudolphi, he was sitting on an upturned cart and when he caught sight of Otto Soumar he told him to run across the street and get him some ginger water. Then he added: "If you so much as take a sip, you little squirt, I'll tan your hide," and Otto said that he wouldn't taste a drop and ran off to fetch beer.

We went on carrying water and I watched the elephant drinking and was amazed at how much it could put away. The caramels drank lots too, but less than the elephants and the horses drank even less but in all it was still quite enough. Then Alphonse Kasalický went by like little Lord Fauntleroy with his hands in his pockets urging us on all the time saying: "Come on, lads, chivvy up, get cracking, get weaving, get your skates on," and so we were hauling water for all we were worth. And Eve carried water too.

I said that the caramel was the caravel of the desert, because I'd read this in a book, but the boys said: "Leave it out, we know all about that," and I said: "I wasn't telling you, I was telling Eve," and Eve whispered to me that I was the brightest of the bunch and so she was going to bring me another candy stick.

In the meantime Otto brought the beer, the circus manager drained it and said: "Hits the spot nicely!" and Otto went straight over to us, ready to put all his energy into shifting water. But it never came to pass, because his governess suddenly came rushing over, moving so quickly that her hat was all lopsided and she started shouting in a strange accent "Heaven forfend!" and something besides and Otto was splashed all over and she started to scold the circus manager, speaking in a rapid voice.

The circus manager doffed his cap, held it to his chest and pushed a leg behind him in order to bow and scrape. Then he said in a solemn voice: "Madame, pray forgive me, forgive me. I did not realize that this was a young gentleman of good family. That was of course an error of mine and I am most distressed by such unpleasantness." But the governess spoke in an even faster voice, saying that it was scandalous and the authorities should be told about it so that nothing like it ever happened again. Then she seized little Otto by the hand and dragged him away just as the waterworks started.

After this the circus manager was really riled and said in a terrifying voice: "That's what you've done, you scamps, you scoundrels, you scallywags. That's another fine mess you've got me into. Shove off! Get away from my circus or you'll see a side of me you won't like." So we all took off and we were a handful.

Away we went, slowly at first as if we couldn't care less but then we started running and when we were far enough away Chris Jirsák began cursing: "Bengal booby, Nubian nitwit, first-class flop, epileptic elephant, blunder of the world, we are not scallywags, we are your esteemed public and you're the fattest Indian Rock Python there's ever been!"

The curses came out really quickly as if beaten out with a whip and there was no stopping them so we were really amazed and so was Eve and it made me furious that I didn't know how to curse like that myself.

While he was swearing the circus master flung a big stick at us but it didn't hit anyone and Christopher Jirsák made a really horrible face at him and added: "You're Kismet the thoroughbred mare, on display for just a few days."

Then he took out his notebook and wrote something in it. We asked him what he was writing and he said: "Gentlemen, I will have a really great sin to take to the holy confessional. Swearing at a circus manager. No one has committed a sin like this before and the reverend father won't even believe what I tell him. But if needs be you are my witnesses."

We said that we'd swear to his sin if we had to, and this made Chris Jirsák ever so proud.

A few days later I went to school, passing Bejval's place on the way as I always do so I can pick up Tony and we can go to school together. But I looked at that horse's head there and it wound me up with its bared teeth and that malicious grin on its face and I said to it: "You needn't bare your teeth at me. And you're no fun to be with." So I didn't wait for Tony, but thought I'd rather go on alone.

And so I went on alone and then it occurred to me that I could use a stone to hit one of those porcelain bulbs on top of the power line, but my aim was no good and so I let it be. It was Tuesday and that's a day I really like because we have reading, religion, drawing and PE. Reading is a cinch and in Religion we have loads of fun with the catechism teacher, because he's always taking a pinch of snuff from a tin box and then saying: "O thou pagan horde, O Romans in your armour, O ye hosts of Amalekites, there will be no lunch break for any of you until you learn how to behave like Christians!" It goes without saying that PE is fab, but what I like most of all is drawing, because we use crayons and can draw from memory.

But it didn't feel like a Tuesday to me at all. It felt more like a gloomy Thursday when we have to do our sums, study grammar and do history and geography. All the time it seemed like a Thursday to me and I was down in the dumps. I saw Chris Jirsák ahead of me in the square and I thought of catching up with him and saying "Hallo" and then walking on with him, but then I felt sick of Christopher Jirsák. I suppose I must have slept in the wrong position and ricked my neck. I stopped as I always did in front of Mr. Svoboda's sweet shop and saw a gigantic cake there. It was a chocolate one with fancy cream trimmings and I asked myself whether I'd want a cake like that and straightaway I replied: "No way, because it looks like the hat Aunt Vařeka wears when she's off to church."

And when I go past the policeman who stands in the square looking to see if disorder will break out somewhere, I always feel like creeping up on him from behind and pulling out his sabre in order to take a good look at it, but this time I didn't care and just walked politely past and paid my respects to the policeman and he replied: "Good day to you, worthy citizen!" which I didn't take to at all as I'm certainly no citizen.

I ambled into school at a really slow pace while my mind ticked over, thinking that it would be good if the school building suddenly packed itself up and went away and I could just go home and if my parents asked me what was going on I'd tell them that there was no school any more and I'd sit in the courtyard and stay sitting there staring into empty space and with an empty head.

When I got to school the caretaker had already rung the bell for lessons to begin, but there was mayhem in the classroom because the teacher hadn't yet arrived. But I didn't join in the mayhem. I sat in my place and got my work out.

It was a Reading lesson. One pupil was reading from a primer about how 'Winter's woes are not so great, as I've heard them say of late.' I asked myself why there was all this talk of winter when it was so hot and I looked out of the window and saw a man pushing a wheelbarrow full of sand and I wondered at how the man could get any pleasure out of it. I'd have left the wheelbarrow where it was and gone away to lie in the shade on the grass and I daydreamed that I had a mouth full of sand. I also spotted the notary's maid, who was singing while she did the washing, and her wide mouth opened to show incredibly red gums that looked like rosehip jam. I found this disgusting and so I waited impatiently for her to stop and go away. I didn't need to look but I had to because otherwise I'd be looking straight ahead at Andy Špoutil and his scabby head.

Someone sitting at one of the desks at the back sent me a picture he'd made of a person with ass's ears and a message underneath saying "This is Charlie Páta, pass it on," but I crumpled up the piece of paper and chucked it under the desk because it was a stupid joke. My head ached and there was a ringing in my ears as if I was underwater looking for pebbles. I wanted to drink some ice-cold water which would set my teeth on edge. I wanted a drink really badly and I shut my eyes and dreamt of being a mottled jaguar going to drink from a stream. But I wasn't a jaguar and I wanted school to be over so that I could go home.

To cheer myself up and drive away unhappy thoughts I tried to think of the circus and the good times we had had there. But the circus had already moved on, leaving behind it in the square a circular area sprinkled with sawdust, some torn-up tickets, bits of posters, piles of dung and otherwise nothing, not a shred. It didn't make me feel any better and it even seemed as if there'd never been a circus and I'd just read about one in a book or somehow or other I'd been told about one and I half believed that this was true.

So I said: you must turn your thoughts elsewhere, but where? For example, perhaps a travelling salesman might come to us today and Pa would order something from him or say: "I don't need anything, I've got all I want." Or maybe Bejval's stable boys would bring a box that had come from the train and then I heaved a sigh and thought: "Why would a box turn up right now? In any case, even if it did there wouldn't be any pictures in it." And my head went on hurting.

Suddenly I saw the clowns in the circus throwing their coloured wheels. First in the air was the red wheel, behind that the blue one and then the yellow. They moved very slowly, as when the mayor walks with the notary and the reverend and then the pace quickened until the mayor, the notary and reverend were themselves racing round, flying headlong onto the railway in order to catch the train. At that very moment the teacher called my name. I didn't know where we were and the teacher said: "Bajza, Bajza I am going to a lot of trouble and your mind goes wandering off out of the classroom," and his voice was so mean that my head started hurting even more and he was looking over his glasses and lifting his forefinger in a way I didn't like at all. I wanted to tell him to stop raising his finger at me but he turned away and called someone else's name.

The caretaker rang the bell and I realized that it was only the first hour of school that was over and it was break-time. A great shout went up but I didn't join in on purpose. I stayed sitting and staring and everything was green as if I was underwater. And then I saw how Charlie Páta pulled out a bun and began to nibble at it. He had greasy lips and it put me off so much that I began to shout in a terrible voice: "Get rid of that bun or I'll sock you!" I kept shouting at him and I wanted to snatch his bun away from him but I started to feel really unwell. I think it was Bejval who tidied my things away into my bag but it was definitely someone else who stuck my cap on and yet another person who said: "I'll go with him," and all at once we were out in the corridor where there were pictures of scenes from Czech history and the pictures were hanging all askew. The strangest thing of all was that the corridor which leads to the gym had always been on the right side but now it was suddenly on the left. The windows too weren't where they should have been but were on the other side instead. This all made me feel even worse.

The pictures seemed to be sliding off the walls and the teacher was also sliding and spilling himself on the floor and bubbling as if he was on the boil and out of the bubbling a voice issued saying: "Bejval and Kemlink!" "Yes sir!" "The two boys whose names I've called out will come here and take Bajza home. Careful now, do it carefully. The rest of you back to your places. Bejval and Kemlink, you're grown-up boys and I rely on you to manage the situation with due care. I hope that this nasty illness will pass without any unfortunate consequences."

The voice sounded very clear now and I kept hearing it all the time, even when I was already sitting on a stool and Christina was taking off my boots and she had an enormous face. Ma was lighting the stove and Pa was touching my brow and saying: "This lad has a fever, he must have eaten something that disagreed with him," and then I heard the chicory in the shop saying: "That's the last thing we could do with," and then I was already lying in bed, shivering in some terrible cold and jabbering freely "carrion crow, curd cheese, old Nick, Rampusite, rusty tyre," the words pouring forth from me faster and faster and someone was stamping loudly as they moved around the house and I was lying in a sort of green brine and drifting along like a pickled gherkin in a jar and everything was floating, everything was going round and round and billowing out and out.

I didn't even know how long I lay there. I just felt hot with cold waves rippling across my back. I looked through the window at the courtyard and I saw the sun rolling over the roof of our woodshed and there on the woodshed sat Honza our tomcat and he was looking as worried as Pa when he's looking for his pipe and doesn't know where to find it. I didn't like the way Honza looked so worried and shut my eyes.

A little while later I heard some rapid footfall and a loud voice said: "Where's the patient?" and from this voice came the sweet-smelling wind that blows over the red and pink sweets that you find in those round glass jars at the chemist's. I've always wanted to have some of those.

The visitor brought a small case with him and I wanted to know what he had inside it. He breathed over my chest and his beard tickled me under the chin and he stuck a thermometer under my armpit and said: "It's really stuffy in here, my good people. Air, air, air and lots of it, dear people. That's the main thing." Then he looked at his watch for a while and said "Goodness me!" Then I heard the clink of the scales in the shop as they said: "Let me have a pound of coffee as well. This is the fourth case of scarlet fever I've been called out to. Do you have some embrocation? I'll take a small bottle. Just keep calm, keep very calm Mr. Bajza, I will come and take another look at him later today, now how much does that come to? Most kind, I take my hat off to you, sir."

I plunged deep into green brine and swam and kept swimming all the time and little Victor Štěpánek was swimming too and it made me wonder at a tiny tot like that already knowing how to swim and I went home and was well-behaved for quite a time. I was walking slowly, looking like a goody two shoes, pronouncing all my aitches and saying things like: "Without a doubt, naturally, nevertheless, should it so happen that, accordingly and likewise." And when I decided that I'd been well-behaved for long enough I asked Pa, in the politest of voices, whether he would go to the Circus Rudolphi and buy me Jumbo the elephant, because I really needed him.

When Pa heard me ask for this he gave a horrible chuckle and said: "Ha! Jumbo the elephant, we'll see about that! When I was your age I had to fend for myself and no one asked me what I wanted."

But I didn't give up. I pestered him in a pleading voice, saying I had to have an elephant because we were learning about them in our biology lessons and I needed one so I could do my schoolwork properly.

Pa snapped back: "And just who can afford to buy an elephant these days? Just where will it end? It depends on how well the business does. Now skedaddle!"

He spoke in such a grumpy voice that it sounded like "kebabble" and I started to cry.

But Ma took Pa to one side and had a quiet word with him and when I saw this I promised in a loud voice that I'd never skip a single violin practice, that I'd show respect to every grown-up, that I'd run all sorts of errands without making a song and dance about it and that I'd tidy up and mind Mirabelle all the time, never leaving her on her own and telling her fairytales in a soft voice.

And Ma said: "Why can't the child have a bit of pleasure once in a while? You're already becoming a skinflint like Uncle Vařeka. Go on, buy him the elephant. When all's said and done it's not going to break the bank, is it?"

This started Pa flapping his hand, and saying: "If it's got to be an elephant, so be it, an elephant it is. This will show you what I'm like but I wonder whether you'll remember what I've done for you in days to come."

With a loud voice I made it clear that I'd never been so happy and kissed Pa's hand. And then I suddenly saw Jumbo standing there, this enormous Indian elephant, right in front of our shop. He was standing there patiently, his ears like huge leaves of burdock, his skin tough as tarpaper, smiling through those clever little eyes of his.

I gave him a marshmallow which I'd nicked from the shop and he took it with one of the fingers fixed to his trunk, and I asked him: "Are you content, Jumbo?" and then he nodded his head to tell me that he was fine.

Then I said to him in a firm voice: "Rules are rules, dear Jumbo. Nothing to be done about that. Time for school."

Jumbo replied: "If we've got to go to school then let's go to school. Duty before pleasure. Rome wasn't built in a day. True happiness is known to the scholar. So come hither, my boy, and learn thou wisdom."

Then he carefully put his trunk round my waist and lifted me onto the back of his neck. And Christina handed me the bag with my schoolbooks in it and Ma and Pa were standing in front of the shop to see what was going on and I greeted them politely and gave the order: "Forward march!"

And the elephant set off at a slow and majestic pace with everyone watching and I felt very proud. As for those who were looking on: there was Jodaska, who sells earthenware, Trojna the barrel-maker, Rychtera the strap-maker,

Bednařík the shoemaker, Svatý the tailor for men and boys, Mazura the haulage contractor, Jaroš who's a butcher and sausage maker, the bleating greengrocer and even Mr. Fajst, not forgetting Mr. Podlena who's a clerk in the district office.

The whole town was looking on in wonder.

And when I turned the corner the onlookers were: Preclík the chimney sweep, Laušmanka the threadmaker, Dušánek the sign maker, Vobořilka the barley dealer and Homoláč the glazier, and then there was Netuka the soap maker.

The pigeons circling the dome of the church were amazed too, and so were Bejval's horses and Jacob the groom. Even the dogs were amazed, and that includes Patch.

Creatures one and all were goggle-eyed and went "Wow!"

And the mayor and the whole town council were staring out of a window of the town hall lost in wonder. Mr. Letovský, our local constable, stood to attention and saluted me, saying: "All hail to thee, son of our native soil!" I thanked him with extra special politeness.

There was a great crowd of people by now and the fire brigade saluted me with their siren. Several people said that it should be in the papers so that people could read all about it.

And the elephant walked on with regular steps, and when I looked down, what did I see? Two men were walking on the right of me and another two on the left. They wore scarves about their dusky loins, turbans on their heads and each held a spear in one hand while the other hand held a bag with my schoolbooks. The men were called: Anthony Bejval, Edward Kemlink, Christopher Jirsák and Zilvar from the poorhouse, whose first name was Joe. When I counted them I saw that there were a handful of us in all. I was the bigwig and the other four were my bodyguards.

I arrived at school to a racket of trumpets and drum rolls and the teacher, looking out from a window of the school, said: "Let's have some order, boys. We don't want any complaints from our good citizens."

Jumbo let me down in front of the school and then handed me my reader, grammar book, arithmetic book and writing things.

Then the caretaker came out and folded his arms across his chest and asked: "What can I do for you, great sir?" I bade him take good care of the elephant during school hours and bring him some refreshments.

The caretaker bowed and said "As you wish" before disappearing into the school. Shortly after he was back out bringing a bottle of lemonade which he gave to Jumbo.

The elephant lifted the bottle to his mouth and drank down the lemonade saying: "Yummy! Just the ticket! Praise the Lord."

When I saw the elephant drinking, I got terribly thirsty myself and opened my eyes and for ages I couldn't understand why I was lying in bed. Where was the crowd of people? Where had all the splendour gone? Where were the trumpets and the rolling drums?

It was already late. The shop was shut. Pa was sitting at my bedside staring, Ma was propping me up with one hand and holding a glass of raspberry lemonade in the other and saying: "Drink, dear little Peter, it will do you good."

I wolfed it down. It was gurgling inside me and when I'd finished it I said: "Thanks, dearest Ma, for putting in a word to Pa about buying me an elephant. Jumbo and I talk to each other, you know, and we're always going around together."

"That's fine," replied Ma, "but I want you to have a good sleep now so that you can sleep off what's troubling you."

"And a hundred thanks to you too, Pa," I said, "for letting me put you to such expense."

Pa smiled a little and said: "Don't mention it. You know I'm not one to count the pennies when something has to be done."

Christina was standing at the bedside too. She was looking at me and I said to her: "When I get up I'm going to tell Jumbo that we're off to the land of the Rampusites. Do you think they've ever seen an elephant there?"

Christina sniggered, but Ma said "Ssh!" to her in a stern voice. And as I dropped off to sleep I heard myself saying in a weak voice: "Ma, give Jumbo some rice, because elephants love rice, it's their favourite food," and then I heard the scales in the shop saying in a tinkly voice: "A kilo of rice. Anything else I can be getting you, please?"

"Wherever would those mountain-dwelling Rampusites see an elephant? Elephants live on the vast open plains of India, irrigated by the mighty River Ganges, which you see, Christina, is a sacred river to the people living there."

The only thing is that I don't know any more whether I said that or the teacher did, because we had biology that day, but in the courtyard rather than the classroom. The pupils were standing around our Jumbo and the teacher was pointing at him with a ruler and holding forth:

"Now then, pay attention, boys. Follow what I'm saying with care, and you will have something to take away with you into the rest of your lives. If you do not pay attention, then you show a lack of consideration towards myself, given the way I exert myself on your behalf, not sparing my own health as I do so."

"Well now: the elephant which you see lives in large herds which romp around in the immensities of the Indian pampas and live for the most part off plants. Melichar is not paying attention. Melichar, give me that piece of string, you wretched boy. Now then, the elephant is easily domesticated and renders valuable service to people because it is a diligent animal unlike Šabata, whom I have just caught dawdling. It helps in the work of building, towing huge logs with its trunk, I have just this moment had to admonish

Melichar, but it is all water off a duck's back to this wretched boy. Melichar, Melichar, wretched boy, I shall invite your father for an urgent consultation. That also goes for Klema, who does not pay attention and distracts others too. Now then, young scholars, the elephant is an immensely strong animal and lives to a very great age. I can see that with some of you boys I may speak with the tongues of angels or devils and still you will turn nothing but a deaf ear to my words. Vašátko and Klenovec will be kept in detention, I cannot be bothered with them now."

The teacher told us many more gripping things and we all hung on his words. When lessons were over and it was time to go home Anthony Bejval joined me and chatted and looked around to make sure that everyone could see that I was talking to him more than anyone else. But I hardly spoke to him at all and just walked beside Jumbo.

Bejval said that he had invented something really big, and when I asked him what sort of invention it was he said that it was that Jumbo could live in their stables. It would be a way of teaching equine wisdom to an elephant and elephant wisdom to the horses. The two species would make friends and get on together.

I replied: "That's no invention and I don't want anything to do with it. Horses can stick to horses and I'll go round with the elephant."

However, he wouldn't get off the point and kept telling me that Jacob would provide the elephant with hay, oats and rice and would make sure that Jumbo had all he needed.

I said: "That would suit you down to the ground. You could then tell everyone that it was your elephant, not mine. No way! You'll be waiting till the cows come home. I'm not that stupid and you're not such a brainbox either and anyway who wouldn't lend me his bike?"

When Bejval heard this he was ashamed about having been so stingy with his bike and letting no one ride it because at that time he didn't know that I would have an elephant and so would be able to lord it over everyone else. But he pestered me for so long that I eventually said: "All right, then, just so you'll learn your lesson for another time," and I let Jumbo go to the stables at his place.

Jacob was happy and said: "By Jove, we've got an assistant!" and he set about cleaning the elephant with a brush.

It so happened that soon after this Mr. Kukrle moved to our town and got a job as a clerk in the post office. He wanted to hire Mr. Bejval to move his furniture.

I told them at home that I wasn't going to school that day because I had to help with the moving of Mr. Kukrle. Ma said: "Move him then, if you have to, but make sure you're home in time and I'll put your elevenses in the oven for you." I replied "You bet!" and ran off and Ma called after me: "Look after yourself, Pete, you know that you're not at all well," and I replied: "No worries!"

And as I hurried there I was joined by Zilvar from the poorhouse who ran along with me, as did Eddie Kemlink and little Victor Štěpánek, so that made us a four. When we got to Bejval's, Tony was waiting for us so now we were a handful. I sat in the driver's seat next to Jacob who handed me the whip and this made me very proud. Jumbo walked solemnly behind the furniture waggon, nodding his head and smiling through his bright little eyes.

When we reached the place the removal men started packing while Mr. Kukrle leaped about like a monkey shouting in a pleading voice: "Oh Jesus, fellas, you've got to be holding it crossways, you'll smash the lot to pieces, why should I suffer a loss like that?"

The removal men replied: "Honourable sir, please be so good as not to fidget like a flea in a jar. Just sit tight and look on."

And Jumbo said "I'm really keen to see how you go about this, young sirs."

The removal men replied: "This is hard work, hellish hard work," and Jumbo said "Out of my way, I'll deal with this myself." The removal men smiled and said: "We'll see how you make out, Jumbo."

However Jacob, being the most senior of them, said: "Now then, lads, just follow Jumbo's lead, because he'll have the best idea of how to do it."

And so it was: first of all Jumbo got hold of a sewing machine, lifting it with his trunk as if it was light as a feather, and then he took hold of a curio cabinet, followed by a cupboard, a mirror and beds, bringing them from the waggon with the ease of a baker feeding buns into an oven. Anyone else would strain their body and sweat, but to Jumbo it was nothing and he kept smiling with his clever little eyes.

The removal men stood beside themselves in amazement, frozen like statues. They spoke in an unusually wondering tone as they said: "Well, well, there you are, you've got what it takes, lad, a real tower of strength, God bless you, we wouldn't have got through it before evening was coming on and you've done it in a flash."

Jumbo said nothing, keeping his thoughts to himself, but I was really proud of him.

When we had done the whole caboodle Mr. Kukrle gave the removal men a tip so that they could buy a drop of the hard stuff to drink to his health, but elephants don't have an appetite for such things so he gave Jumbo a sackful of apples. Jumbo thanked him politely and was pleased as punch.

Then we went home and Jumbo sorted out the storeroom for Pa. He arranged the empty crates in the yard to look tidy and Pa said: "And you'd think elephants were just animals. Only a dumb animal, but anyone could learn a lesson from him. He's obviously been well brought up ever since he was tiny."

And he thanked Jumbo for everything in a lordly manner and Jumbo said: "Don't mention it, Mr. Bajza. I'm happy to put my shoulder to the wheel, or at least my trunk, whenever I get the chance. It's no skin off my long nose. As the saying goes: 'To work and to learn, salvation to earn.'"

Then I sat in the courtyard with Jumbo and read him a brilliant detective story called 'The Sign of the Four' and the elephant hung on every word and nodded his head knowingly and said: "There are things it is hard to believe happened even once. I'm curious to know whether they'll catch the murderer. It would serve him right and see that he didn't do it again."

I read for quite a long time and then felt my energy draining away. The book slipped out of my hand and I fell asleep. While I was asleep I saw the doctor coming back, bringing his little case once again full of the things doctors use to stop people being ill.

He sat at the bedside next to me, breathing heavily and examining me carefully, and then he said: "So how is our patient doing today, then?"

I replied: "Before you came I was reading a book to Jumbo."

The doctor threw a look of astonishment at Pa, and then another one at Ma and then he asked me in a steady voice: "To Jumbo? A book? Who's this Jumbo?"

"Ah," I said, "You've never laid eyes on our Jumbo. So I'll explain. Jumbo's the name of my elephant. We go round together all the time. You can't see him at the moment because he's in a stable at Bejval's place chatting to the mares. When I get up again I'll show you him. Don't worry about it, he's not causing any trouble."

The doctor adjusted his pince-nez, smiled and said: "Ah! So there we are. Now I see what you mean. Hm. To tell you the truth, I've heard a bit about Jumbo already. He's the talk of the town. When I've got a bit of spare time I must meet him. For my part it will be a pleasure. Hm. Well, well. Shall we take a look at your temperature now?"

He took the thermometer from under my armpit, looked at it, shook his head and said something in a soft voice to Ma and Pa. I overheard him saying something about a Crisis and I knew at once who this Crisis was.

I should say that Mrs. Crisis walks around in a thick, shaggy fur coat and has ears like a dog. She wears blue gloves and her hands lean against two shields with the coats of arms of cities on them. And she has an acorn for an ear on either side of her head. She's easy to make out by her broad mouth full of awfully big teeth. And she lives in a house across the river and comes out when it's dark to catch small children and put them in her sack and then she sells them to the tinkers.

I'm well aware of what Mrs. Crisis is like, because I've seen her portrait on a poster hanging at Žaloudek the to-bacconist's. I remember the fact that there was a notice in capital letters on the poster saying: Piatnik's Playing Cards.

When the doctor talked about a crisis Pa fiddled with his moustache and his hands trembled, while Ma's face was a picture of deep concern. But I said: "Don't worry, she won't catch me, because I'm clever and know how to run really quickly. And if anything happens I'll tell Mr. Letovský the constable and he'll draw his sabre and cut her down."

And then I went on: "And anyway have no fear because all this is just a dream. There's no Mrs. Crisis and no doctor who took my temperature, nothing like that. Just wait for me to wake up again. I'll be out of bed in a jiffy and off to the Bejvals, where I'm meeting the boys."

And so once the doctor was out of the house I jumped out of bed and ran to Bejval where I found all the boys already waiting. There was Anthony Bejval, Edward Kemlink, Chris Jirsák, Joe Zilvar and little Victor Štěpánek, so when I arrived that made us half a dozen.

And when all six of us were together, Bejval said: "Fellow braves! The Ješiňák tribe is once again on the warpath and spoiling for a fight with us. We won't start anything with them, but they won't leave us alone. This morning Ma asked me to go for milk, so I took a can and on my way I ran into that carrot top Leo Ješina, the whole of whose freckly face looks as if flies have been doing their business there. Meanwhile I'm just minding my own business and my Ps and Qs, going on my way and doing what I'm doing. But he stopped me in my tracks saying: 'Give me that can, scoundrel!' and began a scrap. I replied in a slow voice: 'Let me go, you low fellow, I've done nothing to you.' But he didn't want to stop and kept trying to tear the can out of my hands, so I bashed him on the bonce with a stone and he yelled like blazes.

But then lo and behold, his terrible screeching meant the Ješiňáks began to gather round, so I ran like the clappers while Leopold Ješina was yelling behind me: 'Just you wait till you're passing our place!' It was clear from all this that we had to drop everything and go to war with the Ješiňáks in order to give them a beating. Otherwise the town would be too small for the two of us until the crack of doom. I came out with an Indian war cry of Yeeeaaaah!"

"Yeeeaaaah!" we all repeated in loud voices, of which mine was the loudest.

A fighting spirit gave us strength and we were eaten up with desire for revenge, though we knew that it was going to be a conflict full of hard knocks, because the Ješiňáks were very well armed. Our spies informed us that the Ješiňáks had asked Rudy Venclík and Johnny Pivec to come and work us over. I've already told you that these two men are married. Venclík manages a cutler's while Pivec has a soft drinks factory. But this doesn't make them ashamed about getting into fights with boys. They're both terribly strong and each of them can thrash boys at least five at a time.

So we talked over what to do. Eddie Kemlink's idea was that we'd do better to give these battles up and think of something smarter. Tony Bejval told Eddie that if he spoke like that to Jacob he'd take his whip to him. Jacob heard this and said "Fiddlesticks!" This made it clear that Jacob didn't want anything to do with any battles.

But Jumbo had been listening to what we were saying. He gave a faint smile and said in a slow voice in his elephantese: "What are you afraid of, gentlemen? I'll come along with you and you'll see just how I sort out these Ješiňáks. Just leave it to me. I'm not scared of thousands of Rudys and not even of millions of Johnnies."

These words took the faintness out of our hearts and we were no longer afraid of anything but trundled off to war with a spring in our step. Jumbo walked ahead and we marched behind him in military formation while the whole town looked on. Everyone said what dashing soldiers we were and there was no denying that.

So we kept marching until we reached a farmstead which was already in the land of the Ješiňáks. Next to a dunghill Jumbo gave the order for us to halt and so we stayed standing there, waiting to see what was going to happen. Jumbo roared in a booming voice that echoed all around: "Ješiňáks, come out of your holes!"

At these words the Ješiňáks came dashing forward from all sides, each one armed with a club studded with nails to make it hurt more, while they opened fire with stones from their pockets. And there was a great host of them, more and more coming all the time, thousands of Ješiňáks, millions of them, swarming through the surroundings, while we stood there alone, gripped by fear as our ranks began to waver. But Jumbo stayed calm and surveyed the scene with a lofty smile.

Rudy Venclík and Johnny Pivec stepped forth from the ranks of the Ješiňáks and began cursing and swearing wildly at Jumbo. They called him a circus vagrant, a buffoon, a grubby gypsy, they taunted him about his trunk, his great big ears and all the outside of him, they insulted his appearance and in a voice of mockery they called on him to pass the hat round so that everyone could pay something for his keep.

When he heard all this abuse Jumbo became very angry and said: "I am already nearly a hundred and eighty-eight years old, but I do confess that I've never seen ill-bred riff-raff like this. If it was children of school age swearing at me, I'd think: 'It's just that there's no brain in their heads. When they've grown up they'll be the wiser for it.' But then you get a pair of beanpoles like this – one in the cutlery business and the other with a soft drinks firm – both of them married and paying taxes and acting as if they'd just been cut down from the gallows by mistake. This should be passed on to the newspapers as the example set by some of their local citizens whose names they would rather not mention at such a moment. Shame on you, gentlemen!"

By way of reply to this lesson in manners one of the Ješiňáks threw a brick at the elephant. Jumbo flew into a rage and said: "Look here! You've just exhausted my patience."

With these words he bent down and scooped up a trunkful of manure from the dungheap. Then he sprayed Johnny Pivec and Rudy Venclík from head to foot in liquid stink.

You should have seen the way the men ran away with all the other Ješiňáks behind them. Terrified screams came from Johnny Pivec and Rudy Venclík, while people closed their windows as an incredible pong spread far and wide.

So off went the two who'd been drenched to their homes, and when they got to the door each called out in a piteous voice: "Oh wife, run me a hot bath and fetch clean clothes, because I stink to high heaven! Oh how I stink! Never did a cutler or a soft drinks maker stink like this!"

When they heard this Mrs. Pivec and Mrs. Venclík grabbed whatever was to hand, in the first instance a broom, and swept their husbands off the porch, yelling in loud voices: "I took an oath of fidelity to my husband before the altar, not to an inescapable stench. Get away from the building! You can take that stink right back to where you got it from! Yuk! It smells like the dog-catcher's sack! Clear off before you pollute the whole house!"

So Rudy the cutler was not allowed past the entrance to his workshop and Johnny had to give a wide berth to his soft drinks factory, until the stink oozed away from them, a reeking recounted to this day by the people of our town.

We boys, who go everywhere together, laughed at this with our high voices while Jumbo laughed with his low voice. My voice was the highest pitched, two pitches above Jumbo's. We laughed till the sun went down, till my insides hurt and Ma said: "What are you laughing at, little Pete?"

I opened my eyes and was amazed to see that I was lying in bed. And I said: "How could I not laugh when they were running like that, dripping liquid manure and shouting their heads off? We were all laughing so, and Jumbo was laughing too, till his eyes shed tears."

Pa came over from the shop, felt my forehead and asked what was going on.

Ma gave a sigh and said that I'd been dreaming about something.

"It wasn't a dream, Ma," I said, "it really did happen. How could it have been a dream, when I saw it with my own eyes? What about the spray, didn't I see it myself? You wouldn't say you were only dreaming if you'd smelt that incredible pong coming off them and spreading everywhere."

Ma asked me whether I was thirsty and when I said I was she gave me a glass of raspberry lemonade.

I drank it right down and Pa looked at his watch and said that the doctor should have been back and perhaps he'd been held up somewhere.

And I said: "You know, Pa, I really like being ill, because it means I get raspberry juice. When the doctor comes, ask him to prescribe me something very sweet as medicine. If I can have raspberry lemonade I'll stay ill for as long as the doctor wants me to, it's all the same to me."

Pa smiled and said that I was a real clever clogs. Ma smiled too and I was glad to see them happy and I added: "Let Christina come and see me, I've got something I must say to her."

Christina came in from the kitchen and stood in front of the bed drying her hands on her apron and I said: "You know something, you should have seen this. They thought they'd beaten us."

"Who thought they'd beaten you?" asked Christina.

"The Ješiňáks, of course. How can you ask such dumb questions? Jumbo came up with this terrific invention which made them stink to high heaven."

"What invention? Who's Jumbo? And who stank?" asked Christina as she began to chuckle horribly.

Ma sent Christina back to the kitchen, straightened the pillow under my head and said: "Don't speak, Petie, get some rest."

So I didn't say any more but closed my eyes and thought of how I must buy Jumbo a nice red hat.

This was the nice red hat that Jumbo had always wanted, and when I thought that he'd forgotten all about it he started stomping about, belly-aching and pestering all over again. "I want that nice red hat. I need it. I've got to have it." He went on to say that it must have a black tassel and gold fancy work round the border, like the one worn by the publican at 'The Golden Crow'. And he kept following me around and muttering: "Let me have a red cap, Sahib!" until I got annoyed with him and said "Stop grovelling, Jumbo, you're not a baby elephant any more."

On the other hand I must admit that I'd put the idea into his head, because I wanted him to tell me stories about India. I could see that he somehow didn't want to, but when I insisted he spoke about it, though without much liking for doing so.

"Why are you always going on about India?" he asked in a huffy voice. "There's nothing there. Just dust and gruelling heat and diseases which are all very catching. And no skating or sledging."

"But they do have bananas," I protested.

"Yes, they have bananas, but what of it?"

"Bananas and pineapples and all that sort of thing."

"They do have pineapples too," Jumbo admitted, "but that sort of fruit you can get here in all the shops."

"We don't have them in ours," I said, "we've only got figs, dates, carob bread and liquorice. India's a wonderful place with amazing butterflies."

"Yes, they have butterflies, Sahib, but what's that to me? I don't collect them. Of course they also have all sorts of flower species, with colours and shapes you'll never see elsewhere. For someone doing a project for their botany class, that would be all to the good, but I am not such a person. I never did botany. What interests me in plants is whether they can be eaten."

"There are also tigers in India."

"What's that to me? I don't speak to tigers. I don't make friends with every scoundrel in town."

Jumbo scowled and went into a sulk. To lift him out of his bad mood I began asking him about his family.

This put a swagger in his step and he told me proudly that his father was the best worker in the docks and that his word was law there because he was put in charge of all the other elephants.

"And what about all your other relatives? Uncles and aunts, girl cousins and boy cousins, sisters-in-law and brothers-in-law?"

Jumbo mumbled something about all his relatives not being worth a pipeful of tobacco because they didn't treat him well. There were some elephants who only lived for themselves and nothing good was to be expected of them.

When I asked him about his grandpa, Jumbo blushed, lapsed into a glum silence and fiddled with his trunk as if he was doodling in sand. I wouldn't take 'no' for an answer and kept asking him about his grandpa, because I guessed there was some family secret there.

In the end Jumbo leaned over and after looking carefully round in all directions whispered into my ear: "My grandpa, Sahib, was a wild elephant, but please don't tell anyone this or there'll be gossip."

Then he started telling anyway off his own bat and I was fascinated by what he remembered. Jumbo's grandpa frolicked around in the jungle with the rest of the herd like a marauder, causing damage wherever he went, living off forest fruits and drinking from a stream. He was ignorant of the higher things in life and the arts and sciences meant nothing to him, seeing that he'd never had any education. Jumbo's father was the first to feel a pang for something higher and a desire to learn about the world. He went to school himself and supported the education of his son.

Jumbo went on speaking for a long time and I hung on every word. When he'd finished he gave a sigh and said: "You wouldn't believe all the tribulations I've suffered in my time."

I said that I'd like to see what India was like, because I could send our teacher a postcard from India and he'd make sure it was passed round the whole class. Jumbo didn't want to hear of this so we squabbled and I said that if that was how he felt I wouldn't be friends with him any more. This made Jumbo's lip curl and he said: "I don't give a hoot."

Then I carried on talking about India with Eddie Kemlink, but not until I'd talked about it with Tony Bejval, who was all for it and said that we should form a club and we'd hunt tigers and other wild animals in India and bring their skins back.

Then one day I began speaking to Jumbo about this again and he said that he wouldn't be totally against it after all, but if he was off to India I had to buy him a red cap.

"Just why do you want a red cap?" I inquired in an amazed voice, because it really did surprise me.

Jumbo replied: "I want a red cap because my family was always making a lot of my starting to work in the circus which meant going far away. They said that people valued me a lot and claimed I'd made a pile of money. And they went on about how when I went back home I'd buy a bungalow and want for nothing and no longer have any worries."

I said that I didn't follow what he was saying.

"Why ever not?" answered Jumbo, "what is there that can't be followed? If I went there in my birthday suit like Adam, then everyone would laugh at me and say: 'Aha! There we have it! Mr. Jumbo turned up his trunk at us, nothing was good enough for him with his swollen head. And now see him, coming home looking like a vagabond and without a penny to his name to sponge off his family some more.' O Sahib, you've no idea what my family is like. Each one is worse than the next and envy alone will have them counting the hairs on each other's backs."

"That sounds like the Vařekas," I said, "they are forever green with envy as well."

"They don't even come close," was the firm response from Jumbo. "How could these Vařekas get a look in? My family's a million times worse. They're the talk of India."

I said: "If it's really how you say it is, Jumbo, I'll get you that hat."

Jumbo was over the moon and jumped for joy as he said: "That's the ticket, Sahib. With a nice red cap I'd be game for anything. A nice red cap with tassels and a black pom-pom on top and some gold embroidery all the way round it. Oh I'm cock-a-hoop, quite cock-a-hoop!"

So the very next day I set out with Jumbo on a red cap mission to Mr. Jirsák. I told the elephant to wait outside because there wasn't room in the shop for swinging a cat if he was there and I went in alone. I greeted Mr. Jirsák nicely and he tilted the glasses on his nose while saying in a friendly voice: "A warm welcome to you, young man, what will we be having now?"

I offered Mr. Jirsák another nice greeting and asked if he'd be so good as to make Jumbo a nice red cap.

Mr. Jirsák replied: "Whatever has to be made I will make – that's why I'm a cap maker. And where might he be, this elephant?"

I said that Jumbo was waiting in front of the shop, because he was unable to enter it on account of his size.

Mr. Jirsák said: "If the mountain won't come to Mohammed, Mohammed must go to the mountain." Then he said to Chris: "Come along, boy, your Pa needs a hand."

Then they both went outside and I went with them. Chris had to lean a ladder up against the elephant so that his measurements could be taken and Mr. Jirsák climbed up it. Chris passed him the tape measure. And Mr. Jirsák went round the head measuring and calling out numbers, while Chris wrote everything down in a notebook. At the same time Mr. Jirsák inquired of Jumbo how he would like to have his cap so far as colour, shape and design were concerned.

The elephant said: "I want it to be a red cap."

"Red will suit the gentleman very well," said Mr. Jirsák.

And Jumbo said: "And it should have tassels round it."

"Then tassels it will be," said Mr. Jirsák. "Tassels have been much in demand this year."

And Jumbo said: "It should have a black pom-pom on top too."

"A pom-pom goes without saying," said Mr. Jirsák. "What would a cap be without a pom-pom?"

"I would also like," Jumbo continued, "some gold embroidery all around it."

"Plain as a pikestaff!" said Mr. Jirsák, "What else but gold can go with black?"

"Above all, Master Tailor," said Jumbo, "it should be modern."

"You may rest assured, Honoured Sir," said Mr. Jirsák, "that we make our hats according to the latest Paris fashions. Honoured Sir will be one of the swells, an eminence to turn heads and win success in the world of women. Every female elephant will surely fall in love with His Lordship. It will be something most singular, the like of which has never been seen before."

A lot of people crowded round while Mr. Jirsák took Jumbo's measurements and gawped at what was going on.

And Mr. Jirsák said: "It will not be a cap, it will be a work of art. His Lordship will see that for himself and will thank me for it."

Jumbo was overjoyed and then said that he would wish the cap to be ready the following week, when he'd be celebrating his one hundred and eighty-eighth birthday.

Mr. Jirsák attended to an itch behind his ear and said: "Holy smoke, you really mean next week? That's a deuce of a rushed job! One might call this a cap but it's a cap like no other. It's as if I had to produce caps for a company of dragoons. After all this blessed cap will require at least five yards of red felt and it's not ready-made either. Hell's bells, dash it all! Never mind, if there's no other way then we will work after hours. I am much obliged, Your Honour, we will have the first fitting the day after tomorrow. Chris, hold the ladder!"

Chris held the ladder while Mr. Jirsák climbed down. When he reached ground level he rounded on the people standing around goggle-eyed.

"What the devil is the matter with you lot? Have you never seen an elephant being measured up for a cap? What strange folk."

And the people went away.

Then I told Jumbo to take himself home and said that I'd follow a moment later. And off home Jumbo went. However, I followed Mr. Jirsák into the building and there I asked him to take care that, God willing, he didn't make a mess of the hat in any way because Jumbo had a sensitive nature and he would take something like that badly.

Mr. Jirsák said: "Bear in mind, young man, that in all his years old Jirsák has never bungled a thing yet, because old Jirsák is a name you can rely on, old Jirsák could show you a thousand letters of thanks for the talents he holds in such abundance."

I said that I believed him, that I put my trust in him whatever the circumstances and had only mentioned this to be on the safe side.

Whereupon Mr. Jirsák asked me what the red cap was for and I told him that it was all to do with India.

Christopher muscled in on the conversation and said that he would also like to see India because there were many lessons to be learned there, but such a thing wasn't going to happen. That was because at such a distance and in such a hot climate he might commit a sin, whether from anger or absent-mindedness, from pride or from greed, because such a wild landscape gave rise to many of the vainer forms of worldliness. And the worst of it was that he couldn't even go to confession, India being a land of heathens, where nothing grew but spices, pagans and creatures of the wild. Besides all that he had to help out at home.

But Mr. Jirsák said: "So far as helping out is concerned, don't worry your head about it. It's not as if you're such a great help and your mother and I can manage just fine if needs be. And as for these sins, perhaps there's a parson to be found somewhere out there, and if not then it's not the end of the world either! Somehow you'll muddle through bearing the weight of all these sins, and when you get back then you can hop along to confession. Contrary to what you'll be imagining, I'd like to see you experience life, pay attention to the way things actually are and get some education, so that you'll have a better idea of what it's all about than your pa. If you took twenty years off me then I'd break the yolk myself and wild horses couldn't drag me back again."

Chris was awfully pleased at this and said: "You mean you'd let me set off on my travels with Bajza, Pa?"

Mr. Jirsák said: "Off you go, lad. A youngster should learn about the world and its ways. If you're wise to the world, you will value your home all the more. Pack all your belongings in an orderly manner so that you don't overlook anything and when the moment comes set off for this confounded India. You have my blessing on your expedition."

And Mr. Jirsák went on to say: "But don't forget to pack your tuba so that you don't get out of practice. Then if you should happen to feel homesick you can play something merry and at once lighten the load about your heart."

"How did you sleep, Petie?" I was really puzzled when my mother asked me this question while stroking my hair, so I replied: "How could I have been sleeping, Ma, when I had to be off to Mr. Jirsák with Jumbo on account of the cap?" Ma gave me a thoughtful look and said nothing.

Even Pa turned up from the shop. He sat on the bed beside me and I asked him: "Pa, how much do you think Mr. Jirsák will charge to make a cap for an elephant?"

Pa stroked his chin, twirled his moustache and then replied: "There are all sorts of caps and no one cap is like another."

I said: "It should be a cap with a pom-pom on top and gold embroidery right round the rim and with tassels down below."

"When there are tassels and all the trappings," said Pa, "then it could be very pricey. Jirsák is a good worker, there's no gainsaying that, but he swallows money like a pharmacy."

"Pa," I asked after a while, "will you give me some money in case I don't have enough?"

Pa seemed to fill himself with air like a tyre at a pump as he said: "If that's the way it has to be, I can foot the bill. It can never be said of me that I don't delve into my pockets. I did so for the elephant, so I will not bemoan the loss of a few pennies on a cap. Let bankruptcy stare me in the face."

I didn't say any more but just reflected on the fact that Pa was the nicest of them all because he paid for everything. A moment later I thought that Ma was even nicer than Pa, but in two shakes of lamb's tail it seemed to me that Pa was back in front as the nicer one. I considered the matter for a long time but I couldn't decide the winner.

And Ma said that the boys who went round with me had been there asking how I was. This was strange to me, because I'd been speaking with Chris Jirsák just a moment beforehand and he hadn't asked me anything, but then I reflected: Perhaps I'm asleep and it's all a dream.

I was scared by the thought that Pa had promised me money for the hat in a dream, and that when I woke up he wouldn't want to know anything about it and would yell at me horribly about not being everyone's bank. So just to be sure I asked him once more: "So you'll really pay for the cap? You're not just saying it?"

And Pa replied: "Touch my nose and see if I'm lying." I did as he told me and the nose was hard. I saw from this that Pa was telling the truth and he said: "Now you know, slyboots. Just you remember that if your pa gives his word that word is law."

At this moment the bell tinkled in the shop and Pa got up to serve a customer, but Ma said: "Sit down, father, I'll do it myself," and Pa said: "No way, mother, I'll see to it," and then they argued for some time about who should go to the shop, which meant no one went.

But then it transpired that it wasn't a customer at all, it was the Vařekas, and Ma said: "Look who's come to see us," and Pa said: "Hell's teeth!" and Uncle Silas said: "We've come to see the malingerer," and Aunt Emily said: "What do you think you're doing? Such a lazybones, how come you're allowed to be ill in times like ours? Who can afford the doctor's bills anyway?"

Uncle sighed deeply and said: "These doctors, what a shower! They only know how to take piles of money off you. That's the only thing they understand."

And my aunt said: "We never call a doctor. It's neither here nor there. Where would it get us? When something's wrong with anyone, I give them herbal tea with valerian to take at night. It makes them sleep and the next day they bounce back fresh as daisies. That's the best thing to do. If we had to call a doctor for every complaint we'd have to pack our bags and go straight to the poorhouse. Only rich families can afford to be ill, where there's good money waiting to be thrown after bad."

Then they spoke quickly and in loud voices, saying that it was better to be in sound than in ill health, and then they spoke slowly and in a very low voice to say that our doctor was already buying a second home, it goes without saying, he was always busy feathering his nest and their eyes lit up with envy as they spoke till they looked like those of our tomcat Honza.

Ma said that health was more important than property, and Pa said that he never regretted a single penny that went on his children and Uncle Silas said: "Don't talk like that, brother-in-law, who on earth can toss money out of the window these days?"

Pa said that it wasn't a question of tossing money out of the window when a doctor was summoned to the bedside of a sick child, and that in any case he wasn't expecting anyone to help him out with the bills and my aunt said in a terribly reedy voice "Even so there'd have been no need for young Peter to be ill if he'd been properly brought up and looked after," and Pa said in a deep voice "You seem to think it's our fault that the child's sick," and my aunt went on in the same thin voice: "I'm not speaking of that one way or another because I'm someone who keeps her thoughts to herself," and Uncle said everyone's entitled to their own opinions, there's no offence in that, he had his opinions too, whether they liked it or not. And he went on: "How can the boy be anything but sick, what with your cooking being so rich, far too rich to do his stomach any good?"

As I listened I became furious at the way my uncle and aunt talked and I thought of what nasty things, really nasty things, I could say to them to stop them going on and then I said that Pa was coughing up money to buy a red cap for an elephant. It would have a pom-pom and tassels all around it and Mr. Jirsák would need four yards of cloth for the making of it, not to mention at least a hundredweight of gold. And I went on: "And the hat will cost one million, one thousand one hundred."

When I'd finished my aunt fixed her eyes on my uncle who fixed his on my aunt. They screwed up their mouths and looked at each other for a long time. Then they suddenly broke the silence together: "And then one wonders what you spend your money on," and after that they said the child couldn't have thought of this himself, they knew now just what we were like, we simply treated them as the butt of our jokes.

Ma asked in surprise: "What jokes, Em? I don't follow you."

My aunt rose to her feet smoothed out the folds in her dress and remarked: "I, on the other hand, follow what is being said only too well." To Uncle she said: "Up you get and off we go." To me she said: "I bet you're only ill because of the sort of things you get up to. We shall never set foot in this house again."

Pa said: "Well good riddance to bad rubbish."

Off they went at great speed and red in the face, my aunt's boots making funny noises as if they were saying: "Serves you right! Serves you right!"

And when they'd gone Pa gave a guffaw and went "Ha! Ha! Ha!" and he said to Ma: "What lovely relatives you have, Mother, you should put them in an exhibition." And Ma guffawed with a "He! He! He!" and said to Pa: "How could I send them to an exhibition when they're your relatives, not mine?" And Christina heard all this from the kitchen and she laughed in the highest voice of all going "Hee! Hee! Hee!" and Ma told her off saying "Shhh!, you scatterbrained girl, there isn't a scrap of sense in you, the child wants to sleep."

But I didn't want to sleep, because I had to go to Mr. Jirsák's with Jumbo so that he could try on his red cap.

And so I jumped out of bed and straight away said to Jumbo that he must try on the red cap to make sure that it was a good fit, and off we went, Jumbo and I, and we were a two. And all the way there I could hear Pa's deep guffaw going off "Ha! Ha! Ha!", Ma's highish voice going "He! He! He!" and the Rampusite squeaking "Hee! Hee! Hee!" in the highest voice of all until I was sick of the sound and thought to myself that the Rampusite should save her 'Hee! Hee! Hee!'s for when she was out walking with her boyfriend.

On we went, Jumbo and I, until we got to Mr. Jirsák's and he said: "The top of the morning to you," and straight away stood his ladder up against Jumbo and climbed to the top of the elephant, seizing hold of the red cap with Christopher's help and setting it down on Jumbo's head. Then they took a look and Mr. Jirsák said in a voice triumphant: "Call that a cap? It's a heavenly poem written in cloth. With such headgear Your Honour can frequent the most select society. In a cap like that Your Honour could go directly to the Financiers' Ball, seeing that He looks the very picture of a baron." And down the ladder he came, Chris with him, and the three of us stood back to see how the cap fitted.

Jumbo asked me if I could lend him a pocket mirror, because he too wanted to see what a fine figure he cut. So I held the mirror for him to take a look and he screwed up his left eye and then a little later screwed up his right eye before lifting a leg and doing a twirl and all the time looking rather smug and pleased with himself.

Then he asked Mr. Jirsák to make the hat lopsided. Mr. Jirsák said: "Whatever you wish," and climbed up the ladder once more in order to oblige his customer. Jumbo said that it had to be very lopsided since this was the latest fashion. Then he took another look at himself in the mirror, saw his manly appearance and how majestic he looked, turned pink with pleasure and said that it was the cap of his dreams.

I asked Mr. Jirsák what it would cost and he replied: "Ah well now, as and when, a bit here and a bit there, mind you and heavens above I don't suppose this is a matter to make us go to the magistrate for a judgement, wouldn't you say?" And then he said that some day he'd be calling at our shop and choosing some merchandise to make us quits. I said: "Right, then."

And when we'd left the place Jumbo strutted around like a milord and took a peek in all directions to see whether people were looking at him and when he saw that they were indeed looking he flushed with pride. Then he said: "I'm very elegant but I'd be more elegant still if I had a cloth on my back and a bow on my tail."

But I told him he must think I was made of money to want all this. I went on to say that he should wait a bit because you can't have everything all at once. He didn't say any more but I could see that he was running over even more frills and finery in his mind.

This was the day on which we met together in front of our shop because we were off to India. There was Anthony Bejval, who came with a bike, Edward Kemlink, Christopher Jirsák and Joe Zilvar from the poorhouse. I counted us up and we were a handful. Bejval had a suitcase in which he'd got a change of underwear, a torch, a catapult with a rubber band and a bun filled with poppy-seed. Kemlink brought a briefcase in which he had two pairs of socks, a scarf to prevent him from going down with a sore throat, a bag of lozenges, a firecracker, an insect exterminator in the form of a powder, a map of India and its outskirts, a compass and the address of a certain Mr. Brabec, who is a tailor in the capital city Calcutta. He got this address from Mr. Kemlink, since he said that Mr. Brabec would give us a hand if needed. Chris Jirsák turned up with a rucksack in which he had a whole pile of Cowboy and Indian books and a starting pistol with five caps. He also had this powder which can be used for a Bengal light so we'd be able to make one ourselves. It's something really amazing. He had turmeric seeds too, which would take the pain away if we ate something that was bad for us, and a thermos flask which his ma had filled with coffee. And Zilvar turned up with a bundle inside which he had a loaf of bread and a piece of cheese, as well as a clasp knife and a snare for catching hares, if we saw any hares, and he'd also been given a clip round the ears for the journey by Mr. Zilvar, in return for which Zilvar nicked a packet of tobacco which will be going up in smoke during our trip.

And when we were all together Jodaska, the widow from across the road, came running up to say that if we met a certain Mr. Mothejzlík in India we should pass on to him the fact that she'd have to put his goat up for sale, since it was off its food and she couldn't cope with it on her own. We'd be able to make out Mr. Mothejzlík from his flannel waistcoat and the cotton wool in his ears, not to mention the fact that any change in the weather made him lisp. I said that we'd pass the message on.

Mr. Letovský the constable also came along and wished us the best of luck, a safe return and good weather. And he looked up at the sky as he spoke and said: "I somehow think it's clouding over where we are." And he went on to say that if we came across a tiger getting ready to spring at us we shouldn't be scared but make sure to give it a thump on the head with something and then it would lay off.

The mayor also came over from the town hall. He shook us all by the hand and said that if our paths crossed with a maharajah's we should pass on his kind regards, because our town has had the best of relations with India since time immemorial, and the closest ties of friendship between our people and the Indian nation go at least as far back as the Přemysl dynasty.

Our teacher came dashing up at the last moment and hoped that he was speaking from the hearts of all those present when he wished us lots of luck on our journey and that we would weather the dangers and surmount all the obstacles placed in our path without meeting disaster. And with great emphasis he urged us not to forget, even when we were in tropical climes noted for their rampant vegetation, that we were sons of our own soil who should set an example wherever we went. He also impressed upon us that we should try to improve our knowledge, and that if we saw anything worthy of note we should write it down in a special exercise book.

And many other people came too, among them the bleating greengrocer and Mr. Fajst. Mr. Fajst urged us to greet everyone we met in India politely so that the Indians did not think of us as the insolent bratlings we were. Zilvar said that we wouldn't give anyone our regards on purpose and that if anyone in India asked us who we were we'd say our last name was Fajst. Then Mr. Fajst called us louts and went away.

Ma and Pa came out in front of the shop. Ma had her hands full of Mirabelle, who kept screaming for the elephant so that she could cuddle him, and Christina was there too, wiping her hands on her apron and giving horrible little squeals of excitement. And Jacob came too, making his way from Bejval's place. He patted Jumbo and said: "Well, old chap!"

And when the hour struck in the tower, Jumbo held out his trunk for me and I climbed onto his back and called out in a loud voice: "Onwards and upwards, men!" and then we all started to move forward. And as we were passing the sweetshop Eve Svoboda came running out in front of us and said that she'd really like to come to India too, but back home they didn't want to let her go, with Mr. Svoboda saying: "I've never been in India and somehow I've survived anyway," while Mrs. Svoboda said: "I've never been in India either and I found myself a husband all the same. If you stay at home you'll also find a good catch." Thereupon Eve told them at home that she was going to her sewing class and arrived with a handbag stuffed with heaps of sugar candies which she dished out to all of us, though she gave me more than anyone else.

So I said she could come with us, which was really kind of me since we were setting out with tremendous adventures in store for us, death lying in wait for a man of daring at every step of his journey. This was not the sort of thing for girls as they don't know how to look death in the face. The elephant put his trunk round Eve's waist and sat her down on his back. She was so happy to be on high, but I told her that when she got into trouble for it at home it would surely be me who'd get all the blame, because everything was always made to be my fault, even though I didn't do anything and the others were much worse than I was. But Eve said that there'd be no trouble at home, because when she didn't get back in time for dinner they'd think she'd gone to her aunt's place and this would please her parents because they were looking to inherit money from this aunt.

So I kept quiet and nibbled at the sugar candies, white ones first and then the pink and then the yellow, but I left the brown ones to the end because they're the best. The other chaps sucked at their candies too and kept it up as far as the station. Anthony Bejval went to the booking office and bought tickets to India for everyone and the clerk asked him to bring back some Indian stamps for his collection and Bejval said: "Why not? Consider it done."

And then we were well on our way with the train going 'Clickety clack, clickety clack – oh what a stupid Ješiňák'. It spoke really quickly saying rude things and when we went into a tunnel the train gave a piercing shriek like a pig carried in a farmer's sack. I wrote down the names of the stations in my notebook so that I'd know them when the teacher quizzed me. Eddie Kemlink was studying maps, Bejval was looking at the scenery and Zilvar from the poorhouse was filling his pipe, puffing at it and spitting all around. People got on and Zilvar spoke with them like a grown-up, saying that time and tide waited for no man, that it all made one think, that the weather was nothing to write home about, that a poor 'arvest was in the offing and the cost of living was going through the roof and some people were worse than the beasts of the field. And we were amazed at the way Zilvar could talk like a grown-up while he puffed away and put power into his spitting. Eve on the other hand was looking at a mirror and squeezing a pimple which had turned up on her chin.

Suddenly the train came to a halt and a man let out a terrible yell from the track: "India, all change please!" So we all grabbed our luggage and got off the train and there we were in India.

We looked all round us and saw these giant houses, at least a million times bigger than the count's castle back home, and there was a great horde of people there going hither and thither. They were chocolate-coloured and spoke to each other really quickly in the Indian dialect.

We didn't know our way about there because everything was different and then we spotted a policeman. So Eddie Kemlink went up to him and greeted him nicely and asked him where Mr. Brabec was staying.

The policeman replied: "If you want to pay your respects to Mr. Brabec, Sir, you must head for Mahatma Gandhi street, which is close to George of Poděbrady square. If you take my advice, you'll go down the hill, proceed across Colliery Court and then take a right before side-stepping to the left and taking a short cut through a passageway. When you come out of there you'll see a porter. Go round the good man and then you'll spot a chemist's. Change direction at this point and carry on further. Whereupon your eyes will fall upon an ironing room and a machine-operated mangle. Mr. Brabec lives right opposite. However, I do have some concern, Sir, that you will not catch him at home. I say that because at this time of day Mr. Brabec is to be found in a public house where he engages Mr. Mohammed Ali in a game of billiards. The public house in question is known as The Edible Fruit Bat. You may care to recognize it from the likeness of a waiter standing in front of it. The gentleman has been cast in metal."

Kemlink thanked him politely for his information, advice and guidance, after which we had a pow-wow about what to do. Bejval said that it would be best to go to Brabec's home and wait for him there.

"After all he can't be in the pub the whole time, at some point he's got to go home," said Bejval.

We said he was right and so that's where we went. And while we were on our way we spotted a man sitting on the ground who was almost naked and had a wicker basket at his feet.

This half-naked man was playing a very mournful tune on a pipe and we stopped next to him for a look. When we'd been watching for a while we saw snakes come crawling out of the basket, each of them wearing a pince-nez. And as the nearly naked man played his pipe the snakes moved to the tune as if they were dancing.

When I saw this I couldn't stop laughing and said: "Look at that, chaps, these snakes are real idiots. They think they've got to dance when the man plays his pipe."

One snake heard this and crawled right out of the basket. It stood right in front of me like an upright stick and made a terrible face after which it said in a loud voice: "Who are you calling an idiot? Just say that again."

I didn't want the retarded reptile to think that I was scared of him, so I came back in a lofty voice saying: "You are an idiot and these other snaky chums of yours are idiots too but you're the biggest idiot of all."

The snake eyed me through its glasses and hissed terribly. Then it went for me saying: "You'll pay for that, you no good son of a no good father, one day I'll give you what for, just you see if I don't."

I got really angry at this: "Who do you think you're calling names, you birdbrain?" I seized hold of a stick and said: "Come on then! If you feel up to it."

Then the other boys grabbed hold of stones and I saw that all hell was about to break loose.

But by now all the snakes had climbed out of the basket and there was a great crowd of them and the nearly naked man was egging them on against us saying: "Have at them, lads, bite their calves!"

One of the snakes had a spiteful smile on its face as it lunged at Eddie Kemlink and bit him and Ed cried out in a terrible voice: "Heaven help me, I'm at death's door!" and fell to the ground. Eve let out a shriek, because she hated snakes, and all the boys ran away leaving me to win the battle on my own but there were too many snakes for me to overcome on my own and the half-naked man was urging them on all the time with his Indian voice saying: "Get to work, lads, see that they don't dare take you on again!" and I threw stones one after another but there were more and more snakes making me yell my head off.

And Ma said: "Calm yourself down, Petie. I'll give you some medicine and it'll make you feel better."

She gave me some medicine in a teaspoon. My teeth were chattering and I was shaking from the battle to get the better of the snakes. It was night time and Pa hurriedly began to put his shoes on so as to rush off for the doctor and get him to take my temperature. But I told Pa that he wasn't allowed out on a night like this because it was teeming with snakes out there and they'd all been whipped up into a fury. And I went on to say that those snakes didn't scare me. I'd given them what for and the name of Peter Bajza and his titanic strength would be remembered in India for a long time. The snakes would pass the word on to their grandsons about the great hiding they got.

I came out with lots of boasting so that Ma and Pa didn't think I was scared, but the truth was that I had plenty of fear in me, because there were so many of these snakes, each one of them wearing a pince-nez just like the one our head of school wears, and their eyes glared at me through the glasses as if they wanted to say: "Bajza, Bajza, you dirty little sneak, you black sheep who spreads his poison among the whole flock."

And I felt sorry for Eddie Kemlink, seeing that everyone bitten by one of those snakes had to die and so much poison had got into Eddie that he died and had a funeral.

The bell tolled in the church tower and Christopher Jirsák walked ahead carrying a cross. Being stuck up, he didn't want to let anyone else hold it. And Mr. Rektorys, who gives us violin lessons, led the musicians and played the carrynet. When he wasn't playing he was waving his arms around as if warding off flies to make the musicians keep to the tune, and Mr. Jirsák blew his trombone and his face filled with puff.

And Eve Svoboda was there as a maid of honour, dressed in white with a garland on her head which she thought suited her really well. You could see how proud she was from the dainty little steps she took. And we lads, who go around together, were all sad, because just a while back we'd been a handful and now we were only a four.

So we made our way to the cemetery with the band playing something mournful and Eddie was stuck in a coffin and the coffin was inside a hearse which was black. The horses drawing the hearse were also black and the driver wore black clothes and on his head he had a top hat which was black too.

And people looked on, lots of them, and I was the saddest of them all and I was thinking that I'd lend Eddie a book called 'The Ghost of Llano Estacado' so that it wouldn't matter to him that he was dead. I told him this but Eddie grinned and answered: "You can lend me 'The Ghost of Llano Estacado' if you want, because I'd really like to read it, but in any case you needn't be sorry that I'm dead, it's all a load of rubbish but you're so easily fooled, you believe anything they tell you."

I was so happy to hear him say this and I knew at once that Eddie wasn't even a little bit dead and that it must have seemed to me he was because he was normally red and round, with a fat face and the cheeks of a cherub. And he wasn't dead at all, not even a little bit.

Then I went on: "If you're really not dead but still living normally as you say you are, then we'll have to go and see Mr. Brabec."

So we went to see Mr. Brabec and all the lads came along. Eve Svoboda and Jumbo came too, so all in all we were a seven.

It was terribly hot because India is a tropical latitude, which is something we've learned at school. As we went along we kept asking people for directions and they told us the right way to go.

When we reached the place we saw a two-storeyed building with a porch where the words 'Victor Brabec, esquire, Tailor to Men and Boys' were written on a notice board. We knew from this that we'd come the right way. So we knocked on the door, wiped our shoes on the doormat and went inside.

Mrs. Brabec was singing something sorrowful while she ironed clothes. When she caught sight of us she asked what we wanted and we told her.

Then she said: "Take a seat, young Sirs, my one and only will be here at any moment."

Then she went on to say that she was fed up to the back teeth with everything, that she was worn out, that no one would believe her, that her head was in a muddle, that she'd lost all feeling in her feet, that no one was sorry for her, that she didn't deserve this, that she had a cross to bear, that she'd never had any luck, that other people knew how to come into this world with a silver spoon in their mouths but she'd never had anything from her life except for a scrap of food to live on, and that she hadn't slept a wink all night because her youngest had teething troubles.

Zilvar told her that this was life and about as good as it got.

Then Mrs. Brabec said that Mr. Brabec was partial to the hard stuff and it knocked the sense out of him.

Once again Zilvar said that this was as good as it got.

And Mrs. Brabec went on to say that her man spent all his time in the pub and preferred his drinking pals to his home and hearth.

And Zilvar came back once more to say that this was as good as it got.

And Mrs. Brabec said that she wouldn't put up with things for much longer because she was going to hit Mr. Brabec across the face with a wet rag so that he'd learn his lesson once and for all.

Again Zilvar said that this was as good as it got and one must learn to live with such things.

And Mrs. Brabec asked: "Tell me this, what have I done, that I have to be so unhappy?"

And Zilvar replied: "There's food for thought in all this."

And Mrs. Brabec said to Zilvar that he was a well-educated young man, who knew what it was all about, and that she'd known herself from the beginning that he must come from a good family, because he spoke in a bookish manner. Zilvar said that he was from the poorhouse, where he'd picked up all sorts of things to do with a proper education.

Mrs. Brabec said: "I knew that from the moment you started to speak," and this made Zilvar very proud.

Then Mrs. Brabec treated us to raspberry lemonade and we drank it down greedily because we were all under the sway of a raging thirst.

While we were guzzling down that good red raspberry lemonade, footsteps sounded in the hallway and soon after the door flew open and a tall, strong and hefty man came into the room. He had a huge moustache and a turban on his head and I knew at once that this was Mr. Brabec because he had a tape measure round his neck and a small cushion full of needles over his chest. He remained standing in the doorway and folded his arms in front of his chest while he bowed deeply three times and said: "Welcome, distinguished guests." And he turned to Mrs. Brabec and said: "Your good health, my Maharani."

Mrs. Brabec said: "It's high time you were here, my Maharajah, my noble husband, who doesn't even know what time he's supposed to be back home, where his faithful slave-girl Julia, his dear wife, has been thinking to herself that he'd linger on in that pub forever, stuck there like an ingrowing toenail, preferring his friends to his wife, while in the meantime his lunch has burnt to a cinder in the oven. I can't bear the sight of this any more and I'm off to my mother's...." and so she went on for some time.

Mr. Brabec replied: "Oh hold that tongue of yours, woman, it's sharper than an Indian sabre. Please calm yourself down in front of these distinguished guests of ours. Allah is my witness that you bring shame upon my head and do so without knowing when to stop and it muddles up my brains. Saint Procopius was right to say that a woman's tongue moves faster than a messenger bringing bad tidings. I'd rather you told us what we had for our lunch."

"There's mutton with rice," said Mrs. Brabec.

Mr. Brabec made a face and said: "Rice yesterday, rice today and rice tomorrow. I'm sick to death of it."

"Then be off with you to a hotel, since you're such a fine gentleman, I can't always be serving up haute cuisine, not in times like these, if you would only stop your blaspheming, one day you'll be glad of a meal like this, it's the best mutton, Brahmaputra the butcher puts the best piece to one side for me, seeing that we're good customers of his, not like the others who buy on tick."

"That's enough!" shouted Brabec the tailor, "bring it to the table."

Brabec the tailor ate his lunch with relish and as he was doing so, he asked us for our names, where we came from and what our line of work was. Eddie Kemlink passed on greetings from his father. When he heard this the face of Mr. Brabec lit up and he beamed with pleasure and stroked his moustache, which was glistening with grease from the mutton, and started to recall the years of his youth.

And he said: "Kemlink was my closest friend, because his inventions were the best. He had the most brilliant brainwaves about making mischief. The whole town prophesied that he'd die a pauper's miserable death, but Allah decreed otherwise and brought it about in his unfathomable wisdom that Kemlink is now a pen pusher in the tax office and for that reason is held in high regard by people. Kemlink and I were thick as thieves and always going around together. You never saw one of us without the other."

He thought things over for a while and then asked: "So what's new in your neck of the woods? Are there still snowstorms?"

"Loads of snow," we told him.

"And are there snowstorms in Lukavice? And in Javornice, are there snowstorms there too? What about in Drahý? Or Lána? Dubinka? Habrová? Do they all get snow? Oh the beauty of it when everything's white, when snow flurries gather and spread across the fields and the frost draws fantastic plants and trees and mountain ranges and strange creatures on the windows. Here in India it never snows. The sun beats down incessantly and sadness holds sway."

Thus spoke Mr. Brabec while we sat there in silence and listened to him talking and drank the good red raspberry lemonade because we never stopped being thirsty. Then Mrs. Brabec brought sweets for us, heaps of them, blue and red and green and yellow gobstoppers and among them maroon glaciers with cream which I really love. The other boys went straight for these candied chestnuts, but I thought I'd save them till last and I said to myself that the boys would scoff the candied chestnuts and then try to scrounge mine but I won't give them any, I'll just say: "You could have saved them as I did, that's why I kept eating the gobstoppers", but the gobstoppers weren't nice at all and I had to keep eating them and hurrying through them so that they went away but there were more and more of them and they dried out my throat and when I wanted the glaciers they'd gone and I looked for them, hunted for them a long time and everyone was jeering at me, Christopher Jirsák was grinning horribly and I was shouting at the top of my voice "Ma! They've eaten my glaciers! Ma, tell them to give me my marrons glacés, I want them!"

Ma put a cold compress on my forehead and Pa stood over me looking sad and Christina dried her eyes on her apron and had a red nose and I looked at them all and then I said: "They guzzled down those splendiferous chocolate chestnuts. I'm not going round with that lot any more."

Pa said I should leave it to him, he'd bring me as many marrons glacés as I could possibly want if I'd stop being poorly. I promised Dad that if he did I'd get better and that it was mean of those boys not to leave me a single glacier. And I said: "The gobstoppers weren't very nice, they've left a tickle in my throat, Mrs. Brabec could have kept them to herself."

"Who's this Mrs. Brabec?" inquired Ma.

"How come you don't know her?" I asked in amazement. "She's this lady in India, her husband's a tailor. And we have to pass on their regards to Mr. Kemlink. There aren't any snowstorms in India ever. It's always hot there. A moment ago we were drinking raspberry lemonade with them. It was good but we stayed thirsty."

Ma passed me a glass of raspberry lemonade and supported my head so that I could drink it, and when I'd drunk it down I said in a sleepy voice: "Leave me now, because I've got to go into the garden with Mr. Brabec."

As I opened the door onto the garden I could still hear Pa saying: "Shouldn't we call another doctor?" and Ma replying: "I think we should, or we'll only blame ourselves," and there were these tall trees with bushy tops in the garden, and growing inside them in the way of blossom were some really big red and white cones. Jumbo stood there leaning against the fence, sporting his dashing cap tilted to one side. He was amusing himself with some other elephant and they were both laughing at something. When they spotted me they stopped laughing and I thought they might be laughing at me. I wouldn't want elephants to laugh at me but in any case they went away.

Mr. Brabec led us to a gazebo where we sat down on a bench while he went on talking and we went on listening. He told us how as a poor apprentice tailor he'd set out on his travels around the world with a loaf of bread in his bundle and had visited many foreign parts. He'd caught a glimpse of a large part of the world, being tried and tested on many occasions but also having a lot of fun. He'd visited a tremendous number of pubs where he'd ordered a bite to eat and something to wash it down with. He'd hobnobbed with members of every nation and although he only spoke Czech he still managed to get along with everyone, because he was a decent fellow who was straight with people and couldn't tell a lie to save his life. His employers were full of praise for him because he gave his work the attention that was due to it. He was a man with a head on his shoulders and skill with his hands. His travels took him to India where he saw a girl who was pretty as a picture. He took her as his wife and established his own business there and then.

"And now we come to today," he said. "I make clothes for gentlemen old and young. Even the big shots know the way to my door, because my products are in the latest styles. I do not skimp on cloth and my linings and trimmings are always the finest. Take the lowest tramp who's spent a week rolling in the mud. Let him make his way to me and he'll leave looking the picture of a perfect gentleman. However it's not my habit to blow my own trumpet, because good work speaks for itself. You can ask whomever you like about me and each one will come back with: 'Brabec the tailor? Oh yes!'"

We listened happily and the closest listener of all was Eve Svoboda, and this made me dislike the fact that Brabec the tailor was so vain.

Then Mr. Brabec went on to say that he made clothes for the local maharajah too, a man who ruled beneficently over one million, one thousand and one hundred people and lived in a splendid palace which had fifty thousand rooms, each with a chiffonier, a divan and a piano-forte, not to mention a gramophone, an aquarium full of fish and a host of other fabulous things.

The maharajah was a good customer who paid up front, never in instalments, but he stood out for his severity and if anything was not to his liking he'd treat the whole palace to his awful bellowing. If any tailor messed up an item of clothing then he'd lose his head at once, with no questions asked and no fuss. The maharajah could do that sort of thing because he had no one above him in rank.

And furthermore, Mr. Brabec went on, he was going to deliver something to the maharajah that very evening. His

Excellency had ordered a new uniform and the final fitting would be that very day. He even asked us whether we'd like to accompany him to the fabulous palace and we replied that of course we'd love to.

"That's all right, then," said Mr. Brabec, "as soon as darkness falls and the Southern Cross appears in the sky, we'll be on our way."

And when evening came and it grew dark over the whole land and great stars were shining in the sky, we set out on our journey. Mr. Brabec walked in front, with the maharajah's new outfit draped over his arm. It was red with gold braid and buttons. It was a magnificent uniform and Mr. Brabec moved with great care in order to do it no harm. And I rode on the elephant while the other boys walked beside me and Eve Svoboda rode on the elephant too, because I gave her my permission, and she held on to me. And that's how we were, we boys as a handful and Eve and Mr. Brabec too and we kept talking.

And so on we went and further still, until we saw this huge palace which was many times bigger than even the count's castle back home. The palace was in the middle of a park, where palms, sycamores and eucalyptus trees grew, and all kinds of plants which we hadn't yet studied at school and so we couldn't give their names. And the trees had a wonderful fragrance which was like vanilla sugar.

When we drew near we heard someone singing 'La-la-la' in a tinkly voice, like the sound of glasses singing in a kitchen cupboard. I wanted to ask Mr. Brabec where the beautiful sound was coming from but then I made out for myself that it was a singing fountain whose spray reached up to the sky as it sang, and this made me very happy.

Two massive lions lay on either side of the entrance. They eyed us up with severe expressions as we went past, but didn't say a word. There were loads of monkeys leaping around in the treetops and pointing their fingers at us and chattering ten to the dozen, probably tittle-tattling about us, and they made faces at us too and were mischievous in all sorts of ways. The way they made fun of us threw me into a terrible rage and I thought: "I'd like to get hold of some stick and tan their hides. That would stop them making faces and gossiping." However, seeing that we were paying a visit to His Excellency the Maharajah I knew that I had to be on my best behaviour so as to avoid getting into trouble as usual.

Passing through that gate we entered the first courtyard where everything was in red like Friday when the street organ's playing and Ma is making cakes. Two soldiers were there on sentry duty, sitting on red horses and wearing red uniforms with red tassels on their helmets. And their sabres were unsheathed, ready to strike at once if need arose.

Then we entered the second courtyard which was in a beautiful blue like Saturday when we have no school in the afternoon and can romp around as we like. Blue soldiers were on guard here, sitting on blue horses and they had blue beards which I really liked. They also had their sabres at the ready but they didn't strike us because we kept to a slow pace and looked really respectful.

Even so our journey didn't even end in the blue court-yard, for all at once we were in a third courtyard, which was all golden like a Sunday when there's no school whatsoever, none at all, and I can laze about in bed and cut out paper silhouettes and Christina has a huge bow on her head and the pork is in the oven going 'sizzle sizzle'. There were sol-diers on guard once again, golden ones on golden horses and with golden beards which I envied so much because in our town not even the Lord Mayor can have something like that. I even decided that I'd ask Pa to let me grow one of those beards and I'd promise him that I'd be good as gold and as no boy before me has ever managed to be.

However, I'd left Jumbo standing outside. He didn't think this was right, but I told him that a snout like his just wasn't suitable for a royal palace. He took to snivelling when I said this, but I explained to him: "That's enough. It's just not on. Just how would it look if a snout like that were to walk into the maharajah's official quarters?"

We were welcomed at the door by some gentleman with gold stars on his coat and a gold pipe tucked away in his high boots. He spoke in an Indian dialect which sounded like clothes being scrubbed on a washboard: then he went 'rub-a-dub-dub' and led us up a marble staircase. It was so splendid that I can't find the words to describe it. It was even more amazing than the Soumars' place, oh yes! – Mr. Soumar just can't come close to it, not by a long chalk. I knew from all this that His Excellency the Maharajah must be incredibly well off, he probably has pockets stuffed with hundred crown notes, thousands or even millions and a sackful of five-heller pieces besides. He must be able to buy imprints and firecrackers and one of those knives with six blades, a nail file, corkscrew and scissors and then again he can buy himself liquorice sticks, candy and a mouth organ and a horse and an automobile and he can spend all day sitting around at the cinema.

And when we reached the top we found ourselves standing in this large circular room with a gold clock under a glass cover and all I wanted to do was get hold of it and if no one was looking I'd have liked to open it and look at all the cogs inside. The only problem was that everyone was looking.

And then the gentleman with the gold stars and the gold pipe in his high boots asked us to wait just a jiffy and so we waited to see what would happen next. All of a sudden the sound of a helicon came out of nowhere and a loud voice boomed: "The tailor has arrived for the fitting."

Straight after that came a roll on the drums and trumpets blared and there was a great hullabaloo and then the doors opened suddenly and some gentleman came through them into the room and I knew at once that it was His Excellency the Maharajah. I couldn't even make out what he looked like, because Mr. Brabec had flung himself to the ground, banging his head on the floor, and we did likewise only I missed out on the banging.

When we were upright again I saw that the maharajah was a sturdy and handsome gentleman with a sabre and golden pistols at his waist and big holes in his nose which sprouted whiskers.

With a stately smile he fastened his gaze in our direction and said in a loud voice: "Whose boys are these, Mr. Brabec?"

The tailor replied: "Bringer of Enlightenment to India, these boys are with me."

Then His Excellency the Maharajah praised us: "Fine young men, washed behind the ears, and the lassie with them is also very nicely turned out."

Eve Svoboda blushed all over and curtseyed a good four times and then hid herself behind me.

"And I'm sure that they are doing well at school as well," His Excellency the Maharajah went on, "I take it, boys, that you know your multiplication tables, geometry and the history of your own part of the world, not forgetting your catechism?"

"We know them," we replied and I said: "And I know them better than anyone."

I don't know what came over me to make me lie like that. The whiskers of His Excellency the Maharajah twitched in a terrible manner and he said: "Be quiet, you! I've had my eye on you for some time, you are the worst of the lot and you have a bad influence on the others."

I went quiet at once but I was in a terrible fury about the way I'm always picked out for blame even though I've done nothing wrong, nothing at all.

His Excellency the Maharajah continued talking about this and that, while Mr. Brabec went ahead with the fitting. He tried him in the coat first, marking the cloth with chalk and then, hey presto, he was pulling the collar off the coat and then pinning it back on, saying in an anxious voice: "Might it not be too tight under the arms, Enlightener of the People? Given that it ought to leave a bit of room at the waist I think it will fit you to a T as it is. It's the fashion nowadays to wear a jacket that's well tailored and a bit on the long side. Of course there are customers who still insist their jackets be on the short side. We'll draw it in a bit at the back, the trousers can do with some shortening, just right at the neck, I think, if you would be so good as to turn around, Enlightener of the Indian People, that's it, that's right, I'm so grateful that it's worked out so nicely. This suit will be a real work of art. May Allah above grant his Excellency the Maharajah a long life and the best of health to enjoy it."

When the fitting was over, we sat down at a table and swapped scuttlebutt. And His Excellency the Maharajah spoke first to all of us together and then to each of us separately, asking us about everything. He began by speaking to Zilvar saying: "What trade is your father in, Sonny?"

Zilvar stood up and answered with a whole sentence: "If you please, One and Only Sir, he is in the begging trade and goes from house to house collecting alms, seeing that he's got a wooden leg and is not too well in other ways besides."

"That is immensely interesting," said His Excellency the Maharajah. "And does he come by much money doing this?"

"If you please, One and Only Sir, that depends. He wheedles the most out of people at funerals."

"This really is most fascinating," said the Maharajah. "In the light of this you must pass my greetings on to your esteemed father."

Then he summoned Kemlink and Kemlink replied in a strong voice that his father did all the writing in the tax office and His Excellency the Maharajah observed: "That must mean a lot of work for your father."

Bejval explained that his family ran a haulier's business, and His Excellency the Maharajah asked him how many horses he had and how much one of those horses needed in the way of oats and Bejval replied that he didn't know and he'd have to ask Jacob for the answer to that one.

Then it was my turn and I was very brave in saying, as I looked His Excellency the Maharajah straight in the eyes, that we ran a general store and could provide our customers with all kinds of goods because our storeroom was well stocked. His Excellency the Maharajah said that it must be hard to make a living from this, seeing that there was so much competition, and he asked how many children there were in the family and I replied that we were a three, that Lawrence was already a shopkeeper's assistant and well on his way to growing a beard, that I came next and Mirabelle was the smallest and was already catching at things and would soon be running around.

His Excellency the Maharajah came back with an "Ah ha!" and then said: "Three children – your father must have a lot of work on his hands looking after you all," and I said that he didn't have work on his hands at all, he just stood behind the counter serving people.

Christopher Jirsák replied to His Excellency the Maharajah's questions by saying that they made caps and slippers at home and that his pa played the bass tuba and the helicon with a group of musicians and that he himself could play the helicon and the violin and that he served in church for the Reverend Father.

Then His Excellency the Maharajah said in a solemn voice: "It pleases me to hear that you serve in church, my son, and that you go in for music, because music brings enrichment to the soul."

Then he turned to Eve Svoboda and asked: "And what does this pretty little girl have to say for herself?"

Eve said that they owned a sweetshop, and His Excellency the Maharajah said that he'd known straight away that Eve was from a sweet line of work, because she was such a rosy-faced young lady who looked as if she'd been made out of almond paste. Eve blushed to the roots and started chirping in the way little girls do.

So we swapped scuttlebutt while we ate exotic fruits, though Mr. Brabec drank drops of the hard stuff and was proud of us for giving answers in the proper manner.

Then purple and white dots came flying out of nowhere, which is what happens when I think too hard. They were swarming around me like ants and I shut my eyes so that I could work out in my mind what I'd been seeing and hearing.

When I opened my eyes again I saw Pa standing over me and Ma was looking at me too and the doctor was holding my hand and saying something which I didn't understand, it sounded like 'glug glug glug' or the sound of water boiling on the stove.

And I asked Pa: "Is it really true that you face lots of competition?"

Pa threw a look at Ma, Ma threw one back at Pa, the two of them threw looks at the doctor and the doctor gave a nod. Then Pa replied in a very slow voice: "No doubt about it, there's competition everywhere nowadays."

I said nothing, because I had to think about what this competition was that you couldn't get away from. Then I fixed on the idea that it could be one of those huge green beetles that dart here and there ever so rapidly making a loud whirring sound as they go. My mind was full of Mr. Whirring Beetle, but I didn't know where he could be found. I hadn't even seen him in the shop or in the store-room or in any of the boxes or one of the sacks. Maybe he was hiding behind a shelf and was going to fly out at some time and Pa would have a lot of work on his hands to avoid being bitten because Mr. Whirring Beetle is one of the poisonous group of beetles.

And I asked Pa: "So you do have plenty of work on your hands?"

Pa replied: "I wouldn't mind about that if I didn't have other things to worry about," and Ma heaved a sigh. In order to please Pa I said to him: "When I grow up I can help you with the work and when there are two of us we'll mow down the competition."

Pa laughed out loud and said: "I'd like that, it would be right up my street to have such an assistant." Then he whispered something to the doctor and they both looked at me. After a while I inquired: "Would it be in order for me to go tiger hunting with His Excellency the Maharajah? I'll behave myself while I'm there and I'll always go to my violin lessons."

"Of course you can, but take care of yourself," said Pa.

"I'll be very careful. His Excellency the Maharajah promised to lend me a double-barrelled shot gun to shoot with. I'll pick them off one by one and it'll make them mad. Bejval thinks that he can bring down a tiger with an airgun. But that's not true is it, Pa?"

"Bring down a tiger with an airgun? That's a ridiculous idea."

I told myself that Bejval was just a big show-off and that I would tell him this to his face. Then I closed my eyes and thought about how I'd bring Ma a tiger skin which would make her very happy. It was with this thought in mind that I made my way back to the maharajah's palace.

So back I went to the maharajah's palace and all the other boys came along. Eve Svoboda joined us too and so did Jumbo, who was very happy to be coming along this time. But Mr. Brabec didn't join us, because he had to do some tailoring at home and he explained to us: "Boys, you wouldn't believe how much work I've got to do, I have to stay at my post all day long and I can tell you that I'm out of my mind with work." We expressed the wish that he wouldn't lose his mind and let him be. I hadn't observed Mr. Brabec out of his mind, he just seemed to be his usual self, but I didn't say anything. Mrs. Brabec told me that he was always out of his mind when he started missing his drinking friends, so I learned from this that Mr. Brabec must really have been out of his mind but it wasn't visible.

These were the thoughts in my mind as I arrived at the maharajah's palace along with the other boys and Eve. There was a hustle and bustle both in front of this stately home and inside it, with everyone rushing round and speaking in quickfire voices, while all the time the roll of a drum or the sound of a trumpet was coming from almost every part of it, creating a great hullabaloo. Servants led the maharajah's white elephant in front of the gates. The elephant was all dressed up in a fabulous harness set with precious stones and with a howdah on its back that I could only wonder at. Then they led in another elephant which was also decked out in splendour and it too had a howdah on its back.

I could see Jumbo casting an envious eye at the elephants and I caught him out muttering to himself: "I can see that they live the life of Riley!" I told him off for saying things that were mean-minded and so he went silent. When His Excellency the Maharajah arrived and took his seat in the howdah, I said: "Why, I should have brought the little summerhouse we've got in our garden so that I could have a howdah to sit inside too, that would be a smart thing to do."

The second elephant was for the royal princess who arrived with her chambermaid. She was wearing white silk harem pants and a beautiful red camisole with golden tassels and on her head she wore a turban with peacock feathers. I had the feeling that I must have seen her somewhere before and I said to myself: it all looks to me as if she's the acrobat rider at the Circus Rudolphi, but I didn't say a word out loud because I could have been barking up the wrong tree. Eve was really excited as she looked at the princess and said with a sigh in her voice: "She's as pretty as a picture. I'll be her friend. What do you think, Pete?"

"No doubt about it," I replied.

And they brought still more elephants but they weren't dressed in finery and the other boys were sitting on these elephants. It turned out, however, that Zilvar didn't have any elephant because he came too late on account of having been to the toilet. The royal princess smiled at him really sweetly and then told him to sit with her in the howdah. "You bet," said Zilvar, and he climbed onto the elephant and sat down in the howdah with the princess and her royal train and he lit a cigar and looked very pleased with himself. The princess had a gun and Zilvar had one too but the chambermaid didn't have any guns because her job was to make a breeze around the princess with a fan attached to a long stick so that the flies kept away from her.

Zilvar puffed away and swapped scuttlebutt with the princess who swapped some back with him and Eve sat on Jumbo with me and kept looking around at the princess and at Zilvar and paid no attention to all the scuttlebutt I was trying to swap with her, and this made me furious.

After a while His Excellency the Maharajah made a signal with his hand and the trumpeter made his trumpet blazon forth with a stupendous sound and the procession set off into the distance until it reached the jungle.

You might like to know what a jungle is.

A jungle is like the forests we have at home, except that it's not the same as a forest because a jungle is terrible untidy. There are no signs to say that you shouldn't frighten the animals, light fires, pick mushrooms or other fruits of the forest under pain of a fine. You don't get those signposts showing you how to reach the best views and places of historical interest. You don't even have benches for people to sit on when their legs get tired.

There's nothing like that in a jungle where the undergrowth does what it likes and all the plants are tangled up with each other and nothing is where it should be and it's as if in our class the teacher has suddenly been summoned to the head's office and there's no one there any more to watch what we're doing.

In the jungle tendrils hang down from the tops of the trees to the ground and the trees are all dishevelled, because they don't look after themselves. But on the other hand they're lush with flowers of fantastic beauty which come in all colours and various shapes. Some of them look like stars, others like balls or boxes made from silk paper, and yet others resemble bottles or saucepans or meat-mincing machines. You look around some more and you see flowers shaped like small boats, while others look like shoes or hats or trousers or packets of chicory. We even saw a flower that was shaped like a human face, with two eyes and a nose in the middle and it was sticking out its long red tongue.

And there was so much noise all around us, a terrible racket which was more than we made when doing gym or in the swimming-pool or anywhere else! – you just couldn't compare the two. It was a place where the wailing, cheeping, squealing, droning, growling, mocking, grunting, singing and crying never stopped. It was the monkeys that were the greatest nuisance. They wanted to see and hear everything that was going on and made somersaults in the branches and even did handstands. There were many fabulous butterflies there too which went flying hither and thither and there were also tiny birds, really minute ones that looked like coloured lights and I thought that if I caught them I could decorate the Christmas tree with them; they'd sit tight and everyone would look at them with their mouths open.

I also wanted to know what all the plants and trees and animals were called but I didn't know their names because no one explained them to me. This made me afraid that when I got back home and had to tell them about everything, they'd all say to me that none of it was true and that I was making it all up but it was all true and His Excellency the Maharajah was a witness to the fact and so were all the other boys.

And so we went further and further and it was awfully hot and I was really thirsty and the natives went in front clearing a path for us with their sharp knives and above our heads the monkeys were forever leaping around and chattering about us and laughing horribly at their own chatter. A good hour went by before we came out of the jungle and a huge plain opened up ahead of us, all of it covered in tall, thick grass. His Excellency the Maharajah turned round and announced in a low voice that the tigers had their lair here and so this was the place to hunt them, and he ordered us to be ready. So we all checked our rifles were in working order and waited for a chance to shoot.

Some native beaters were crawling through the grass groping around with sticks and at the same time breaking out into terrible roars in order to frighten away the tigers. Tigers like absolute peace and quiet and cannot tolerate such roaring which they find hateful, so they became enraged and dashed forward out of the grass in order to find out who was making such a scene and stopping them having a moment's peace. And when they saw that the nuisance was caused by Indians kicking up a hullabaloo, they went after them in order to teach them a lesson. But we had our rifles at the ready in a moment, and then we took aim and started firing and I bagged about sixty tigers myself, if not more, and His Excellency the Maharajah praised me saying that I was a stalwart among hunters and that made me very happy.

Each of the boys scored a hit except for Zilvar, because he spent the whole time talking to the princess and smoking his cigar and the princess said that she was afraid of tigers and Zilvar told her that she shouldn't be afraid because he wouldn't let any harm come to her, seeing that he was incredibly strong and could get the better of any tiger.

I would have known nothing about this, since all my attention was on the hunt, but Eve kept nudging me and whispering: "Look at the way they keep talking," all wide-eyed in wonder.

It was already getting dark when we set out on the return journey, and when we reached the maharajah's palace it was pitch black. I was tired and homesick, seeing that I was in the dark among people that were strange to me and so I didn't speak a word to anyone, not even goodbye. I put Jumbo in the stables and made sure that they gave him food and drink and then I simply got going and popped off to Ma and Pa so that I could tell them about everything I'd seen and been through.

The only thing was that I couldn't say anything, because it was already after dark and I wasn't allowed to wake Mirabelle, so all I could do was lie in bed looking around me. There was a night light on the wardrobe and it kept flickering and I saw the shadows jumping from wall to wall, always springing up and then hiding again as if they were playing hide and seek. And the clock went on ticking and

I was amazed that it never stopped and went on working through the night. And always such a slow and serious tick tocking like our notary strutting his way back from church, and the shadows moving around stealthily like mice so I tried to get hold of them with my hands but catch them I could not.

Ma was sitting at the bedside with her hands leaning against the chair and her head resting on her hands while she slept and I would have liked to tell her all about the jungle and those tigers of which I'd shot at least sixty. And my head ached and I had a dry mouth and I don't know any more whether everything really happened or whether it just seemed that I was hunting and all that.

But how could it be nothing but seeming when just a moment ago I was sitting on an elephant with Eve Svoboda sitting right behind me and pointing at Zilvar who was sitting beneath the howdah with a princess? I can't have been mistaken about all that.

And I can hear Eve whispering to me perfectly clearly: "Hey Pete, listen – are you listening to me or not?"

"Of course I am," say I, "what's the matter?"

She says: "Joey Zilvar and the princess are having words with one another."

"So let them talk," say I, "what's the big deal?"

Eve is all goggle-eyed and hot under the collar about it and she says: "But, you nincompoop, this surely means they're going together."

"If they're going together, let them go," I said in a voice that didn't care.

"Jesus, Pete," yelled Eve, "how can you talk such rubbish! What I'm telling you is that they're going out together for real!"

"What!" I was amazed. "You mean that Joey Zilvar would throw himself away on some princess, that can't be right. I know him too well to believe that."

"What have I just been telling you! I was taking a good look. He gazes at her, she gazes back at him and they go on gazing at each other as if they were seeing each other for the first time."

So I took a look at them and sure enough: Joey was gazing at the princess and she was gazing back at him and they went on and on gazing at each other. So I told all the boys about this and they also took a look and saw them gazing at each other and talking together, and therefore everyone knew that they were sweet on each other. Chris Jirsák managed to howl with laughter and make a sneering face at Zilvar at the same time. Zilvar secretly showed him a fist to make clear that he'd fight it out with him. Chris nodded to show he understood and kept making a sneering face all the same. Zilvar said to the princess: "Hang in there a moment, Miss." Then he climbed out of the howdah, found his way down the elephant and went up to Chris and asked him what he thought he was doing making a horrible face, let him make horrible faces like that at his grandmother but not at Zilvar, if he didn't want his mug beaten to such a horrible pulp that his own mother wouldn't know who he was.

Chris replied in his vain way saying that would be the day, he wasn't scared of some incy wincey bridegroom and no bridegroom would ever take him on.

Then Zilvar said that Chris should turn up towards sundown the next day by the petrol station at the square in Calcutta and there they'd fight it out.

Chris replied that this suited him to a T because he wouldn't yet have been to confession and so he was free to fight.

Zilvar said: "Good, so it's agreed." Then he went back to the princess and smoked a cigar and went on talking to her while she went on gazing back at him.

Ma woke up and was startled at the fact she'd dropped off and she asked me: "Are you not sleeping, my Petie? It's night-time now and all people of goodwill are fast asleep."

"One and only Ma," I said – I sometimes call her 'One and only' because Ma was an only child and never had a little brother or sister as she told me lots of times – "One and only Ma, did you know that Joey Zilvar from the poorhouse and the royal princess we saw in the circus are like bride and groom?"

"Get away with you!" said Ma in surprise, "I've never heard of anything like that."

"Cross my heart and hope to die!" I assured her, "they're really together, I mean going together."

"He's a slyboots all right! Only yesterday Joey Zilvar was in our shop buying vinegar and never a word passed his lips about it. He just asked how you were and passed on his best wishes."

"Yes," I said, "you know how it is. He wouldn't exactly shout from the rooftops that he was dating a princess. The boys would laugh at him and he couldn't be seen outside his own home for the shame of it."

"Why would the boys laugh at him?"

"Why would they laugh at him! Because it's totally embarrassing when a boy has a serious girlfriend."

"But Petie! You have a sweetheart of your own. Little Eve from the sweetshop."

This made me really angry: "That's not true, so just forget it! She's not really my sweetheart at all. We read books together and she gives me some sweets she's pinched from her shop and that's it! Whereas Joey's really dating a princess and so he's in terrible disgrace."

Ma smiled as she stroked me and told me not to be annoyed any more and that she hadn't meant it. Then I stopped being angry and said: "All the boys have seen the way they look at each other and Chris Jirsák made horrible

(173)

faces because of it. So they're now going to have a scrap about it at the petrol station."

"Where are they going to have this scrap?" Ma wondered.

"Where?" I said huffily, "I keep telling you! At the petrol station. The one by the square in Calcutta, right opposite the shop where they sell venison. Don't you know it?"

"Oh yes!" said Ma, "Now I know where you mean."

So we chatted away, but it seemed to me that Ma somehow didn't want to believe what I was saying. I could see it in the way she kept looking at me, and this made me sorry and I said to myself: Maybe she thinks I've never been to India and that would really take the biscuit.

And I couldn't really get my head round the idea of Zilvar buying vinegar from us this very day, when he was supposed to be scrapping right now at a petrol pump in Calcutta with Chris Jirsák, or why he'd pass on his greetings to me when I'd been speaking to him a short while beforehand.

So I was all mixed up in my mind and said to myself: "It's your own fault! If only you'd sent a postcard from India to your teacher and to the family back home, as well as to your brother Lawrence, which is what you promised to do, then it would all be put beyond doubt and everyone would know and then you wouldn't need to get headaches wondering whether it's all true or not."

All of a sudden everything became clear as day to me and I told myself: "Ah ha! That crafty character Joey Zilvar came to the shop for vinegar on purpose, so that no one would squeal on him about his getting flirty with a princess. And he was afraid that it would be the talk of the town and Mr. Zilvar would find out about it and would get mad and soon be removing his belt for whacking purposes. He was owed some whacks anyway for the fact he'd nicked his pa's tobacco when we went to India." So now everything was properly accounted for and I was glad about that. And I made up my mind that I'd definitely send those postcards so that everyone would be in the know.

And I also decided that I'd have to bring something back for Mirabelle that would make her happy, the only problem being that I didn't know what. I'd think the matter over and come up with something. Then I closed my eyes so as to rest a little, because I was dog tired.

The fact that Joey Zilvar was hand in glove with a royal princess became the talk of all India. Brahmans, Mohammedans and Hindus, all castes from the untouchables to the top notch, chewed the fat over it. Malayans and Chinese, arriving at the ports in their junks, had nothing else on their lips. Even the white people got excited about it and the whole of India was a hive of gossip. Everyone knew that Joey Zilvar and the princess were always talking together and that they were really sweet on one other.

They stuck together like birds of a feather and from that moment on Zilvar never went out with the lads any more. They had picked out a large fig-tree in the maharajah's garden and there they used to sit on a bough while Zilvar read to the princess from books, some of them funny and some of them more like instruction. What bothered me most of all was the fact that he'd borrowed my 'Leon Clifton and Monte Carlo', the detective story, and he never told the princess that the book was mine and when he gave it back to me four pages were missing and he said that they'd always been missing and that just wasn't true. So I called him a brainless bridegroom and he said just let me try saying that once more and so I did say it once more but he behaved as if nothing had happened and went back to his princess.

He didn't want a scrap for all the world.

He walked slowly, never hurrying himself and looking pious and delivering his words of wisdom in a written rather than spoken style. He was the most awful bore.

Sometimes he sat with the princess at a little attic window of the maharajah's palace and there they would sing together 'Under the Greenwood Tree' and other songs, while Zilvar sang his part of the duet in an unusually deep voice. And they'd also go walking round the garden, where the princess picked flowers and Zilvar puffed a cigar, his hands clasped behind his back to make him look fully grown up. I also know that he bought her an ice-cream cornet and a lucky dip which had a ring in it and its precious stone was a piece of red glass. And she bought him a cane, some braces and a mouth organ.

There was one time when all of us boys and Eve were sitting with the princess on some logs in the red courtyard and playing at having different trades. First of all Eve and the princess were travelling wayfarers and made up some riddles and Zilvar got them all right. Then they asked him: "What would you go for, a violet or a rose?" Zilvar went for the rose, because he guessed that the rose was the princess. Then Zilvar and I were the travelling wayfarers and the princess did the guessing. We asked her: "What would you go for, an oak tree or manure?" The princess replied "manure", because Zilvar gave her a secret sign that he was manure. At that point everyone saw that they were going together, really going out together, and that it was no game they were playing and so one after another we said: "Count me out! I'm not playing on!" Eve also gave up and said she wasn't playing any more.

And the princess also gave him a real clock which went and Zilvar kept taking it out and looking at it and saying in a loud voice that he was amazed at the way time was flying, just so we'd notice that he had this timepiece. But when he did this we kept looking somewhere else on purpose.

They were also sending love letters to each other all the time and Bejval said that he'd never seen such nonsense in his life and he went on to say that it would be better if we went off on our own and we said: "Dead right!" and then we were a four with Eve thrown in.

Everyone there knew about it, all the servants knew and the maharajah's Indian relatives knew too and the maharani must have known something about it too, because the relatives spread gossip and made nasty remarks about it. But Her Excellency the Maharani said:

"Never mind, the girl's not old enough for it to mean anything, it's the madness of youth, and when all's said and done we know all about it because we were young too. Let them sow their wild oats and get some wisdom." His Excellency the Maharajah was the only one to know nothing, because he didn't spend much time talking with his relatives.

And Zilvar spent several days all on his own, walking round the garden, having a smoke and a spit with his cigar and talking to himself like a lunatic. Then the walking and the talking came to an end and he had his hair cut, washed his neck, had his suit pressed and cleaned his shoes and then presented himself one day at the maharajah's palace and let it be known that he had a really important piece of news for His Excellency the Maharajah.

When His Excellency the Maharajah heard what was going on he said: "I'm really eager to know what this is all about," and received Zilvar in his chamber. To find out more he sat down on a divan and sat Zilvar in an arm chair. His Excellency the Maharajah smoked a Turkish pipe and Joey Zilvar puffed at a cigar and a long time went by while they sat and said nothing. We were all crowding round behind the door looking through a peephole and straining to find out what he was going to say.

Nothing happened at first and then Zilvar said that there'd been no change in the weather and the sun beat down very strongly, making it hot, and His Excellency the Maharajah said that the monsoon season was approaching and that would be a very different kettle of fish and Zilvar said: "Could be, I don't want an argument," and His Excellency the Maharajah said that he didn't want an argument either and that he had no taste for arguments and Zilvar said: "My view entirely."

A long time went by with nothing happening, while they sat quietly and puffed mightily. Suddenly Zilvar broke into a torrent of words, saying that his heart had spoken to him. His Excellency the Maharajah said: "Why is that?" and Zilvar said that he and the royal princess had been courting and therefore he'd made up his mind that it was time to get hooked.

"Hooked to what?" asked His Excellency the Maharajah.

Zilvar said that he wished to ask for the hand of the royal princess in marriage.

His Excellency the Maharajah removed the stem of the pipe from his mouth as his eyes opened wide and he came out with: "What's that you said?"

Zilvar repeated that he wanted to marry the princess. His Excellency the Maharajah shook his head and said "Strike a light!" in a voice that died away slowly and Zilvar had to repeat himself yet again.

And His Excellency the Maharajah went red in the face and in a terrible voice that shook the chandelier beneath the ceiling he roared out: "A numskull like you as a suitor for the princess? You, the low-born son of a low-born mother, just what gives you the right to such a thing? How dare you say such things in the presence of a sovereign! I will teach you a lesson!"

As he clapped his hands two armed guards appeared and His Excellency the Maharajah pointed to Joey Zilvar and said to them: "Remove this rapscallion to our deepest, darkest and dirtiest dungeon! That'll cure him of any ideas about marriage with a royal princess!"

The guards seized hold of Joey and cast him into a pit with nothing in it save for a foul stench. And we lads went with Eve to look at him through a barred window and we spat at him now from this bar and now from that bar and Zilvar said: "Cut that out, can't you?" So we left him and instead we enjoyed just watching him sit there. For the most part Zilvar took no notice of us but just played games with his knife skewering it to the floor, or else he tried to see whether he could do a handstand with his hands manacled. When he managed one he was very proud of himself and said: "What do you think of that, lads?"

Even so we took pity on him, because he was a nice enough lad in other respects and he was being made to sit in jail with the worst criminals just for being stupid. So we went up to the window and stuffed something to read through it. We brought sweets for him and Mrs. Brabec came every day to slip him something to eat so that he wouldn't get bored or starve. And the whole town went to catch sight of him as he sat there smoking his cigar and reading the paper to catch up with the latest news. Word went round that the wrath of His Excellency the Maharajah had broken out against the boy in a mighty torrent of rage. It was said that he'd issued a command for the boy to be delivered up to the executioner and all the people of the town felt sorry for Zilvar, who although still a spring chicken was soon going to be a headless one.

It was also rumoured that the royal princess was making an incredible song and dance about the affair, that she was in tears wherever she went, that her eyes were red with crying, that she refused to eat, in fact that she took nothing in at all and was in a state of headlong decline. And Her Excellency the Maharani was worried to death and summoned the leading doctors of the land to her and they declared that the princess needed a proper diet and a change of air, otherwise they couldn't be responsible for what happened to her, and so Her Excellency the Maharani said to His Excellency the Maharajah: "You're a fellow without an ounce of conscience in his body. Don't you see what it's doing to the child? And just who's going to get the blame if she does something to herself?"

His Excellency the Maharajah frowned and with a flourish of the hands declared: "Just leave me in peace, all of you. I haven't got time for you."

"You are only interested in yourself. Everyone else can go hang," said Her Excellency the Maharani.

"Whatever she is now you brought her up to be. Get out of my sight," said His Excellency the Maharajah.

But Her Excellency the Maharani wouldn't give in and kept going up to him in order to settle the matter. One day she made yet another attempt and found His Excellency the Maharajah sitting on his throne and governing. Her Excellency the Maharani asked: "So what is to be done with this little girl, oh stubborn mule of mules! How are you going to meddle in the affairs of these two young people? You've dug in your heels so that you'll get your way, but you won't get your way."

His Excellency the Maharajah said: "Don't start your jabbering now. Can't you see that I'm governing?"

"The child is more important than your official business," Her Excellency the Maharani answered in a loud voice.

His Excellency the Maharajah flew into a rage and began running around the room yelling in a terrible voice that he never had a moment's peace, but Her Excellency the Maharani took no notice of his yelling but stuck to her guns saying that he must sort the matter out. And then finally His Excellency the Maharajah's spirit was broken and he relented and said: "Very well, let it be as you wish. I will try to see what can be done with this young fellow. He will be put to the test in a most demanding manner and if he does not come through with flying colours he will find himself shorter by a head and no messing!"

Her Excellency the Maharani said in a soft voice: "My dear husband, I see that I have not been deceived in you. Sometimes you are wild in the head, but your heart is in the right place after all."

And His Excellency the Maharajah sent out messengers to the far corners of his realm and ordered all the noblemen and knights, counts and chieftains, commanders of fleets and armies, princes and parish council leaders to be in attendance at the royal palace. And when this had taken place and all the bigwigs had been brought together he bade the prisoner's manacles be removed and that he be tidied up and brought before the assembly.

And when this had come to pass and two armed guards had brought Zilvar, His Excellency the Maharajah began to address him as follows: "Young man! As a warning and example to others, the unheard-of audacity of your actions should be met with the executioner's axe. However, because I am, as everyone knows, a merciful sovereign, I have fixed upon another course. I am going to give you another chance. But you will be put to the trial in a most challenging manner. My grand counsellor and schemer-in-chief will present you with three riddles. If you guess them correctly, you will have the hand of my royal daughter in marriage. But if you do not stand the test, then woe betide you! You will be handed over to the executioner, from whom you will learn the fate of the foolhardy."

Joey Zilvar replied: "No worries, mighty King, I'm up for anything."

Whereupon His Excellency the Maharajah nodded to his leading advisor and schemer-in-chief, who had glasses on his nose and a beard that reached down to the ground. This man went up to Zilvar and said: "You will be given three very taxing questions, so that we can test your mental powers and determine whether you are to enjoy the royal favour or be handed over and condemned."

Zilvar said: "Ask away to your heart's content. I'm ready for you." And he smoked a cigar and boldly looked him straight in the eyes. Meanwhile we kept our own eyes on him. Eve kept her eyes on him too and so did the princess.

Then the grand counsellor and schemer-in-chief rose to his feet and said: "Well then, prisoner, listen carefully and pay attention. My first riddle goes like this: Its stomach is the size of its head, and its head is the size of its stomach and it's nothing to write home about."

"Easy peasy," came the conceited reply from Zilvar, "everyone knows the answer to that, it's getting the bottom grade for behaviour, a 3. You'll have to find more difficult questions to ask than that, my dear sir, or it won't be a proper game."

Everyone present was overcome with amazement and even we boys were taken aback and Eva too was taken aback and the princess was a bundle of joy.

The grand counsellor and schemer-in-chief tweaked his beard and said: "Very well then, I shall move on to the second riddle, which is much harder to solve. We will see how you fare with it, foolhardy youth. Listen carefully: It goes by but it has no legs. What might it be?"

Zilvar laughed and answered: "But what else could it be, my dear friend, apart from time? Time has no legs and yet it passes by. You must give me something harder than this, or you'll start to annoy me. These are not questions for people where I come from."

Everyone looked on in wonder, none more so than His Excellency the Maharajah who said: "This really takes the biscuit. Mark well what this boy has between the ears. Minister, you must give him something harder to stop that head of his swelling."

"He will find that it has swollen too soon," said the grand counsellor and schemer-in-chief, "when he hears the third riddle. I spent a sleepless night preparing something specially for him. I am already sorry for the boy. Very well then, ill-fated youth, listen carefully and tell me quickly what this is:

> *I don't come from far*
> *So tell me my pa,*
> *And where will I stay,*
> *Though I've still got to pay?*
> *I don't come from far*
> *So tell me my pa.*"

"Even a small child knows the answer to that one," Zilvar answered him with pride. Then he began to sing:

> *I'm from Praha, Ha! Ha! Ha!*
> *The oakum-picker is my pa.*
> *My three homes in Prague are fine*
> *When I buy them they'll be mine.*
> *I'm from Praha, Ha! Ha! Ha!*
> *The oakum-picker is my pa!*

When Joey Zilvar had finished singing he was greeted by astonishment on all sides. Heads nodded and necks twisted, hands waved and applause rang out. Then His Excellency the Maharajah said to Zilvar: "I can see that you have a head worth keeping on its shoulders and that you'll make your way in the world." And all the ministers, the knights and the nobles, the dukes and the councillors, not forgetting the mayors and the barons, also said that Zilvar's head was worth keeping. And we boys were proud of him too and pleased that Joey had put one over on the old schemer-in-chief, and we yelled "Bravo!" and "Hurrah!" Eve yelled too and no one yelled more than the princess.

And Zilvar said nothing and puffed away at his cigar, paying no attention to what was happening around him and looking straight at the princess who was looking straight at him and indeed the two of them were looking straight at each other.

His Excellency the Maharajah left his throne, got to his feet and slowly lifted his hand up high as he declared in a strong voice: "Those who have come can return to their homes, for this audience is over." Whereupon all the big-wigs gathered there mounted their horses and set off for their homes. We, the lads and Eve that is, also went off and swapped scuttlebutt on the way home, saying that Zilvar was a superstar because he'd run rings round that grand whatever with the beard.

The only ones who stayed in the palace were His Excellency the Maharajah, Her Excellency the Maharani, Zilvar from the poorhouse and the royal princess. They drank coffee and talked together and Her Excellency the Maharani talked most of all, saying that she was glad at the way things had turned out and then she said: "We've paid for the girl's education and she won't be wanting for a penny or two and the money we have we can't take with us..."

So word soon spread through the whole Indian nation that a royal princess would marry Zilvar from the poorhouse and that there was going to be a great wedding. It was the talk of the markets and of sailors on the high seas, of commuters in their trains and clerks in their offices, of bricklayers as they built and of seamstresses as they sewed, of children in school and even of their teachers, of miners in the depths of the earth and of everyone who could open a mouth and speak. It was also written up in the newspapers. It was rumoured that His Excellency the Maharajah was getting on in years and that Joey Zilvar would take over the reins of government from him, which would be a great advantage for all the subjects of his realm because the arts and sciences, not to mention industry and commerce, would flourish under the rule of Zilvar. This was because Zilvar from the poorhouse was supposed to have an open mind and to know how to deal with anything that came his way.

I thought for a long time about how things might turn out with Zilvar on the throne and whether the royal crown would suit him and whether he'd always be away from home ruling the country or only sometimes and for the rest of the time would hang around with us as he used to. And when I opened my eyes I realized all at once that it was Wednesday, because pigs were squealing in the market-place, geese were cackling 'honk honk honk', hens were clucking, people chatting and horses whinnying. This was because Wednesday is always our market day and there were loads of people in the shop. And a lovely sun was shining and there were dancing fairies on the walls and I wanted to catch these flecks of sunlight and shut them up inside a box so that we could keep hold of them.

And I called out in a weak voice: "Christina, fetch me pen and paper and some ink."

Christina came wanting to know why I needed them.

I said: "Don't ask too many questions and fetch them quickly. I've got to write a letter of apology for Zilvar, to say he can't come to school."

She wanted to know why he couldn't go to school and I told her: "Because he's going to get married and he doesn't want this to mean he misses classes without permission."

This gave Christina a fit of the giggles and she fell about from one corner of the room to another till she caught hold of the table and yelled: "Oh dear! Oh dear me! He'll be the death of me!"

"What are you laughing at, you Rampusite, you daft Rampuss?" I snapped at her. "Instead of this 'oh dearing' would you please bring me my writing things so that I can pen the note?"

She ran off to the shop without replying. Soon afterwards Pa came in and asked what this letter of apology was all about. I told him all about it, and that Zilvar had asked me to write the note and I'd promised him that I would, and I said that Joey was the biggest superstar of them all. And I explained that he was afraid of being away from school without permission because he was getting married. And I told Pa everything, leaving nothing out.

Pa heard me out and grinned so broadly that the handlebars of his moustache reached his ears. Then he said: "So Zilvar's getting spliced. That's news to me. The crafty devil's surprised us there! And never a whisper about it. But my dear chap, I don't know whether the teacher will allow him leave of absence. Perhaps a pupil is not allowed to miss school in order to get married. Well all right, then. It's not our business. Let old Zilvar sort it out."

"Does Mr. Zilvar already know about Joey getting married?" I asked.

"Well as to that, to tell you the truth I don't really know," replied Pa.

"What will he say about it when he finds out?"

"Who can say, lad? Old man Zilvar is rather strange a lot of the time."

So we had a talk and then Ma arrived and she had a talk and so we all three started talking together and I bragged that Joey Zilvar was a brain box and that he guessed all the riddles without a moment's thought and everyone in India was looking on in amazement and Pa said: "As for that there are some real smart alecs here in the Czech lands who know all the answers and are able to field anything you throw at them. It's been scientifically proven that no one can come up to their level."

And Ma said: "Right that's enough talking because Pete's got to get a bit of rest. And why is Christina always chuckling to herself in the kitchen?"

"The thing is, my one and only Ma," I explained, "I told her about Zilvar and the fact he had to get married. And you know what women are like. When they hear there's a wedding in the offing they either dissolve in tears or in mad laughter."

Pa laughed heartily and said: "The lad's seen through it all."

And Ma caressed me and said: "You're my Mr Clever Clogs but you should have some shut-eye now, so you'll be fit and well again."

And then I dreamt that the doctor came and went, leaving behind him an aroma of something Latin. He took hold of me and turned me onto my side and then onto my other side. He gave my tummy a press and said "Aha! Aha!" and then he turned me again and went "Aha! Aha!" again. He had really cold ears and kept saying something and Pa was talking too and Ma was looking at both of them while they were speaking. And I pushed the doctor away because I was impatient to be back in India and I knew I couldn't go there while the doctor was around and so I said: "Go away!" and pretended to be asleep. They began whispering 'swish – wish' and then they tiptoed out.

And I buried myself in the duvet and before long I knew that I was no longer lying in bed, that was just what the others were thinking, but I knew perfectly well that the bed was really an aircraft with thousands of horsepower and as soon as Ma and Pa went to see off the doctor I got the engine going and then it was full speed ahead with the joystick and the plane slowly took off from the ground and flew up and over the roof of our house. I circled over our town a few times and looked down at all the houses and I saw our school looking as tiny as mum's sewing box and I saw Mr. Letovský the policeman standing in the square and there was Bej-val's furniture waggon going by and I could see it was Jacob leading the horse and then I saw the village of Habrová and flobbed downwards so the spit would fall onto my enemy and send him into a towering rage. And I kept flying up and up so that our town became minuscule below me and then I headed south.

Back in India the lads were waiting for me and Eve was waiting too and she said that there was lots of tittle tattle about what had been happening in the royal palace, and Bejval asked me where I'd been all this time and I replied: "I had to see how things were back home, nothing to be done about that." Jumbo was waiting for me too and said he'd missed me and now he'd joined up with an elephant gang and they were all splendid young bulls. Jirsák asked me if I'd seen his ma and pa and I told him that I hadn't because I'd not had much time and Jirsák said: "That's a shame, you could have dropped by and brought me some news from home." Eddie Kemlink said that we ought to go to the maharajah's palace at once because things were happening there. So we went straight away to take a look.

The palace was a real hive of activity and everyone was dashing hither and thither. The hustle and bustle was biggest in the kitchen because this was where they were preparing the wedding feast. There were loads of monkeys there and they all had their hands full and were being rushed off their legs. There were other animals there too, all of them at work doing something. There was an elephant turning the mincer to make rissoles, and another elephant had a coffee mill between its legs and was grinding coffee with its trunk. Plucking poultry was the job of one small monkey while another was washing the vegetables and a third peeling the potatoes. A huge snake called an Indian rock python was kneading dough for apple strudel and a couple of parrots were sorting peas. A ginger tom who looked like our Honza was whisking egg-white and never even took a nibble for himself on the sly. I found this odd because Honza would wolf down everything and then Pa would hurl a shoe after him because of the way he goes for everything he can lay his paws on. There was a bear chopping wood, a dog stirring thickener into the soup and it looked as if the whole place was there for one thing only – work. An old tiger was picking through some raisins and another one was slicing up noodles. An aroma of spices, vanilla and chocolate was everywhere. Small monkeys were tossing plates, pots and pans all over the place but nothing was ever broken. The only one there doing nothing was an old orang-utan who went round with a grave look on his face, sniffing everywhere and tasting everything. He was wearing a white apron and a high cap on his head, which meant he was the chief cook.

Eve tugged on my coat and asked me in a whisper whether I'd go and see another room where she'd have something interesting to show me, because this was the room the dressmakers were sitting in, making the wedding dress for the princess, but I said that I wasn't interested in knowing about this and the other lads said they weren't interested in knowing about it either and Eve said that she found this very strange of us, because the dress was made of fine silk and for the bridal train alone they needed over thirty feet of fabric.

But we were happy to go into the garden where Joey Zilvar was taking a walk in a brand new outfit. He smelt of eau de cologne and his oily top showed he'd been at the hair lotion and he had a new bowler hat on his head. He was swinging a cane, walking at a slow pace and had a smug look on his face. When he spotted us he touched his hat with the cane and announced in a grand voice: "Allow me to bid you welcome, chaps. What's cooking?"

We started talking to him but he didn't say a word more. He just turned away and started walking on, swinging his cane and singing 'Ta-ra-ra- boom-de-ay.'

Bejval grumbled that Zilvar looked down on everyone and Eddie Kemlink said that he needn't think so much of himself and I said that God only knew what Zilvar thought of himself and he should think of himself less, and Chris Jirsák turned his eyelids inside out and made a horrible face at him.

Zilvar stopped and shook his head with a proud look on his face and said in a slow voice: "Such are the morals of today's youth. Huh! It's clear to me that you were brought up in a barn. You should be ashamed of yourselves."

Kemlink yelled "Rubbish!" and thumbed his nose at him.

Zilvar said in a solemn voice: "If it was someone else I'd have their block knocked off, but I can't be bothered with you."

"I'm not talking to you anymore," said Kemlink and went on: "But I know you'll come crawling back again, little bridegroom!"

Zilvar said nothing more. He just lit a cigar and went away looking full of himself. We said to Kemlink: "You sliced him up nicely there and we're not going to have any more to do with him."

And I added: "Let him go off with his princess."

Then we went to sit on some logs and we started a game of hide-and-seek and Jumbo was forever wanting to play with us, so we let him. It was a real hoot because he could never find anyone and he spent the whole time shuffling about searching for us and we laughed at him and this made him angry.

When it grew dark we stopped the game and sneaked up to the windows of the palace and looked into the rooms. We saw Zilvar sitting next to his princess, looking all grown up and from the way his lips were curling and pouting and his eyebrows going up we could see that he was speaking in the proper manner so that everyone knew he was a little bigwig. And His Excellency the Maharajah was speaking with him and so was Her Excellency the Maharani and they were all in cahoots.

So we went away from that window and we said to each other that Zilvar wasn't the mate of ours we thought he was but just another of those people with big heads and big mouths and we agreed that we ought to make this clear to him so he'd realise it for himself.

Bejval said that we should think up some way of getting back at him, and the rest of us all said: "Do some of your inventing," and he said that he'd come up with something but he'd have to think very hard first.

The day of the wedding was getting closer and as it did so a cheerful commotion arose. Kings and Queens and all sorts of nobles from all over the realm and from other lands were invited to the wedding and now gathered together. It was like Corpus Christi Day in town, with crowds of people streaming through the streets and loads of people everywhere making a terrible crush. Houses were decked out with flags, flowers and fresh floral sprays, while several had given the front of their homes a lick of paint to make them look nice, and caretakers were sweeping the pavement and looking full of pride. And whatever your eye was drawn to had nothing else to say to you except that the royal princess was going to marry Joey Zilvar and that His Excellency the Maharajah had let it be known that he was going to splash out. So everyone was really keen to know what the wedding was going to be like.

All sorts of people came together in the capital, especially those bringing merry-go-rounds, see-saws, slides, shooting galleries, puppet shows and other artists, not to mention the people selling Turkish delight, grilled sausages and groundnuts. Then there were the gingerbread sellers and those showing off squirrels running about in cages. The best part of the nation could be found walking among the stalls and shouting loudly on all sides in order to be heard. We were also there having the time of our lives shooting at targets and I was the best shot of all and I won a porcelain dog, a mirror and a notebook with a pencil and a bar of chocolate which I gave to Eve who kept munching at it. And wherever you went from the square to the forest you came upon the organ grinders who kept playing nineteen to the dozen.

The best thing was a troop of monkeys sitting in a tree in the park. They were all dressed in the same uniform and had musical instruments with them so that they could practise some numbers for the wedding. An old male wearing a pince-nez was in charge of the band and was waving his baton madly to get the monkeys to keep up their playing. It struck me that the bandmaster looked very much like Mr. Rektorys, the man we go to for violin lessons, but I knew it wasn't Mr. Rektorys because that would mean something had gone really wrong.

At one point a great hubbub arose while the band was playing. Several monkeys had crawled into the maharajah's sideboard where they'd stolen a bottle of spirits. So they started drinking and then they started squabbling and finally they started fighting and one monkey clobbered another monkey on the head with a coconut and the monkey that was hit fell down and had to go to the doctor where it was patched up and told to lie down. This monkey was the trombone player and the trombone had fallen down and was broken too. So the band asked Chris Jirsák whether he could help out and told him there was good money in it so he said: "Why not?" and played the trombone.

It was a strange sight watching Chris sitting on a branch with the rest of the monkeys, puffing out his cheeks as he blew into the trombone. People went to take a look at him and pointed at him with their fingers. We went to look at him too and had a good laugh about it and Chris got into a terrible rage at this but there was nothing he could do because he had to pay attention to the bandmaster so that he didn't get out of synch.

When he had a long break, he called down to us from the branch: "Look here, you swine, just leave me alone if you don't want me to jump off this tree and split your gobs open from ear to ear. I'm a trombonist above anything else and I play whenever I get the chance. If that means monkeys, monkeys it is. I'd never waste a musical opportunity."

And when the monkey band moved on through the town playing the Castaldo march, everyone came to look and a bunch of tiny tots ran along behind them. The monkeys were banging on the big drums and rat-a-tat-tatting on the hand drums and blowing at the brass and whistling on the carrynet. And Chris went along with them and kept looking closely at the score to avoid looking at the people while they were ogling him.

The band arrived at the main square where they played merry and mournful pieces while people walked around. We lads who always go round together were there too having a laugh and Eve had a laugh and Jumbo had a laugh and got so excited that he used his trunk to trumpet a tune.

They went on playing for a long time until a fanfare of bugles from the soldiers at the palace announced the fact that the marriage ceremony was under way. Eve Svoboda was squealing terribly saying: "Heavens above, the wedding's starting and we're going to be late," as she tugged at my sleeve.

"Fiddlesticks! We're not going to be late," I replied in a lofty voice, "we've time enough."

But Eve came back at me in a voice full of worry: "But we'll be all squashed up between loads of people and I won't even see how the bridal pair look in their finery."

"Stuff and nonsense!" I came back at her huffily. "What's all this about finery?"

But Eve wouldn't leave me in peace and said: "Maybe it doesn't suit them, but I have to know how it doesn't suit them. O Pete, let's not stand here lounging round and hanging back. Let's run like the clappers!"

What else could I do when she was forever pestering and wouldn't leave me alone? So off I went with her to the palace, and all the lads came too and the monkeys stopped playing their music and so Chris Jirsák joined us and went to the palace too, taking his trombone along with him. And as we went there he said that we could have left off earlier and that we needn't have taken the mickey out of him.

I asked in a voice all sweet and innocent what he meant by taking the mickey and he said: "I'll give you an example – when the band was going down the street, which one of you shouted at me: 'Monkey features'?"

I said that it couldn't have been any of us, and that was why it must have been someone completely different, and Chris said: "Lucky for you that it was someone else, because otherwise I'd have beaten one of you to within an inch of his life."

We had doubts about his being able to beat one of us to a pulp, but Chris said that he would do it anyway because when he was in a fury he was mean as hell. So we chatted away while we kept up a smart pace, until we got to the royal palace where we saw the bridal procession getting into line. Maybe a million or at least a hundred elephants and maybe even more, at any rate it was more than I could count, were standing in a never-ending line. A terribly fat fellow with a plumed and golden helmet on his head was sitting on the first elephant while he waved his sabre hither and thither, and he rolled his eyes and had a moustache. He was the top general in the maharajah's army with decorations on his chest to mark the massacre of all his enemies.

Yet more generals were sitting on elephants behind this one, but they were more run-of-the-mill generals without so many decorations because they'd only massacred their enemies now and then. Even so every general had a sabre, a gun or an evolver and a proud look on his face. Some others had less or even nothing but an open umbrella as they sat there, but even these had a proud look like the others.

Right in the middle was a white elephant with a howdah which had curtains in red and gold. These curtains came open when the wind blew and so we could see the princess sitting there. Some gentleman was sitting beside her, it must have been her best man. He was wearing a high and shiny top hat and a black tailcoat with blue undergarments and red slippers on his feet. I had to burst out laughing because he was such a funny sight, and I pointed him out to Eve Svoboda but she only had eyes for the princess and she kept on saying: "She's picked the best of the best, the heaviest satin for the dress, that much was clear from the first glance at her," and she went rabbiting on about these clothes and I said that they didn't interest me.

Eve wanted to take me on about this but at that moment they led out His Excellency the Maharajah's elephant which was the biggest one of all, the most beautiful white elephant which had a howdah on its back with gold and silver lattice-work and a weather-vane on the roof of the howdah which turned with the way the wind was blowing. The elephant's back was covered with a brightly-coloured carpet.

While we were gazing at this Jumbo was having a good look too. He was wearing his red cap so he would cut a dash himself and kept his eyes fastened on the Maharajah's elephant and they never left it for a moment. I asked him what he thought of it but he just gave a snuffle and mumbled something to himself. I told him off for the snuffling and said he should use a handkerchief but then he suddenly started snivelling. I said that a grown-up elephant should be ashamed of himself crying like that and asked him what had brought it on and he replied that he'd thought he'd also get an invite to the wedding and walk in the procession and he'd been looking forward to this like mad.

I said that we boys, who go round as a group, also thought that we'd get an invite and who'd have thought that they'd leave us out when Joey Zilvar went and got married and all of a sudden didn't know us. All right then! Very well! We weren't going to forget about this. And then I went on to say: "Stop that snivelling!"

While I was chatting like this to the elephant, the band struck up and the procession started to move. Bells rang and cannon roared and there was a great ballyhoo and all the people looked on as the bridal procession made its way into the church.

But then I suddenly remembered that my family had to see the festivities and Christina had to see them too so that they could pass the word on to everyone, and so I stopped standing in the street and started running fast.

Eve shouted behind me: "Where are you running off to, you mad thing? We've still not seen the best bit," but I said to her: "Leave go of me, I've got to run home so that Ma and Pa and Christina see the ceremony and can let everyone know what it was like," and Eve said: "Make sure you come right back."

When I'd scurried all the way home I was out of breath from running so fast and I was sweating and there was a pounding in my temples and my mouth was parched. And I yelled out in a loud voice: "They're off, they're already off!"

Ma coaxed me into calming down and Pa said in a sad voice: "What a worry he is, this is really more than I can bear."

But I had no patience with them at all for making these speeches while everything would soon be over and so I said: "Hurry up, they're throwing cakes into the crowds and people are catching them so we should catch some too, and where is Christina? She has to come along too."

Ma said that Christina was washing clothes in the tub and I yelled back that she should leave everything and hurry, hurry back before everything was over. And Ma wanted to give me my medicine but I pushed away her hand holding a teaspoon and started snivelling, saying that my family never went anywhere and I shouted this to the whole building so that people in the shop stared across, peeking into my room and wondering who was yelling his head off there and among them was the bleating greengrocer who quickly crossed herself and said: "Heaven forfend that it goes to the lad's head, that would indeed be a terrible thing."

But there was no time for prattling on because I grabbed hold of Ma and Pa by the hand and we sprang out of the door and flew up to a great height, higher and higher we rose until our town was as tiny as a box of toys beneath us and the people looked like ladybirds and we were right up on high. And Christina was running behind us carrying a basket of washing with her and as she rushed along she flung away shirts and skirts, long johns and bodices, and the wind blew into them all and items of clothing floated in the sky, but Christina paid no attention to all this and kept hurrying along. And we were already up in the sky, with me running on ahead so that I could show them the way, because I knew how to get anywhere, and Pa helped Ma to jump across the clouds, she put a foot onto one cloud and then Pa reached out a hand and she jumped onto a second one and she was afraid that she would slip because of her high heels and Christina was shrieking horribly because she was afraid to climb to such great heights and we were right up with the sun itself where it was baking hot, sizzling and crackling while we went on jumping, gasping for lack of breath as we rushed along.

And I kept being terribly afraid that by the time we came running along we'd be too late for everything but as luck would have it we got there in time and we even heard the bells pealing and the cannon roaring and some amazingly beautiful music.

We perched ourselves on a box for chicory in the street in order to get a better view and I pointed out His Excellency the Maharajah and Her Excellency the Maharani to the family. They were sitting in a howdah. I also pointed out the bride and Joey Zilvar to them, not to mention the military officers and all the rest, every little thing. Mr. and Mrs. Brabec were there too and the tailor boasted that he'd made a suit of the finest cloth for the bridegroom Joey and that he'd made the lining of his coat from a double weighting of silk and that this suit would last him so long that he'd grow tired of it. And Pa lit a cigar and puffed away merrily and drank in everything around him, and Ma did the same and Christina did it most and said that she'd never seen any show of finery like this among the Rampusites, not in a whole lifetime, and that in India people could get more entertainment for free than they could get for a ten-crown note in the mountains where she came from.

I asked the family whether they were having a good time and Pa said: "I like India more than anything," and Ma said the same so I was very proud and Ma went on to say that I shouldn't take it too much to heart because it could come back to haunt me in my dreams and I told her not to worry, I wasn't going to have any nightmares about it.

And Eve was there with us too on that box, standing on tiptoes, eyes wide open and all lit up and she said she was keen to have a wedding like this too, because it would make all the girls green with envy, especially that Bunty Šebek.

All of a sudden and quite out of the blue my parents were no longer standing on the box but I'd lost them somewhere and I started looking for them and searched everywhere and even sneaked under the bed and went through all the wardrobes and peeped under the fireplace and behind the stove. Then I went up to the attic but no one was there. I was worried sick now, wondering where they could be. I made Christina light a candle so I could take a look in the cellar and I went on searching high and low for them until Eve said to me: "Why are you always crawling about? What are you looking for all the time? I've been watching you for a long while now. Remember we're in church, so mind your Ps and Qs and pay attention while they stand before the altar and say the words that can never be taken back – 'I do...'"

So I forgot about my parents for a moment while Joey Zilvar and the royal princess stood before the altar and the reverend gave them a serious talking to and up in the gallery they sang in very thin voices and the bride was thickly-veiled while the bridegroom had white gloves and looked a model of good manners. Then a heavy silence filled the church and Eve whispered to me: "Now comes the main event, I just can't wait to see it." At this very instant Anthony Bejval yelled in an awful voice: "Here comes the glorious moment of revenge, a little something of my own making for this very occasion." Then he chucked a stinking ostrich egg, which had already spent several days under his shirt to make it just what was needed, in the direction of the altar.

The egg hit the bridegroom on the head and broke, sending yolk running down his face. Presently a stench like no other, one which had never been witnessed before, was coursing through the church.

The whole church was left dumbstruck with no one even breathing a word. Then the bridegroom broke the silence with the words: "What vile wretch did that?" after which he started crying.

The priest was open-mouthed, his words drying up in mid-flow. We said nothing either and didn't move an inch. I'd have been happier had we gone far away from the place, and I grabbed hold of Bejval by the back of his shirt to say we'd be better off outside but he didn't move because he was so pleased with his invention, so I stayed and Christopher stayed as well and Eddie stayed and that went for Eve too and we all watched the yolk streaming down the face of the bridegroom and trickling onto his new suit until he was entirely messed up and gave off a horrible rancid pong.

Once again came the voice of the bridegroom: "What vile wretch did that?" and he was in tears and we didn't say a word. His Excellency the Maharajah went scarlet and reached for his sword and Her Excellency the Maharani went scarlet too and they were both in a rage and the nobles next to them went the same colour. Every one of them turned towards us, but we stood there looking righteous and as if butter wouldn't melt in our mouths.

The voice of the bridegroom rang out a third time: "What vile wretch did that?" and the bride said: "It couldn't have been anyone but Pete because he made such a horrible face at us when we were going up to the altar."

"Is that so?" said Joey in a horrible voice and he went on: "Let me at him, he's got a thrashing coming to him and I'll deal with this in no time at all."

And he rushed at me with the princess hurrying after Eve saying: "She's the one who's always egging him on."

And while she was speaking all the people in the church began to shout that this was a disgrace and His Excellency the Maharajah said in a loud voice that he'd have to deal with this so that it didn't happen again and the fat general brandished his sabre horribly until it flashed like lightning and all the nobles drew their swords and swore that they'd be avenged.

The princess grabbed hold of Eve by the hair and Eve grabbed hold of the princess by the hair too and they tugged at each other's ringlets and Eve shrieked: "Do you really think, you cow, that you can do whatever you like just because you've got a train nearly three yards long?" and this led to an awful scandal, in fact a real scuffle.

His Excellency the Maharajah sprang at Anthony Bejval who said proudly: "Come on, then!" and His Excellency the Maharajah said: "You poxy little brat, I'm going to kill you," and Bejval came back at him full of sang freud: "Go ahead and kill me – your father will have to pay the fine," after which they started boxing. Her Excellency the Maharani said: "Not so fast, please, I don't like to look at this."

Some guardsman gave Chris a huge slap and Christopher slapped him back and the guardsman said: "Looking for a fight are you? Fine with me!" and then he gave him another slap and this time it was an even bigger one, but Chris knew what he was doing and slapped him quickly twice and the guardsman started to snivel saying: "Just you wait, you low-caste boy, come anywhere near our place and my pa will give you what for." Then he ran off.

An Indian verger grabbed hold of me by the collar and dragged me to the door saying: "O thou pagan from a horde, thou host of Amalekites, thou Roman in your armour, come with me to the parish council right now." But I got myself free of his grip and said: "Leave me alone, can't you. I've done nothing to you either," but he kept yelling that I must go before the council because I set a bad example and was the black sheep among all the white ones and I said: "You're an even blacker sheep yourself," and he said: "Just look at this, he's still full of cheek," and he gave me a shove and I said: "Do that to your grandma, you mouldy old man," and he said that was no way to behave in the House of God and kept chasing me all over the place.

I saw how Eddie Kemlink was sitting on a general, and twisting his nose as hard as he could and this general was puffing and panting and yelling: "Comrades-in-arms! Some-one somewhere help me! This rascal could leave a man maimed!" and as I was running around I said to him: "It's your own fault, why can't you leave us be?" and the general replied loftily: "What business is it of yours? It's not as if you're the one twisting my nose, is it? Just clear out of here before I find something to clobber you with!" I wanted to answer him back, but I was still being chased by the verger.

And the yelling and the hullabaloo got louder and louder, with objects flying in all directions in the terrible mayhem all around. Later on all the lads said that it had been the best ding-dong they'd ever seen. And as if all this had been nothing to speak about – a troupe of monkeys swarmed into the church and joined the fray. In the midst of this mêlée I noticed Jumbo socking the maharajah's elephant on the back with his trunk and saying: "I'm out to get you, you scoundrel," and laughing wildly while the maharajah's elephant socked Jumbo across the back with his trunk in return and said: "I'll beat you black and blue, you jackass, you'll be seeing stars," and so they set about each other with a vengeance.

A large tiger, one that was already a bit long in the tooth, came bounding in and laughed saying: "This looks like fun, I'd like to know who'll swap a few punches with me." The words were hardly out of his mouth before another tiger jumped on his back and they were rolling about on the carpet and roaring their heads off. Now the Indian rock snake had to get in on the act and it began beating one of the ministers of state with its tail. It was like being thrashed with a bull whip and so the minister squealed horribly and then seized hold of an evolver and shot the snake in the stomach and the serpent shrieked in a piteous voice: "Oh gentlemen, he has shot me dead as a dodo and all I did was give him a few light strokes."

There was bedlam everywhere. People were skirmishing outside in front of the church, cows and horses were doing battle there too, dogs were at each other's throats as were the birds in the trees and even the butterflies in the garden and the flies in the kitchen; in fact anything that could come to blows did so. And at the height of the fray Her Excellency the Maharani said in a high voice that no one could have missed: "What are the leading lights of the land doing, fighting like this? You leave me lost for words. I'll tell you one thing, though. This is all the fault of that lad Bajza. He's always in at the start of every scrap and he never stays out of trouble." And in a deep voice His Excellency the Maharajah said: "That's the gospel truth, let's be after him!" And all at once a great cry went up and the whole lot of them, nobles and commoners, boys and beasts, all the bigwigs and the priest and the verger and even the princess came tearing down on me as if it was all my fault and I'd done nothing at all and in fact I'd told the others to behave themselves. And now everything was supposed to be my fault all over again. I put up a brave fight to no avail when there were so many of them, it was all against one, so I tried to run away but there was no way I could, my legs didn't want to know, it was as if they'd gone to work for someone else, and I began to yell: "Why can't they leave me alone when I've done nothing to harm them! They started it, I was minding my own business and now I get blamed for everything!" and I shouted more and more until I noticed that Pa had his hand on my shoulder and was saying: "Stop it. That's enough now. We're here with you and there's nothing to be afraid of."

I piped down when I saw it was Pa because he's the strongest one of the lot and can get the better of them all, he'd really give them what for, oh yes, you should see what he can do, and Ma said in her soft little voice: "Now then, my Petie, who's been kicking up such a fuss?" and I went on crying a bit, though only a small bit, and I said in an accusing way: "You went off without a word and left me there on my own to take on all comers," and then the doctor was there as well and he said to me: "Now then, young stalwart," and I said with a scowl: "I am not your young stalwart so just leave that out!" because I had a suspicion that the doctor was also one of my foes and he kept reminding me of that general whose nose had been given a twisting by Eddie Kemlink. So I said: "You can be glad of the fact that your nose is still in its proper place," and the doctor laughed in a loud voice and went "Ho! Ho! Ho!"

Then the doctor took a look at the thermometer, closed his medicine bag and said: "The worst is over now, the main thing is to get rest and then some more rest," and he held out his hand to my parents saying: "My compliments to you all. Glad to have been of service."

What is His Excellency the Maharajah doing now, or Her Excellency the Maharani, and what about the royal princess? What are the tailor Brabec and Mrs. Brabec doing, and what about the snakes, the tigers, the elephants, the monkeys and all the other local inhabitants? And is it possible that Jumbo still has that nice red hat and still remembers who bought it for him? And what about India? Does India really exist, or is it only to be found in an atlas?

I do not want to ask my parents, because they will tick me off straight away and won't want me to talk too much and will make me take my nasty medicine instead. I still thought I could perhaps have a word with Christina about it, but as soon as I mentioned India she burst out laughing so I said to her: "You Rampusite of Rampusites, there's none more Rampusitical than you."

All night I sleep like a log and don't have any dreams. A while back Christina lent me her pocket mirror and I was amazed to see that I had a tiny doll-like face, the sort of doll our Mirabelle plays with. Everyone says that I've been very poorly and our Lawrence sent a letter in which he wrote:

"Here's hoping that with God's help my little brother Pete will get back again the health he's lost and once again with warmest regards as ever your dutiful son Lawrence."

The lads I go round with paid me a visit today, because the doctor allowed them to come, so come they did. They stood around the bed and were a four but with me there too we were a handful. Joey Zilvar was there among them and I would have liked to ask him whether he'd really got married or what he was up to, but he kept mum, I expect because he didn't want to say anything in front of the others. And the lads told me what was going on that was new. They said we had a new teacher who's still hardly out of shorts and so they call him an ansillyary teacher, but on the other hand he knows how to run really fast and plays on the left wing for a sports club called Ctibor. Apparently in the last championship match he broke free and scored three goals, and one of them was taken on the volley.

And they went on to say that when I was taken ill the entire place had to be whitewashed and there was no school for three days and so the whole affair had put a spring in the step of the pupils and they were really happy about it.

I said to them: "I wonder if you're properly grateful to me for all this." They replied that everyone had said good things about me and called me a crackerjack because I'd been down with scarlet fever which was really something and I was ever so proud when I heard this.

But the question of what happened to India kept preying on my mind and I just couldn't get it out of my head. So I made up my mind to find out what I could from the lads. If they spilled the beans about it, all to the good, and if they didn't say anything, so what.

And so when they came to see me again, all of a sudden I blurted out in a loud voice: "India?" and then kept a crafty eye on them to see what would happen next.

Speaking all at once the boys came back at me in another loud voice saying: "India!"

Once again I fixed them with a cunning look and said in an even stronger voice: "Calcutta?"

And back came the chorus in a strong voice of its own: "Calcutta!"

Fastening another sly glance upon them I suddenly said: "Maharajah?"

They were even louder as they replied: "Maharajah!" and Bejval said that this was a really great game which we'd call 'Indian Jaunts' and he said we could play it many times over, and I said: "Yes, we could, because we all know very well what it's like in India," and then I gave them another foxy glance to see what they'd say and whether they'd at last let the cat out of the bag. But the lads didn't say a thing, unless you count Eddie Kemlink saying "You bet!"

So I didn't press them any more and without beating around the bush I asked Joey Zilvar what his pa said to him when he got married. Joey laughed horribly at this and said: "Get lost, you prat." And the other boys laughed too and Chris Jirsák wondered how I'd got an idea like that into my head. And I told them that they should go home because I wanted to get some sleep and they went away saying: "Be seeing you, then!"

And I was in a sulk for a long time because I couldn't get to the bottom of what had actually happened about India, and I was really sorry to think that there might be nothing to all these amazing adventures, that they might be a pipe dream or a will-o'-the-wisp. What was even worse was the fact that I missed India, a place where everything is so lovely and where there is more beauty than anywhere else in the world. I'd hoped that India might at least come to see me again at night, but she didn't let herself be known. And I could never sort it out in my head: India was there and then all of a sudden she was gone.

And when at one point Eve Svoboda came to see me, I pounced upon her right away: "Eve, you've always been a bright girl, haven't you?"

"You can be sure of that," she replied.

"So can you remember that wedding in India?"

"What wedding in India?" she said, her voice full of surprise.

"You know – the one where Joey Zilvar got married to a royal princess."

Those blue eyes of hers opened wide.

"Joey Zilvar? And a royal princess? No, never!"

"Eve," I said in a firm voice, "don't you remember how you said that the princess had a heavy satin dress and a ten-foot bridal train?"

"Heavy satin dress? And you say she had a ten-foot bridal train? That must have been a grand wedding. And were there lots of people there? What about the bridesmaids? What were they wearing? Tell me! Was there music and singing? Did the bride have a garland of flowers in her hair? What was it like when she stood at the altar and said that 'I do!' which can never be taken back? Did the bride weep floods of tears? Come on, you silly thing, tell me all about it!"

"What is there for me to say? You saw it all as well as I did. We were there together. Just cast your mind back."

Eve thought this over for a while and then shook her head sadly.

"I don't know anything about it," she said. "I was never there. I never put a foot outside the house. What a shame. An Indian wedding – that must be like something out of a fairy tale."

When Eve had gone, I took a look at my legs. They're weak as a sparrow's. I tried to move round the room but I couldn't manage it. I was all sticky and my head was in a spin. I don't think that I could even get the better of little

Victor Štěpánek. But I'll soon pick up again and get stronger and then I'll be a match for any of them. Oh well – just for the moment – I think what I really want to do now – is – visit the land of Nod.

TRANSLATOR'S NOTE
AND ACKNOWLEDGEMENT

There is always a difficulty over whether or not to anglicise names. Anglicise and you lose the flavour of the original; fail to anglicise and the names are easily misread, so that the flavour is lost once again.

In this translation I have anglicised first names (and the dog) but have left surnames (and the cat) as they appeared in the original. This may seem like an unwelcome compromise, but it retains both the Czech context and a recognisable peg for English-speaking readers to hang their thoughts on.

At the same time, any reader who doesn't know Czech is asked at least to take note of pronunciation. Peter's friends are more recognisable if the inventor Tony Bejval is pronounced BAY-val rather than the first syllable being treated as something to rhyme with hedge. The pious Christopher is more of a YEAR – SARK, with all the pious resonances that brings with it, than someone who sounds like a cross between a jersey and a sack. A few minutes spent checking on how the names of the main characters are pronounced in Czech will add a great deal to an English-speaking reader's enjoyment of the book.

I would like to thank Martin Janeček for his editorial advice and Lucie Johnová for reading the text through several times. Mary Hawker, Nigel Hawker and Dr Richard Haas also read the text and provided invaluable suggestions. I would particularly like to thank my wife Lenka Cornerová Zdráhalová, murderously meticulous as ever, for all her help in improving early drafts of this translation.

Mark Corner

Central European modern history is notable for many political and cultural discontinuities and often violent changes as well as many attempts to preserve and (re)invent traditional cultural identities. This series cultivates contemporary translations of influential literary works into English (and other languages) which have not been available to global readership due to censorship, the effects of Cold War or repetitive political disruptions in Czech publishing and its international ties.

Readers in English both in today's cosmopolitan Prague or anywhere in the physical and electronic world can thus become acquainted with works which capture the Central European historical experience and which express and also have helped to form Czech and Central European nature, humour and imagination.

Believing that any literary canon can be defined only in dialogue with other cultures, the series will bring proven classics used in Western university courses as well as (re)discoveries aiming to provide new perspectives in intermedial areal studies of literature, history and culture.

All titles are accompanied by an afterword, the translations are reviewed and circulated in the scholarly community before publication which has been reflected by nominations for several literary awards.

Modern Czech Classics series edited by Martin Janeček and Karolinum Press

Published titles

Zdeněk Jirotka: Saturnin (2003, 2005, 2009, 2013; pb 2016)
Vladislav Vančura: Summer of Caprice (2006; pb 2016)
Karel Poláček: We Were a Handful (2007; pb 2016)
Bohumil Hrabal: Pirouettes on a Postage Stamp (2008)
Karel Michal: Everyday Spooks (2008)
Eduard Bass: The Chattertooth Eleven (2009)
Jaroslav Hašek: Behind the Lines. Bugulma and Other Stories (2012; pb 2016)
Bohumil Hrabal: Rambling On (2014; pb 2016)
Ladislav Fuks: Of Mice and Mooshaber (2014)
Josef Jedlička: Midway Upon the Journey of Our Life (2016)
Jaroslav Durych: God's Rainbow (2016)
Ladislav Fuks: The Cremator (2016)

In Translation

Bohuslav Reynek: The Well at Morning
Ludvík Vaculík: Czech Dreambook
Jan Čep: Short Stories
Viktor Dyk: The Pied Piper